DRAGONSPEAK

ISAAC'S BLESSING

AUSTIN VALENZUELA

CONTENTS

Aura Legend

For those who wish to see the Dyra as they see themselves...

- Lilac - Relaxed, Serene
- White - Neutral, Investigative
- Spring Green - Friendly, Communicative
- Midnight Blue - Sarcastic, Skeptical
- Cloud Gray - Sad, Hopeless
- Bright Yellow - Excited, Inspired
- Burnt Orange - Irritated, Withdrawn
- Sweet Red - Hopeful, Important
- Dark Red - Eager, Provocative
- Jungle Green - Playful, Sensitive
- Black - Isolated, Abandoned
- Dark Purple - Worried, Overwhelmed

CHAPTER I

SECOND ERA, 113, HIGH SILVER

Solomon

S olomon leaned on the abandoned pew and observed the cathedral's stained-glass ceiling trying to revive the confused, backward age in his mind. The scene seemed to represent peace and reconciliation with the dragons, as if there could ever be such a thing.

St. Daemonus looked like a dreamland in the first-era paintings, before the Lord's renovations. The designs of that decadent time appealed more to Solomon's taste in decor, he'll admit, yet he would never outrightly shun the Lord's architectural intelligence, or come to think he understood such a complex soul. These depictions merely amused him. The irony could be found in the humans, shown interacting with dragons in suicidal manners.

One pastor stood but a few feet away from a Wyrm. Solomon had trained to recognize the dragon by its lack of arms and legs, most vulnerable to aerial attacks, less it burrow into the ground too soon.

The first-era pastor in the depiction extended an open hand to the grown creature, presenting a green apple, white streaks of glass making the fruit seem glossy.

Naturally, Solomon cringed at seeing an unarmed person so close to destructive power. Everyone knew meeting the creatures' gaze was forbidden unless one wished to lose their mind and soul.

This was the story of the first-era: ignorant, senseless pastors who dedicated themselves to the power of the dragons, not realizing their rightful claim to the Great Spirit—a powerful force that the greedy creatures kept from humans all these ages. The first-era and all previous humanity had never been able to *take* from the dragons. Solomon approached one of the stone columns holding up what was left of the abandoned cathedral, leaning against the dusty support.

Somehow, the columns and glass ceiling survived the cathedral's decay. Most of the walls had collapsed and a thick coat of dust covered every inch of the hallway depths. Solomon couldn't deny he felt something powerful when he'd stepped inside the broken house of worship. He'd become more energized. His vision and hearing improved, too. Being blessed in the spirit, he knew what it felt like to progress in spiritual aptitude. The excitement of overdue change filled the air. The slightest sound within the cathedral seemed to carry up through the columns, into the maw of the largest dragon in the scene—a crystal white Wyvern, piercing blue eyes surveying over the church and his gathered followers.

The cathedral was built during the first era, Solomon thought. *There's a reason why these structures are abandoned.* Even he, the most capable military leader of Jericho's time, hesitated to confront the Tempus forest's evil spirits when they were lugging the dragonic sacrific all the way.

"Right," an eager-to-please Zealot called out behind him. "All scraps are good and cleared, and there isn't another lock in the world that'd do any good with 'er."

Solomon exaggerated a smile and turned from the pillar, convinced the other Zealots sent the dimwitted boy as a messenger just to spite him. *This one will be overwhelmed once exposed to the spirit.* He gave the Zealot no more than a glance as he moved toward the group.

"Magnificent work. Astounding, every one of you." He clapped his hands together and strode toward chains pinned to the floor by robust stakes.

The Zealots quieted.

Solomon placed his hand on one of the spike heads and brushed his fingertips along the connecting chain, and the metal was cold like grazing the surface of ice water. He followed the chain's arc down and up, coming to a stop as it wrapped around faded gray scales.

Exhaling choppy breaths, he acknowledged the dragon for the first time since they arrived. Solomon never knew the Chrysos would be so large given its youth. He wondered what power those scales withheld. Texts claimed the species often brought significant advances to humanity; today would be their most crucial role yet.

Solomon's fingers shook in the scale's reflection. A wave of nervous excitement rushed through him. *I'm becoming a part of history.*

The ground shook, and he lost balance. At the last moment, he reached out his hand and braced himself against the dragon. Icy numbness surged through his arm, up to his shoulder before he found himself able to rip his hand free. The skin on his palm glowed bright red and lacked feeling. Solomon clenched his wrist as the rumbling ceased.

"The touch of the Chrysos... you've suffered worse to get here." Lord Jericho's voice filled the empty cathedral—distant, transient— booming from a darkened hallway across the nave.

Solomon fell quickly to a knee. "I have my Lord."

"Soon, your suffering shall end. The eye of the Silver Goddess is upon us. The equinox moon will soon rise." Red eyes glowed within the dark of his hood, two lanterns above bright golden necklaces. He ambled into the light of dusk and removed his hood to reveal ice-white hair and a face as young as it was wise. Solomon had consistently looked upon the face of his Lord and felt ashamed of his own meager achievements despite old age.

Inside Solomon's cloak pocket, there was a nervous scurrying and scratching at his stomach. With a forceful tap, he silenced the creature. "The sacrifice is in position," he said, standing. "We await your order." A subtle glance at the Zealots made them double over the stakes and chains.

From the corner of his eyes, Solomon watched as Jericho spoke privately with his servant, Haskil. The Lord gestured to a nearby hallway and turned back to the nave as the deformed being ran off.

"Now?" Solomon asked.

Jericho nodded. "The natural way."

Solomon reached in his cloak pocket and wrapped his hand around doughy scales. He pulled out a yawning infant dragon the size of his palm, a bluish silver—its eyes were indigo slits, wide and scared.

He tilted the dragon onto his left hand, careful not to wake it too much. The Wyvern crawled to his other palm and returned to sleep. Solomon hand-selected the dragon for this day because it had not yet learned to stand—the perfect age for transfiguration. Any older and the dragon would be too aware of its surroundings. Any younger and its soul wouldn't have enough natural spirit needed to awaken the Chrysos.

The creature flipped onto its side, exposing its stomach. Within his cold, red palm, the numbness receded and Solomon felt a distant vibration.

A similar turquoise hue as the dragon, Solomon picked a special dagger for this day as well. His father gave it to him on his deathbed when he made Solomon vow to alleviate the world of its suffering. *If only he lived later into Jericho's reign, and could see my progress.* Solomon gave the dagger a trusting look, rubbing his thumb over initials engraved on the hilt's end—S.S., for Solomon the Strong. The familiar steel handle welcomed him. Extending both arms out, calm and comfortable, he steadied his breath.

The events of the sacrifice played through his mind, precisely as he hoped for them to occur. Confident in his preparations, he brought to mind the given spell. The word would carve a path for the spirit to move through. The image in his mind settled on a subdued Chrysos, but awake. He cleared his throat and spoke with intent.

"Expergise." The air around him grew hot and muggy.

Solomon swept the dagger unerringly across the young dragon's throat, slicing clean through the rubbery neck. The creature squirmed, gurgled on its blood, and soon died. Red, melted paste spilled through the pastor's fingers to the floor; the scent sweet as candy.

Previously locked within the little dragon's scales, turquoise color lifted into the air as ghostly wisps. The substance of its soul wafted with intent and direction, as Solomon had imagined, and he watched the streams disappear into the Chrysos' gray scales. As the last of the wisps entered, the famed dragon flashed a wave of gold throughout, its scales brightening like watered flowers. Solomon couldn't believe the radiant changes. Legs shaking, he stepped back.

I've done it. The Chrysos is awake.

Moments passed while the dragon lay unmoving, scales growing in luminosity. Solomon dropped the Wyvern's body, silently thanking the creature for helping him complete his role. Yet, the infant dragon didn't appear to be dead. Something moved within.

It was the stone floor. A growing vibration.

The cathedral shook in a massive quake, the columns swaying left to right, violent vibration thundering up Solomon's legs.

He collapsed to his forearms. The nave a shaking blur, he caught a glimpse of the Chrysos' all-seeing, wide golden eyes as they blinked open. The dragon tried to raise its head but chains stopped it halfway. The movement sent Zealots flying throughout the room like flailing wisps cast from the Chrysos herself. Others hid inside hallways. *Unloyal,* Solomon thought, watching them abandon their post.

Jericho stood unflinching before the creature. A miniature man, more powerful than nature.

The Chrysos' golden color fluctuated to display a near-infinite range before settling back to a sandy yellow. Solomon squinted, watching as the Chrysos seemed to realize its surroundings. Eyes twice the size of himself panned the room. He glimpsed gold irises long enough to admire their sparkling tone. The dragon's gaze paused for a moment on Jericho, though the Lord wouldn't return the favor. *What would he find if he looked into those eyes?*

No one spoke. The Chrysos breathed heavily, tugging its chains with no real effort. The dragon slowly lifted its head and cried out, a long, depressing note. The glass ceiling shattered.

Solomon barely made it into one of the several hallways before shrieks sounded from the Zealots too loyal to be quick. Beautiful glass crashed to the ground and impaled the screaming unblessed, who gave their life for a good cause. *The Spirit will reward them justly in the afterlife.* Solomon watched a piece of red glass, perhaps from the apple, slide across the tile to the tip of his sandal.

And dust eventually settled. Those who were dying died.

The Chrysos laid its head to the side, exposing its throat. Solomon could hardly believe what he saw. It was like a dream come true, helping him ascend to some other life of grace and respect.

She surrenders.

A smirk sprouted upon the Lord's face.

The remaining Zealots began to cheer.

Gray moonlight poured into the nave as day turned to night. The sight could have been a mural scene of its own. Solomon almost believed he could put his hand right through the dragon's scales if he dared step closer.

The Lord's servant emerged. Haskil scrambled up to the Lord and bowed to present a sheathed sword. Solomon recognized the two-handed weapon by its ruby-studded sheath. No one had ever used it before, but legend said the Sword of Daemonus inherited the soul of whoever's life is claimed. A child's tale that Solomon hoped it to be true. The sword embodied the core principle of Jericho's reign.

The Lord gripped the black handle at the sheath's end, drawing out the wide-faced blade, thick near the center and falling off into sharp edges on either side. A ray of moonlight reflected off the center, cutting through the shadows and any remaining doubt that the dragon's time has ended.

Jericho stepped in front of the exposed portion of the creature's neck, dwarfed by its massive size. Mumbling complex, indistinct mantras, he took a wide stance, and raised the sword high into the air.

THE NIGHT BEFORE...

CHAPTER 2

SECOND ERA, 113, UAIR FIVE OF RISING SILVER

Isaac

A candle on the floor beside Isaac illuminated a pile of scattered books and Boyd's pointed face across the room. Moonlight shone through the enchanted glass window, casting a symbol for the time of day on the floor. The resulting shadow took the shape of a full moon with five dashes in the lower right quarter, reminding Isaac they should be in bed.

He would be lying to himself if he didn't admit these books were their last hope for finding a way to pass the equinox test without killing a dragon—a remote one at that. The answers had to be in first-era texts, but Jericho had been precise about stocking only second-era texts in the renovated library; nothing remained about the distant past but slanders. Even here, with each book he'd carefully chosen laid out across the cold gem-studded floor, none seemed as promising as the notebook held in his hands, low before the candlelight.

Caressing the rough leather brought back memories of a simpler time. The notebook was the last gift Isaac's father gave him. Accounts of every first-era story and belief filled the pages, even those tragedies condemned at the time of their release, shared throughout secretive, yet honest circles; maybe that's why his father waited to provide him with the book until their very last day together, waiting for him to mature as much as he could. When he handed the notebook over the day before he boarded the ship to St. Daemonus, he said that one day Isaac would be like the pastors and apostles inside, communicating with the wisest dragons to exist, aiding the world through their worship.

Sadly, he wasn't, and never would be. Not in a place like St. Daemonus, where pastors and apostles sacrificed dragons for their inherent power over the natural world. With the test to become a pastor in this horrid church scheduled for tomorrow during the equinox, he hoped the notebook would reveal a way to free the dragons or convince others they aren't dangerous. None of the second-era books from the library contained any luck.

Isaac hadn't read the yellowed pages in a few years, soft to the touch as he flipped them one-by-one. The notebook's worn appearance didn't make him any more confident. It was not as well-crafted as he remembered, though when his hands gripped the weak spine, he couldn't deny the comforting surge of familiarity that rushed through him. He opened the first page and read the letter there, handwritten by his father—signed, Abraham.

The sentimental words made him sick.

"Here," he said, stopping on a page ridden with scattered bullet-points and slanted, brisk handwriting. He put his finger on the text and squinted. "It says, '*Procidat* is an illusion spell you can place on any creature within a given radius.' We could use it for the rest of the class. The pastors, too, or whoever is testing us. It'll make them think they saw us take the dragons life, and we won't actually have to. After that, we can get our black cloaks and escape to somewhere far away."

Boyd scoffed and closed his book, throwing it into the pile. When they went to the library that morning, he hadn't grabbed anything other than a short volume about daggers. "And how would we make that happen without using the draconic spirit?"

"We could try casting the spell ourselves."

"You think this is the first-era?" Boyd stirred in the flickering darkness. There was a long silence in the upper tower room, one of the few student quarters near St. Daemonus's southern edge. "Couldn't we just refuse to take the test?"

"You know what happens to rogues." Isaac closed his notebook. *Rather, we don't know, and that's the scariest part.* Churches shunned anyone who refused to worship the new Lord Jericho, he who has ushered in a new age and dragged the church out from its prior state of ignorance. Any student who failed to pursue their bestowed role was labeled a rogue, hunted down by apostles who had too much fun with the job. *The only place to hide would be the southern isles.*

"The goal is to get out of here," Boyd said. "Or have you changed your mind?"

"Of course I haven't." Isaac's sunk his fingernails into his palm, quelling his rage. "Do you know of anybody who ever refused to take the test?"

Boyd looked down, admitting to Isaac's point.

Since it finally came to their fifth year and graduation to pastor-dom, Isaac couldn't help but wonder if he had the same beliefs as he stated upon arriving at this forsaken church, when he'd hope to save draconic creatures.

"You only want to run away,"" Isaac said. "You don't want to fix anything. Even if we escape, the church will continue to murder the dragons. It needs their power to survive." He wouldn't let his friend escape church walls and run into the Tempus forest where death awaited him.

Boyd gestured toward the books. "We don't need these. We have two choices: escape, or take the test and kill a dragon. The real question is whether or not you want to be a murderer. The people we swore not to become."

"We refuse to take the test then," Isaac said. "I like that idea more than leaving. I'm willing to suffer those consequences more than I'm willing to run away on some ship."

Boyd laughed. "Look at you, changing your mind like a leaf in the wind. You said it yourself. Times have changed. The church is different than it is in that notebook. We've found out how to harness the draconic spirit and render these innocent beings our magic little wands. I'm starting to think it's the only way anyone knows how to use the spirit these days."

Isaac tucked his father's notebook in his night cloak.

"Besides," Boyd said. "What if we fail the test in front of everyone? You know how badly Jericho treats the unblessed." Boyd had always refused to call the Lord by his proper title.

"That's why we need to figure out how to pass," Isaac said. "They already laugh at us. What harm could a few more laughs be? At least we gave them a good time on our way out."

Boyd's heart didn't seem to lighten, his gaze drifting aside.

But the pause gave Isaac a chance to listen for the servant's footsteps, a sound he'd internalized over the years. If they were caught conversing at such late hours, they'd be forbidden to take the test tomorrow. Isaac knew better than to give up that opportunity just yet. "We'd never survive outside of St. Daemonus walls. You know what kind of creatures are out there."

"You've looked at Tempus as often as I have. There's nothing but a few sheep and dead trees. Don't lie to yourself."

"We can only see the border of the forest," Isaac said. "There are true dangers that Jericho placed inside."

Boyd turned away. "We'd survive."

Isaac's confidence wavered.

"And if we both could make it, I could make it alone." Boyd looked toward the high window, the moon. His face seemed older. By his tone, Isaac knew he'd given up on trying to pass the test.

"There's a reason why Tempus is forbidden." Isaac wanted nothing more than to save his friend. "You won't make it if you go."

Boyd sighed. "The only reason we can't go outside those walls is because Jericho doesn't want us to. Do you hear yourself? You're giving into his lies."

Isaac stood with Boyd, making an effort to keep his voice quiet despite his urge to shout. "Everything you've said is based on the assumption that Jericho's tricked us. You're the one who's believing in fake things. You see Jericho's manipulation everywhere. Yes, he's bad, terrible even, the worst human to exist, but there's no way someone like the Lord could trick an entire church and every single island. He's charming, not smart."

"That's my point," Boyd said. He walked to the window and gazed up, staring into the night sky.

Jealousy overcame Isaac when he noticed how much the upcoming equinox had changed his friend. By morning, Boyd would have the white hair and red eyes of a blessed pastor. It seemed ridiculous that people could change so fast overnight, but he'd seen it in some of the fifth years yesterday as well. Most adolescents naturally transitioned on their fifteenth equinox into the look that distinguished the blessed from those less fortunate—if the spirit deemed them worthy. Soon, Boyd would have the same features as Jericho and everyone else at St. Daemonus. Even his stride toward the window seemed nimbler.

If Boyd didn't want the changes, Isaac would take them. That way, he wouldn't have to feel like such a fraud when trying to sacrifice a dear dragon. It was selfish of Boyd not to do the same, but he seemed too scared to play the part of pastor even for a moment.

Isaac had hoped for some way to take the equinox test and become blessed without going through with the sacrifice. Then he could change the entire church, start a new era and found an island where dragons could roam free, as they had in his father's notebook.

Another reason why Boyd shouldn't leave came to mind. "Let's say the Tempus forest isn't dangerous," Isaac said. "How would we get off Daemonus? The nearest island is Windhaven, weeks across sea."

"Pastors leave on missionary trips all the time. There are trader ships at the harbor. We'll sneak aboard. Who cares where they go."

"You can't expect them not to find us hiding in the food supply. They'll throw us into the sea the second they find out we're rogues. No one wants to risk that kind of punishment by the Lord. And he would find out, too." Isaac realized how hard he was clenching his hands. He loosened them, rubbing damp palms with red pinch marks on his cloak. "The goal is to make pastors care about the dragons. That's how we change things."

Boyd turned from the window, and for a moment, Isaac thought he had imagined the blessed changes in his friend; Boyd looked like he did when Isaac first met him. Innocent and free. "I thought we agreed that's a lost cause."

It struck harder than ever that Boyd could be right. A basic assumption his friend seemed to admit years ago finally came to mind. "You don't think anything in my father's notebook is true?"

"Your father wasn't well," Boyd said, as if sorry to say the truth. "He had an obsession. The spirit makes people crazy. We need to get as far away from St. Daemonus as possible, from every church."

"A few years ago, you would've said everything in there was true." Isaac couldn't help but question everything Boyd said from the beginning. "You lied to me?"

"No... I'm smarter now than I used to be. Your father is no different than Jericho, the pastors, or anyone else who is brainwashed by the spirit. Humans were never meant to have that sort of power. Why else would the dragons have fled whenever we discovered a new island? They could never escape from us, we always need more, more, more, until we took what the dragons didn't want to give."

Isaac walked up to Boyd, speaking through a clenched jaw. "Don't ever compare my father to Jericho."

"Look at yourself," Boyd said. "You're letting the spirit get to you. I'm not your enemy."

Isaac pushed him back into his bed. The wood frame crashed into the wall, splintered. The candle toppled, splashing hot wax, burning and molding to Isaac's leg. The candle flame sputtered out.

Isaac caught a glimpse of Boyd's figure stalking somewhere behind the veil of moonlight.

"Dragons seduce you," he said. "Look into their eyes, and you go insane. Your father is no exception. Dragon-lover or not, the spirit isn't good for you. Let the dragons be."

"My father was a shepherd in Windhaven, part of a settler group." The truth proved Isaac as wrong as Boyd. "He was never in Daemonus. He never even saw a dragon, just studied them."

"He was drunk with spirit, just like all the rest." Boyd coughed. Isaac thought he hadn't pushed him that hard, but the transformation made his friend fragile, trading strength for agility. "Apparently, the fervor seeps into the next generation."

"Have you seen yourself? You're the one who is becoming like them."

Boyd limped into the moonlight, all innocence gone. Red eyes stared at Isaac. He turned, bent under his bed, and retrieved an over-packed bag, the handles of multiple daggers protruding from the top.

"You planned to leave all along?" Isaac asked.

"I thought you might come to your senses after you figured out there's no other option. I guess I underestimated your loyalty to Jericho."

Isaac fell back onto his bed, swearing never to trust anyone again. He felt defeated, worse because Boyd was right. The notebook never had the answers. But Boyd's solution of running away to inevitable death didn't seem any better.

"Listen to me," Boyd said, bag thrown over his shoulders. "If it's the last thing I say to you. Nothing that powerful can be good for anyone."

"There's a way to live with it," Isaac said. Then he caught himself.

There he was, doing it again—using the old stories in his father's notebook as proof. The world had opened up and suffocated him all at once, and he saw himself in a new light. Every test and paper he failed, what they said about him being weak, unworthy of pastordom, became stark truth. *I'm a simpleton dragon-lover.* Every part of him that believed dragons were friendly broke away as one big lie, and he realized no part of him remained. He instinctively reached for the notebook for comfort, and stopped his shaking hand mid-way.

Boyd must've realized he wouldn't convince Isaac to leave. He shook his head and started toward the door.

Isaac wanted to call after him but the words caught in his throat.

For some reason, Boyd still paused. He turned back to Isaac. Perhaps he was having second thoughts.

Isaac found hope again.

Then he heard it himself, the encumbered trot of the servant, Haskil approaching from down the hall.

Isaac shoved as many books as he could under his bed and climbed into covers that barely fit. Boyd shuffled behind him, hesitating, probably trying to decide between the door and his bed. Daggers clanged one another as the bag slammed against the wall, and Boyd's bed squeaked from its breaking parts as he climbed in.

The servant's thumping ran past their door. It stopped at the far end of the hall, and started back. A few quick steps in succession, and as if Haskil jumped across the length of the corridor, their door suddenly burst open. A warm gust blew through, and with it, the musty smell of a torch's burning tallow.

Isaac froze in the crackling heat, struggling to breathe as if he slept, quieter than the servant's steps. He opened his eyes barely enough to see, back turned to the door, watching as the torch dispelled the moonlight. Warmth grew on his neck.

The servant's typical snorts held something stranger, more ferocious inside, sounding more akin to hunger. Haskil craved to find students creating trouble. The torchlight might have burned Isaac's hair when the growls turned to high-pitched yips and quiet curses over the sound of collapsing books. The torchlight waved chaotically across the wall.

Most of his body hid under the blanket aside from his feet, but he left his head exposed so Haskil could see the color of his hair and know who he was. Because Isaac was from the lesser island of Windhaven, most pastors, including Haskil, didn't find him intelligent enough to be capable of bad behavior. Isaac couldn't catch a baby Wyrm, let alone disrupt things on purpose.

"Sinners," the servant muttered. The door opened, slammed closed, and Haskil thumped down the hall using the rhythmic walk Isaac recognized and descended the stairs.

At this rate, Isaac would have no sleep before the equinox test. He rolled over, trying to get his mind to stop the same turning motion.

My father was wrong. Boyd is wrong.

The only options are to kill a dragon or escape.

The only escape is death.

Across the room, he knew that Boyd lay somewhere inside the darkness, yet his friend felt so far away. Their conversation had ended. Whatever decision they made about the test tomorrow, they'd make on their own. Boyd probably planned on being gone by now.

Fine, let him go.

Isaac flipped onto his back and stared up. He felt more tears welling inside, cursing himself for being so fragile. The notebook beckoned from his cloak, heavier than before. It had provided such refuge over the years. When nobody was there for him, to listen and help solve his problems, he'd disappear into the lands his father had recreated, realms where he was a hero.

Realizing his father told the stories so Isaac could escape the real world made him wonder how wrong he'd been. *There's no way to live with them. There never was.* The sooner Isaac lived with that belief, the better off he'd be.

He always knew the dragons had a dangerous side, but he didn't like to admit it. Even the notebook warned of pastors freezing to death and burning to a crisp. But, if this part of his father's notebook was true, why weren't the others? What about the pages that spoke of the wisdom the dragons provided? What if dragons were allowed to grow and prove themselves worthy of trust?

It hurt to think of his deeply ingrained ways and how unchangeable they seemed, swaying his thinking every second. It'd take years to unlearn what he used to be, not to mention proving himself to his peers. No wonder Boyd wanted to run away.

Five years he'd spent refusing to take responsibility. He needed to become somebody in the church if he wanted to make a difference, no matter the means. In the future, when he was more involved, he could give dragons the chance to prove themselves, even if it was only one, in secret.

Isaac flipped over, content enough with his decision to shut his eyes and sleep.

CHAPTER 3

SECOND ERA, 113, UAIR ONE OF RISING GOLD

Boyd

Boyd snatched the dragon-skin bag from under his bed and snuck toward the door as falling grey shifted to high gold. He glanced back toward the depressing room, more like a cell. Isaac stirred, a moving lump beneath his sheets.

He closed the door without a sound.

The effects of Boyd's transformation left him confused. Last night's sleep was dreamless, as usual, but the remaining blessed changes undoubtedly took place. Before he left, he'd been able to smell Isaac's body odor, a familiar smell from years of sparring together, but one he had never detected so fully. In the poignant musk, he sensed an anxious fear.

Anyone who looked at Boyd would mistake him for a faithful pastor. The Spirit chose to bless him. Why, he did not know. Forever, he would lurk in this disguise of white hair and red irises. When the other pastors looked at him, they would see one of them.

He hated that, but for what it was worth, the blessings were his key to escape.

A strange, ultimate silence filled the hallway through which Boyd moved. He descended the stairs three steps at a time, the sound of his leather soles no more than drips of water on stone.

He planned to use his blessings to his advantage once he reached the other islands. The unblessed respect pastors for their inherent Spirit, which meant they'd be easy to trick, believing anything he said. He'd have to stoop to Jericho's level and deceive people, but he saw nothing wrong in using his curse to unravel its wrongful nature. Before he received his role as apostle and Boyd never saw him again, his father once said, "The holy land of Daemonus grants her dwellers the gift of the Spirit. She makes her men better than others." Then he shipped Boyd to the island.

Better because this is where pastors take from the dragons without remorse. Better...

Isaac could never see the bigger picture. He's too trusting of the dragons, and everything else.

Cast on the hallway's walls, circular shadow dials filled with a dull golden light in the upper right segment. A single dash protruded just right of the northern mark, indicating uair one of rising gold. When uair two arrives, a second dash would appear right after, leading eventually to the dash of mid-noon, or High Gold, on the south end, when the equinox Spirit was most potent.

I'll be long gone.

Boyd ducked left at the bottom steps, away from the library and classrooms, starting down the southern path. He walked through their tower's arch, under the location of his room for the past four years, happy to put the memories behind him. Along the southern path, crimson roses greeted him as he jogged toward the outer wall, giddy.

He felt like a wolf stalking silently through the brush, sniffing, turning his head, nose up, looking for a scent. Around him wafted the faint smell of fertilizer paired with sweet rose petals. Throwing his pack over the shoulder-height stone border, it dropped to the other side with a clink and rustle of grass.

Boyd turned back to take a last look at the church.

May it burn.

He jumped on top of the wall in a single bound and dropped over. Catching himself on the stone, he adjusted mid-fall and landed smoothly. Dirt covered his cloak, and he brushed it off, looking for his bag.

It was gone.

He felt a sharp sense of helplessness.

I couldn't have thrown it far...

Looking up further, Boyd staggered at the sight of the immense field beyond the wall. The vast expanse seemed to go on for a distance far longer than he could walk. Despite the many times he'd looked out over this field from their tower window, it just dawned on him that he'd been stuck in a cage his entire life.

Black-fleeced sheep grazed mindlessly amid the brush. The untrimmed grass ticked Boyd's shins, growing thicker further in, forcing him to stop less blades of grass tower over his head. *Please don't let my pack be in there.* The brush seemed to move as one, persuaded by a salty ocean wind. At the far end, the field finally merged with the great white trees of the Daemonus forest, Tempus, dead and decaying as ever. Unsure of where to go, Boyd knew he stood no chance without his daggers.

Along the edge of the wall, he found nothing but vines and overgrown grass. *I have to be careful of snakes.*

Boyd forced himself to search out near the field's infinitude, immediately regretting it. The forest called to him in a dry lullaby, a whispery wind. The hairs stood on his neck. *You are not ready yet,* it said. *Turn back.*

He felt for the sole dagger kept in the hilt along his waist, his favorite, and was comforted by its touch. *The forest is right. I'm hopeless without my other daggers, but I can't go back. Isaac would kill me.*

I'll head for the harbor.

A clangoring thud and the sound of rustling grass came from behind him.

He spun in time to see the brown leather pack ricochet off the ground, nobody around to have dropped it. He tried to sense any movement around him, smell something as he did the church roses, but all he could focus on was the biting stench of sheep dung.

His mind played tricks on him. If it weren't for Isaac's fear of the forest, he wouldn't have doubted himself. *Nothing can harm me out here. That's Jericho's lie.*

His bag had been there all along. Somehow, he overlooked it.

These reassurances turned to doubt as he walked closer to see not his daggers, but a tree branch in the shape of a *Y*, protruding from the open top.

What is this joke? He searched the field.

"Where are you?" he yelled to the grass and Tempus forest. "Show yourself. Give me back my daggers." He tried to sound mighty, but the words felt like squeaks compared to the landscape.

He turned to the bag. Unlike the trees of Tempus, the branch seemed to have been part of a living tree. More than living, perhaps enchanted, as the bark pulsated with fading blotches of purple, blue, and green. It could've been fused with the Spirit in some way.

Boyd reached to grab the branch, planning to lob it into the woods, but the wood felt rubbery, with a fair amount of flexibility for bark. As he lifted it out, a silver band trailed from underneath, connected between the stick's upper ends, the weapon as light as air. *A slingshot.* It made Boyd think of Isaac's notebook and the first-era weapons described inside.

Boyd looked out to the sun rising over the forest horizon, showering the field with gold streaks. The elastic band reached back to his shoulder, spanning the length of his arm, bending the ends of the branch. Closing his eyes and aiming up, he released it.

A high musical note echoed over the field to Tempus like a pleasing bell.

"Thanks," he said to whoever took his dagger and replaced it with this.

The second-era didn't produce slingshots because they didn't provide a clean, prepared sacrifice, but they were still lethal weapons according to Boyd. And without his daggers, he couldn't be picky about what he used to defend himself.

He placed the slingshot into his cloak and counted himself lucky to have a backup weapon. From the waist sheath, he pulled out his favorite dagger, Duskfall, and used his cloak to clean off its distinctive wavy red-orange blade. *You'll never leave my sight, I promise.*

Voices from early risers on the other side of the wall sounded in the distance. Boyd took the hint and fell into a sliver of a shadow near the stone border, the empty bag slung over his back, wondering if forces in the dead Tempus trees grew nearer as he crept through the shadows of the rising sun, toward the Daemonus harbor.

CHAPTER 4

SECOND ERA, 113, UAIR
ONE OF RISING GOLD

Isaac

I saac bathed in the dormitory washroom at the far end of his hall. He dipped his sponge into the bucket on the floor and pulled out a gob of dripping red liquid. Clumps of the sweet-smelling substance fell from the sponge; it'd been here a while, and had time to congeal.

He couldn't control his hands as they reached up and squeezed. The thick liquid poured over his head. Ice cold.

His vision was tainted a blurry red. An irresistible urge to distance himself from the blood and bucket overcame him, and to his surprise, his body spasmed free, the sponge falling down, down, bringing with it the gravity of the washroom's scene to reveal a new setting.

The sponge landed on a gem-studded floor, spreading tiny red droplets across many-hued stones.

No.

Classmates with elated, warped faces pointed and laughed at his nakedness. Their blessed hair glowed so brightly it blinded him. Their red eyes burned with a searing heat. Their laughs sounded more like satisfied screams. He tried to cover his privates, shield his eyes, and run, but he couldn't escape. His legs had become part of the ground.

He opened his mouth to scream—nothing came out. Around him, his classmate's faces melted away, followed by the walls and the studded floor until impenetrable darkness surrounded him.

Suspended in an empty, dark space, Isaac waved his arms and legs, swimming through the void in no direction. He needn't breathe here. The shimmering, stinging purple hue within the darkness affirmed that life didn't go on, not here.

As the thought crossed his mind, a faint light sparked in the distance—dim vermillion.

The light grew, approaching him. Isaac couldn't draw his eyes away.

A series of gentle wisps mingled, danced together, their motion casting a playful spell. Chimes played a light tune somewhere far off; someone rang a bell.

High-pitched, robust bells joined in.

The auburn lights took the shape of a soaring dragon, rendering Isaac puny in comparison. The orange dragon slithered through the void without wings or legs, flaming red eyes staring into him, becoming part of him, all of him.

The heat.

The dragon's mouth opened, the chimes and bells ceased, and a rush of flames engulfed him. In the terror of burning to death, Isaac gasped, and his lungs filled with cool morning air.

—

Isaac shot up in bed, cold droplets of sweat stinging his eyes.
Where am I?

His hands shook as he lowered his soaked sheets. The silk night cloak stuck wetly to his skin. He rubbed his forehead with the back of his hand and looked at the clear liquid, thankful it wasn't blood.

Boyd's bunk across the room lay inhabited and unmade. *He decided to leave.* A few clothes and daggers remained scattered across the sheets.

Isaac got up to look under Boyd's bed. As he expected, the bag from last night was gone, along with his friend's dagger collection. He came across Boyd's black and gold coffer and looked inside. The chest proved empty except for a few game cards from the Shattering Isles, trading islands.

Isaac had declined when Boyd asked to play, saying he didn't know how. His friend never brought it up again, but Isaac thought he might have said yes if Boyd asked today. They'd been friends for five years, and here Isaac stands, abandoned again. Boyd even took the red library book about daggers.

I'll have to explain the missing text to pastor Nim.

Isaac checked the sun dial, hopeful there would be a decent amount of time before training. The color emitting from the glass window shone an almond yellow, its shadow displaying two marks to the right of north—uair two of rising gold, likely soon to be three.

He considered going after his friend. Isaac felt as if he'd lost part of himself, and he could do nothing. *We made no progress last night.* The right decision still seemed unclear. What he settled on yesterday, joining the church and changing it from the inside, didn't *feel* noble, going against everything he once believed about the world. *I'm hesitant about what lies ahead, so I choose to regress to the familiar.*

Isaac shuffled to the far wall, pulling their closet dresser across the room. He positioned it under the window and opened one of the swinging doors, using it to lift himself onto the unsanded top.

He opened the enchanted windowpane.

Fresh air nipped at his cheeks, and he gazed out over the expanse of Daemonus and the Tempus forest. His favorite view.

If he took the test and passed, he'd be moved to the pastors' quarters, and the view would be replaced with the training temple. For the rest of his days, he'd gaze upon the place where he'd been humiliated the most.

A stone path labeled the southern hallway extended out from beneath his tower. On either side lay a garden of plush roses, satin red and packed close together. At the end of the path was the circular wall that fortified St. Daemonus, and further on, he could see the place his father once deemed a blessed land. Wooly black sheep grazed on thick blades of grass, some of them nearly enveloped by the tall blades. Their numbers dwindled near the edge of the Tempus forest, where needle-like trees marked the point of no return.

The sound of a creaky wheelbarrow called Isaac's attention down to the path. A black-cloaked pastor with a prickly beard who frequently cleaned the rooms and latrines came lumbering down. He walked a short distance before lining the barrow up with the path's edge, bending to one side and struggling to flip the barrow over. He succeeded after a few grunts, sending dozens of dead dragons no older than infancy tumbling into the garden, hidden under the red petals. The pastor gave the wheelbarrow a shake and returned up the pathway, cleaning his hands on his cloak.

The disposal process is one of the first things I'll try to change.

Looking out of the tower window for the last time allowed him to get over his fear of pastordom faster than expected. After all, he would've seen this as the right decision all along if he had only been honest with himself. Boyd fleeing would be the first of a lot of lasts he'd have to face today. This view would be the second.

He also knew the third.

Boyd was right. I have to give up my childish dreams.

Isaac reached for the notebook inside his cloak pocket.

This fantasy.

He savored the nostalgic, leathery smell. Flipping through the notebook's heavy pages, the familiar pictures evoked reminiscent love for the famous stories. The Apophis still looked threatening as ever to him, its elegant hooded neck like a cobra; the tale of Vritra, the river dragon, used to make him feel invincible as he read about when the blue Wyrm helped Lord Cerilius end the drought in Tel Lacesh by sleeping in the riverbed for forty nights. The second portion of the notebook, written more hastily, consisted of vague descriptions and mythical drawings of outer worlds his father said could only be visited through accessing one's higher soul, whatever that meant.

Isaac sighed. *Meaningless but entertaining.* It helped to look over the tales and confirm how silly they were. Near the end pages, he forced the notebook closed, not wanting to feed the urge to believe in such things any longer.

In the distance, the bell rang for morning training.

It's time to let go.

Isaac gave the old leather one last squeeze before he threw the book out of the window. The book soared over the wall, some of the yellowed pages fluttering through the air, laying atop the rose petals.

For the first time in a long while, Isaac smiled. With his father and the hopeful past behind him, he could start anew.

He jumped off the dresser, slid it back to the wall, and opened its doors. He chose the cleanest of his white robes to wear. The smooth hood felt right as it blanketed him in safe disguise, but his new hood would feel even better.

The second warning bell rang as he slid his own coffer out from underneath his bed. Training would soon begin. He unlatched the golden clasps. The sleek cover lined with red velvet raised open to reveal a cluttered pile of junk. He grabbed his wooden training dagger resting on top and sifted through the rest of the items he hadn't touched in years. Toward the very bottom, amongst a group of miscellaneous buttons and thimbles, rested the iron dagger every first-year received upon their arrival at St. Daemonus.

He picked up the blade, pondering its dull edge. *Daggers were always Boyd's thing.* That would have to change, he knew, as he holstered both blades into their respective sheaths and hurried off for training.

CHAPTER 5

SECOND ERA, 113, UAIR THREE OF RISING GOLD

Rebekah

R ebekah rolled over in bed, morning light warm on her skin. It took everything she had to keep her eyes closed, but she wanted to feel the gifts of the equinox, to perceive the difference, and know for herself whether or not she'd been blessed before looking in any mirror. Hopefully, today's events would live up to the expectations she built over the last five years.

She stretched, a certain ease to her movements. Her legs felt loose, light, and free. She smiled, extending her arms to the ceiling, and inhaled a deep, full breath. The air had a distinct scent, one she recognized as the saltwater ocean. Dead fish, and the like. A hint of bitterness lingered as well, which she attributed to the aged stones said to exist deep beneath the Daemonus floors.

The idea of exploring the distant isles and spreading the Spirit's message as a St. Daemonus apostle seemed even more exciting if she indeed was blessed. The things to do on islands like the volcanic Raki

Gari and snow-white Windhaven would provide a more amazing experience than she could ever imagine, all in the name of the Great Spirit.

But you don't even know if the Spirit will bless you.

It was often hard to remind herself of the fact. The prospect of the upcoming vernal equinox overcame the forefront of her mind and brought with it anxiety like a dreary overcast.

Rebekah had paid attention to how Damascians spoke of those who weren't blessed. It was secretly her deepest fear, though she may have blessed qualities, that the Spirit would not deem her worthy for some reason, forbidding her from pastordom and shaming her to the life of a Zealot. Her friends would make up some reason for her failure, because of that failed transfiguration test in her third year, or because Balsan kissed her on the lips in her fourth, but the Spirit wouldn't deem her unworthy because of those things, would it? Knowledge of the Spirit is what matters when it comes to spreading the protection St. Daemonus and the church had to offer, nothing as superficial as what she'd done in her years before being a pastor. She was just a child. But of course, Jericho wanted them to grow out of that stage sooner rather than later.

Rebekah opened her eyes. Her sight adjusted with quickly to the early yellow light cascading through the window, approaching light orange.

Training has almost—

A scream resounded through her skull.

A thud came from her right, then another, and the sound of shattering glass followed. The sounds echoed through her head, a terrible crash and thousands of different bells like enormous chimes ringing against the stone floor.

Her sense of hearing had increased, perhaps too well.

Rebekah sat up in her bed and looked across the room, knowing what was wrong with the color of her roommate's blonde hair and how she slouched to hide her eyes. In front of her was their mirror, cracked to pieces. Now Rebekah wouldn't be able to know if the blessings had taken the curls out of her hair and made it as straight as a pastor's.

"It's okay," Rebekah said.

It most likely wouldn't be okay for her roommate Priska.

Raising herself from the bed with a marked absence of effort, Rebekah floated like a ghost to her friend. "I'm sure once you pass the test, you'll see the changes." Even her own voice sounded different now, developed and giving—like her mother. She knelt next to Priska, resting a hand on her shaking arm.

Priska had wrapped her right hand in bloody sheets. "Don't give me that..." Sobs heaved her body. "We both know I'm doomed. I'll be off Daemonus by the evening."

Rebekah struggled to find words of comfort. "I doubt you need to be that extreme." She thought to suggest joining the Zealots, a way to serve in Daemonus as one unchanged, but knew that Priska thought too highly of herself to sail the open sea or wear the same dirty cloak for weeks on end. She'd never have the humility to be amongst such savagery, and Rebekah didn't blame her.

Priska's family had been involved with the church since the first era. There were even rumors of her grandfather having aided Jericho when he fought to establish the new reign. How could someone with generations of familial ties not be chosen by the Spirit, while Rebekah was?

"It's not your fault, maybe you weren't exposed to the Spirit long enough." Rebekah crouched next to her friend, her legs nimble and loose. "Don't you remember how we imagined so many trips together on the distant coasts? We could still do so." *An apostle needs Zealots,* she thought, biting her tongue. "Look at your hair. So beautiful and healthy. With hair like this, my mother would say you'd never struggle a day in your life." She removed her hand, noting the absence of snowy white, even at her friend's roots. "I'll miss my own."

"You should be grateful," Priska said.

It hurt to see her friend so irrational. "You can still take the test.

You might be deemed worthy, receiving your blessed changes then. The Spirit could be testing you by delaying your transformation." Nothing Rebekah said was likely to help. It all sounded wrong. Early physical changes marked the main indication for whether a student would pass during the equinox, but she needed Priska to show up for training. Otherwise, she'd have to train below her level, and her routine would be entirely off. "It's worth a try. Why not show up? If you fail, you would have been shipped away anyway, but if you pass...."

Priska finally looked up. Her blue eyes had retreated into hollowness, supported by mounds of bags beneath. Rebekah couldn't help but shudder at her friend's changes. Come to think of it, she hadn't seen Priska leave her bed at all last evening.

"I trained all my life to become a pastor," Priska said, her voice a mix of hatred and jealousy. "Now that hope is gone. My years of training and dreaming were for nothing. I'll never see the Spirit again. Why would I take the test? Do you want me to make a fool of myself? They'll all laugh. I've been rejected by the Spirit. My life will be alone a-and sad, and...." Priska slammed her swollen hands onto the stone floor.

"You can still have a great life," Rebekah said. "There is the rest of Indus to explore. You're trained in the ways of the church. You can stay here if you please."

Priska laughed, short and snotty. "Once you know the way of the spirit, this world is nothing without it." She sat up straight, seemingly struck by an epiphany, and in an instant, turned onto her hands and knees and reached out from her place on the floor. Her fingers threaded through a wave of Rebekah's ice-white hair.

Rebekah flinched, grateful it wasn't Priska's bloody hand.

Her roommate's light blue eyes stared into hers with cold desperation. Her breath crackled, smelled like she'd been eating and drinking nothing. Nails slid like razor blades along Rebekah's neck.

Her dagger was just underneath her bed, in the coffer.

Priska yanked her hand back suddenly and retreated onto her unmade sheets. "Go," she said. "Leave me alone."

As if on cue, the bell for training struck, officially marking her tardy. The training instructor wouldn't mind her lateness. He favored the blessed.

"You're not coming?" She asked one last time.

"I'll never become a pastor. I can take a hint, especially one from the Great Spirit." Her balled-up form within the morning shadows looked like the epitome of misery. "Go."

Rebekah felt an overwhelming urge to drag Priska out of bed herself. "And who will I spar with? We know the common fighters aren't good enough."

"I forgot you're so good you can only have the best training partners."

She didn't want to give up on her friend, but that did it. Priska had clearly decided to become a mediocre fool. "Fine." She gathered her daggers and donned a fresh new cloak. "Have a good life, Priska."

Rebekah bounded down the hall. She ran past the library into the church's central section, catching glimpses of students within openings of the hallway arches. They gathered in groups and talked amongst one another. Training hadn't started. Relieved, she slowed to a fast walk, her breath as steady as if she'd walked the whole way. She hadn't broken a sweat.

Inside the training area, students congregated at the grass temple's bottom stair, divided by their year and friend groups, united in the white of their cloaks. Every one of them faced toward the training mound, some pointing in awe at the upper terrace.

The temple had been named the Grassy Mount, the heart and center of St. Daemonus, and one of the few monuments remaining from the first era. Each level of the six-tiered temple had perfectly manicured grass and spanned fifteen paces in width; Rebekah had been quick to learn. A sacred river ran down the temple's center, dispensing into a small lake no bigger than a well and recycling underground through way of the Spirit back up to the temple's peak.

Atop the temple's plateau, the black-cloaked training instructor, pastor Zuriel, directed chaotic Zealots as they carried cages in and out of an egg-shaped tent that others fortified. Constructed over the river, Rebekah questioned the tent's bizarre decor. Zealots and even some pastors deliberately applied a slimy substance to the walls that seemed to act as a sticky coating before others handed them colorful slabs. Upon closer inspection, courtesy of her blessed gifts, she realized the slabs were actually dragon scales, some large enough to be from a mature creature.

The legend was true. Today, Rebekah would add a scale to the tent from her own sacrificed dragon.

The tiny creatures gave faint squeaks from far behind the hill, as if they knew they would soon lose their lives.

Rebekah had heard many stories about the day of the equinox; how the blood of the sacrificed dragons flowed into the sacred river as an offering, acting as the necessary force to push the river back up the mountain so it may continue to flow from the peak and feed itself for another year. With the freshwater in front of her again, Rebekah tried imagining its segmented waterfalls flowing over the terrace's grassy steps, the color of red.

"There is the want-to-be warrior," a teasing voice interrupted from her left. She turned and saw her friends, Ezer leading the group. "Good to see you could make it."

She pointed at Ezer's bowl-cut hair. "It seems you've dipped the top of your head in some paint. You know, Damascian hair is white, not grey?" She looked at the others, who smirked. "I've seen little girls more blessed than you."

The group laughed at Ezer, and Rebekah waved shamelessly to Azarias, Uri, and Uri's little brother Oma.

"Where's Priska?" Ezer asked, disrupting the good mood.

Everyone knew Priska and Ezer had a past.

Rebekah could almost feel the air grow awkward as eyes shifted from Ezer to her.

"Maybe she didn't want to train today," Oma answered. He was a second year, and despite Uri's utter annoyance, her shadow.

"That's ridiculous," Uri corrected. "Nobody misses training on the day of the equinox."

"Tell me the truth." Ezer said. "Does she show no signs of change?"

Rebekah paused. She couldn't say it. Why couldn't she say Priska hadn't been blessed?

"I wouldn't want to show my face either." Azarias shrugged. "It's not fun to be a disgrace. Just ask the dragon-lover."

Rebekah turned to survey the field. She wanted to see the student brave enough to show up without any apparent changes.

Until now, she hadn't noticed how over half their fifth year was absent. She wondered how many of those unblessed would choose to join the Zealots or live somewhere on the other islands devoid of the Spirit. Each of the fifth-years who attended had at least a shade of white in their hair or red in their eyes. Except for the dragon-lover, standing alone near the river's edge and first terrace, watching the stream flow into the crystal lake.

She vaguely recognized him. They'd had one or two classes together. The Windhavian boy, Isaac. He hung out with the same kid, another dragon-lover. What was his name? Boy?

Boy must've been smart enough to stay in his dorm.

But Rebekah respected the Windhavian. At least he showed up for training; maybe he'll even take the test. The Spirit had to reward that kind of openness, or perhaps it was simply a lack of self-awareness. The kid had been bullied his entire life. He was probably used to the criticism that would come with failing the equinox test.

Atop the plateau, pastor Zuriel struck the gong, and the sound overtook most of the fifth years, giving them goosebumps or making them shiver. Rebekah felt the energy, too, an urge to move.

Pastor Zuriel bowed at the terrace edge. "Find your partners," he commanded. "We've had minor delays in our preparations for today's events, but that does not mean you may putter through training. On the contrary. We must be more attentive than ever. The Spirit is always watching you, but today, it is your judge."

A hum picked up as students sorted amongst themselves and walked as partners toward their designated terraced platform, first-years to the bottom terrace, and fifth-years to the fifth, nearest the plateau.

Partners...

Rebekah searched the grounds for someone around her skill level. She couldn't be picky, but there had to be someone who could fight.

Everyone had a partner and climbed up the terrace, leaving her helpless.

"On with it," Zuriel urged.

She looked to the pastor, whose gaze flitted from her to the Windhavian. "You two." Zuriel gestured for them to pair together. "Train the poor boy," he said to her.

She looked back in disbelief.

"He dared to show his face, maybe you can bless him yourself. I can assure you, the Spirit will not."

She'd have no other choice but to train with the Windhavian if she wanted Zuriel to respect her. *The quicker we start, the faster we'll be done.* With the grace of her transformation, she walked past him and started up the temple to her usual place on the high terrace.

She reached the position and looked back, aware that everyone was watching them. As Isaac climbed, even the younger students laughed at his lack of ability compared to her swift movements. He looked up with lost brown eyes as he ascended the second step. For a moment, she almost wished to somehow give him blessings of her own.

CHAPTER 6

SECOND ERA, 113, UAIR THREE OF RISING GOLD

Boyd

Like a lizard crawling along on the St. Daemonus wall, Boyd kept as far from Tempus as possible. Inside the forest, screeches sounded and cries of death echoed. The darkness was so absolute the sun's light never penetrated the trees. No matter which way he circled the church, he would eventually reach the entrance and the harbor, where he would board a ship and leave for good. The harbor provided the only way to enter and leave Daemonus.

He had chosen to go left around the church walls, it seemed to be farthest from the forest. Little did he know, the forest encroached this portion of the wall after a few paces, its pressure flattening Boyd against the stone.

The training bell rang in the distance. *It's too late to turn back.*

The grass dwindled into stick-ridden gray ground, dead down to the soil. Dagger in hand, he labored across a soft-flowing river, the water clear as day, sharply contrasted against the lack of life in the woods.

He traversed the river stone by stone. Rocks and the occasional sparkling rubies of Daemonus shimmered in the clear water, but there were no fish.

Boyd landed on a cushion of thick green grass on the other side of the bank. For the first time in five years, Boyd laid eyes on the church entrance.

Memories flooded back, most of them long forgotten. He remembered leaving his home island of Lothal, excited to arrive here. Faint images of his mother and father surfaced, nothing more than gray figures watching proudly as his ship departed.

He shrugged at the thoughts, and they went away.

A thick portcullis of brightened iron masked the church's affairs from those of the outside world, another hint of Jericho's secrecy others mistook for greatness. Two sentry towers guarded either side of the arched gateway. Hooded black-cloaks stood watch in each. They faced the school, probably watching training. In front of the gate and drawbridge, two more pastoral black cloaks laughed over some jest. It shouldn't be too hard to sneak past them all.

Another renovation that Jericho made to the church at the start of the second-era had been the two mounted obsidian statues placed on either side of the drawbridge. The sculptor carved an image of the Lord and High Priest, Usher of the Second Reign, as he slayed the ancient lava dragon, Nyros. Jericho stood triumphantly with his foot upon the last of four slain throats; the statues mirrored one another.

Anger boiled in Boyd. *There are too many lies to change.* He wanted to knock the statues over and watch them shatter. Worst of all, he remembered being scared of those dragons when he first crossed the drawbridge, admiring Jericho for his bravery, seeing him as everyone else did.

If the world knew dragons could live with humans, what would they think then? Would pastors still slaughter them without thought?

Besides, it wasn't as Isaac said. The dragons weren't friends who visited from above with holy gifts. They were creatures just like us. Perhaps there could be mutual respect, but never while humans had anything to do with the Spirit.

Before talking himself out of it, Boyd darted from the wall into dead bushes by the edge of a beaten path. Sharp thorns scraped him, leaving pale white marks as he descended near the forest edge.

The harbor looked different from his recollection. Smaller, absent of bustling ships and passionate Zealots emptying and loading cargo. The dock looked like a nasty sore. On the other hand, its beach remained the splendor Boyd had dreamed about—a pearl strip wrapping around the island, interrupted by jagged rocks and speckled with depleted crevices where jewels used to shine. Water as blue as the sky licked the shore.

The smell of the salt sea filled him with more memories. He'd been familiar with the ocean because of his work on Lothal, but never stepped foot on a ship until he boarded for Daemonus. He puked twice on the trip and gagged the rest of the time because his stomach was empty and refused to be filled. The other recruits said it was unnatural to be so allergic to the sea. They rejected Boyd and seemed to bond over mutual hatred for him and Isaac, the recruit who boarded at their first stop, alone, much further north.

The harbor was practically empty save for two ships at the far end, imperceptible if it weren't for Boyd's newly improved sight. It'd be hard to sneak aboard anything with so little going on.

Near the harbor's end, Zealots garbed in torn yellow seaware with supportive belts and sashes loaded crates of red spice onto two carrier boats, the sails drenched in an innocent yellow with the Daemonus sigil in the center. Boyd used to eat the Rikouwa spice every day when he was in the west isles, but ever since he arrived here his appetite for the tangy seasoning disappeared. If he boarded those ships, there was no doubt he'd end up back in one of the trading cities.

Home.

A bead of sweat trickled down his forehead, and he wiped it from his brow. It wouldn't be so hard to succeed in Lothal. Why did the idea seem so frightening? There were many opportunities to gain wealth in such a prosperous city. With his obvious blessings from the Lord, the citizens would give him everything and a lordship. Lothalite colonies would love a blessed one to usher in a new age— what if he could bring the island together, rich and poor? A part of him felt destined to lead. He'd be able to reveal the true malevolence of Jericho's second-era to the world after he had millions of trusted followers. With the entire west on his side, something would have to change.

His stomach turned at the thought that it had to be him; *he* must be the change.

The future prospects of wealth and power didn't make him feel better about his prospects of escape.

You're going to run away, like a coward? He couldn't stop Isaac's voice from entering his head.

Isaac would probably end up aboard one of these ships as a Zealot once he failed the test. He'd be too proud to leave the island and live a normal life. He'd rather pretend to be a part of history. In comparison, Boyd was actually doing something for Indus.

Even if he was able to sneak aboard one of the ships, Isaac was right. He wouldn't stay hidden for long. He couldn't live among crates of spice for two moon cycles, the least amount of time it would take to reach Lothal, considering that was their destination. What would he eat? He'd never heard of anyone surviving on the stems of Rikouwa's sour red stalk.

There had to be some other way to leave the island aboard one of those ships. Among the unblessed Zealot henchmen, Boyd's transformed snowy hair and fire red eyes would stick out. They'd ask why he wasn't at equinox testing. The only bad part about his blessings, pastors naturally questioned a blessed aboard a Zealot's yellow ship.

But if I acted like the gifted individual that I am.... People might think he'd been waved of the test responsibilities, sent away early, perhaps even by orders of the Lord.

And if the Zealots tried to murder him for his treachery before he reached Lothal, as Isaac predicted, that was what he had Duskfall for, nevermind the odd slingshot. He patted the knife in its sheath, ready.

A wider-built Zealot strolled across the drawbridge and down the path toward the harbor, oblivious to Boyd's watch from the bushes.

Without a sound, Boyd jumped onto the path and mimicked his gait. They marched together onto the cloud-like sand. Hot pebbles whisked at Boyd's feet. He went unnoticed by the man.

Squawks from circling white birds, louder than ever, shot like arrows through his head. *There has to be some way to turn down these heightened senses.* He wasn't sure if they were worth the frail frame he'd acquired in exchange. At the dock, the seagulls fought over wiry red spices spilling from half-open crates.

Zealots from the two ships had caught sight of Boyd, dropping their crates to crowd the rails and shoving one another for a better view.

I am a pastor, Boyd reminded himself. *I'm blessed, but I still refused to take the equinox test.*

I'm too good. That's why I don't have my black cloak. The Lord recognized this, and ordered me sent to the trading isles. Boyd filled with anxious enthusiasm, amazed by his recent bravery and hoping it held strong.

A large Zealot wearing a tricorn hat to match his size, a sole milk-white feather protruding from the upturned brim, greeted them at the dock steps.

"Captain," the heavy-set Zealot said between breaths to the man with the large hat. He bowed before the dock and rose unsteadily. "The ship from the Shatterin' Isle's arrived, and matters have been dealt with at the harbor below. We need move the cargo to the uh, cathedral, captain. I do have word from Qane that... Captain?"

The captain's cold dark gaze was set on Boyd. Scars twisted his face into a contorted mess of divots and long pink streaks. The captain didn't speak, but his lowered eyebrows conveyed one message: he would tolerate no lies.

The waddling Zealot Boyd had followed turned to see what held the captain's attention. He almost stumbled over his feet, jowls shaking as he struggled to comprehend what stood in front of him.

"What're *you* doing here?" The man asked. "Today is the day of decision." He spoke as if assuming that Boyd hadn't known.

There was no need to be afraid. The Zealots felt as unsure as he did. They'd never been blessed, and thought highly of the Lord and those blessed by him, or else they wouldn't have stayed to serve the church. Most Zealots hadn't even been inside St. Daemonus since their failed fifth-year test.

It made sense—the other ships weren't at the harbor because the more trusted Zealots were helping prepare for the equinox. This lot would probably never enter the church again, bound to the sea and their trade ships.

These are the simple ones.

Boyd read the awe and fascination in the fat man's eyes, as well as the eyes of the man with the great hat, though he hid it well. He addressed the captain. "I've come for transport."

"But he's a purebred," the messenger countered. He looked to the sky and put his fingers up to measure the sun. "It's only uair three. Training isn't over. He should be preparing for the test, to serve the Lord and Spirit."

The man filled with disdain and would have continued, but shouts erupted from the two trade ships. "Let the holy one aboard," one Zealot yelled. "Give him a taste of the real world," said another.

The captain silenced the crew with a wave, keeping his eyes on Boyd. "Who sent you?" he asked, his voice deep and tired.

"The Lord, of course." Another bead of sweat trickled down Boyd's face. He suddenly realized how hot it was on this beach, exposed to the equinox sun.

"Highly unlikely, captain," the messenger scoffed. "You know how busy the Lord is. The boy's a runaway, a deserter. An ungrateful one and a waste of blessings. We should push him out to the sea, let the Spirit decide if it needs the service of a betrayer."

"We will do no such thing," the captain said.

The messenger's face went pale and his mouth quivered as the captain descended the dock steps, moving closer to Boyd. He scoffed as he passed by the meager Zealot, resting a firm, heavy hand on Boyd's shoulder. Cracked red burns on the dry skin indicated decades at sea. The man reeked of fish and pungent Rikouwa.

Boyd wanted to shrug the hand off, forcing himself to keep calm.

"I know why you're here," the captain said.

A sense of relief washed over Boyd, followed by confusion. "You do? I mean... the Lord didn't tell me of my purpose. Just to reach the harbor."

A suspicious smile grew upon the captain's cracked lips. "Ah, that sounds right. Such is the way of the Lord and the Spirit. They're mysterious."

The chubby man stepped up between them. "Sir," he whispered. "If I may have a moment. I'm sorry, sir, but this could not possibly be of the Lord's will. You know as much as me. The boy has a duty. A *responsibility*." The Zealot's face jiggled as his eyes darted to Boyd, searching him. He reached out and clutched Boyd by the jaw, tilting his face toward the sun.

Even with his eyes closed, the red sunlight seeping through his eyelids was paralyzing.

"They'll gouge out those red pearls. Sell one for a ship of their own, the other for a crew. Do you want to lose your crew captain?" The messenger muttered something inaudible. He moved to clutch a portion of Boyd's hair and pulled hard.

Boyd gritted his teeth. Upon opening his eyes, the landscape was a mirage of fuzzy blotches. His scalp seared with pain.

He was in their control, but not weak. If he had to prove he had enough guts to make it aboard those ships, so be it. But sell his eyes, was that what the Zealot meant? Nobody would do such a thing. He only tried to scare him.

"A single strand of this would grant them a nice galley. Give them steady money fishing offshore. Otherwise, one finger will make the most powerful brew, filled to the brim with Spirit and—"

"I can take care of myself," Boyd interjected.

The messenger stepped back, looking between Boyd and the captain.

Boyd pulled his cloak to the side, revealing the ruby-colored blade of Duskfall in its sheath. "See?"

The captain's grip on his shoulder tightened.

"The Lord told me to go to the harbor and leave Daemonus aboard your ships. Don't you see that I'm blessed? My word is that of the Spirit, and you should do as I say." Saying this made Boyd's heart wrench, but the hierarchy applied outside of the church as well, for the sake of harmony. Zealots were even expected to give unblessed students their proper respect, and the Spirit would provide equal treatment in the end.

Wrinkles on the outer edges of the captain's eyes indicated regret. "You're right," he said, circling behind Boyd. "You are blessed." His hand trailed down Boyd's shoulder to his arm, then wrist.

Out of instinct, Boyd jumped forward, but the captain had him. With one smooth motion, the captain forced Boyd's arms behind his back and locked them into place.

"But we obey the Lord as well," the captain said.

Boyd tried kicking, throwing elbows, but it was no use. The moment he acquired his blessings, he'd traded most of his strength for speed and enhanced senses. The captain's grip hardly faltered.

"What are you doing? I was commanded by the Lord to be sent here."

The Zealots shouting aboard the harbor ships picked up to a roar. Some descended to the harbor, trying for a better view before the captain demanded they return to their duties. He held Boyd's arms without much attention and whistled out to the boats, a deafening sound. "Zuo, Tia." Two younger Zealots sprinted out from the crowd toward them.

"The Lord sent me. I swear it." Boyd gave a few more tugs, proving he was stuck. All these new abilities, and he couldn't escape a simple hold. If only he could reach Duskfall. *I have the skill to slay a couple Zealots, and the speed to escape.*

"A fighter," the captain said. "No wonder the Lord chose him." *Chose?*

"Are you sure he's the one?" The messenger kept a distance from Boyd like he was some unpredictable animal.

"Didn't you read the instructions?" The captain asked. He lost whatever sliver of formality had been there moments ago. "That's right, tou can't read. That's why you run messages, and I command vessels. Imbecile. The boy's eyes are redder than your blood. Care to see?" The captain whistled again, and the two younger zealots picked up their pace. "The boy just went to the wrong harbor, is all."

Boyd searched between the dense forest and endless sea, his only two options to flee. Either one meant certain death, but that was better than whatever would happen when they returned him to the church and discovered his lie.

The wrong harbor? As far as Boyd knew, there was only one harbor in all of Daemonus. What did they think the Lord chose him for? He wanted to ask about everything but had to choose his words carefully. "This was a misunderstanding. I was sent—"

"Yes, yes. You were sent here by the Lord. We do understand." The captain sighed deeply.

Boyd couldn't contain his fury—never in his life would he submit to Jericho's plans. He screamed.

"Look at him," the captain said to the messenger Zealot. "You can see the flames burning. Let me ask you, do you know why the Lord sent you to the harbor?"

That was the question Boyd needed an answer to. He calmed.

The way the fat man was looking at him, how they held him captive.... *Like some sort of animal.*

"All is well, young one. You should be happy." The captain's words grew heavy as lead. "You're the chosen sacrifice."

The word swam through Boyd's head. *For what purpose?*

The two Zealots paused at the edge of the dock, young enough to have been students with Boyd his first or second year. Each was so like the other they looked like twins—a boy and a girl. Both stared at Boyd, eyes wide and mouths agape.

"Come on then," the captain said. "You'll have your time with the blessed one on the walk to the harbor below."

The Zealots snapped into action. Each one grabbed an arm, their hold more attentive than the captain's.

"Careful," he told them. "This one doesn't know what's best for him." He walked in front of Boyd. "Surely, you won't be needing any of your fancy church weapons come tomorrow."

He prayed for the captain to reach for the slingshot, a useless thing. He wished he'd shown that off instead. But the captain removed the hilt and swirling ruby blade of Duskfall. The ringing sound of the unsheathed dagger almost brought him to tears.

"This one is a true beauty."

Boyd shot his heel at the captain's sternum and connected.

The captain staggered backward a half pace, and chuckled. "I like you." He turned to the messenger. "Never doubt the Lord. He's made an excellent choice." Unsheathing his own dagger, a sad collection of rust, he offered it to Boyd before dropping it in the sand for the tide to sweep away. He smoothed his hand along Duskfall. "No need to worry, young one. I'll take good care of her."

The captain wasn't worthy. Boyd told himself he'd see it again as the captain slipped it into his dragon-skin sheath.

"That's my dagger," was all he managed to utter.

"You think so? Strange, considering I hold it." He nodded to the younger Zealots.

They turned Boyd around and escorted him toward the path and church. Behind them, the captain joked with his messenger and yelled at the Zealots to get back to work. He wanted to go back, steal Duskfall, and use it to stab the captain.

Arms locked behind his back, being escorted back to the church posing as someone he didn't know, Boyd couldn't help but choose to focus on the larger issue.

Who had they mistaken him for? Jericho planned to use a student as some sort of sacrifice. Once Boyd reached the church, they'd figure out he wasn't the intended, and he didn't want to think about what would happen after. The rebel escapee who was friends with the Windhavian would not be treated kindly in his atonement.

He sensed that there was something greater that he didn't know, something the Lord was hiding.

The excitement and fear of his uncertainty filled him with a new purpose. He was right about the Lord all along. Jericho told the students nothing but lies. It seemed relatively common practice for him to sacrifice a student, no big deal to the Zealot captain, just like every pastor did with the unknowing dragon young.

Isaac has to know the truth before it's too late. Once he took the equinox test, he'd become one of them.

"Jericho has manipulated everyone," Boyd said as the lies and deceit took frightening shape in his mind. "All of Indus."

"You shouldn't speak of the Lord in such a manner," the boy Zealot mumbled, leaning close. They approached the thinner white sand. "He can hear you."

"Zuo," the girl whispered.

"We're not supposed to talk to the blessed, remember?"

"Right."

Smiling at him with their wide blue eyes, their teeth had already yellowed from their time spent sailing. They seemed awestruck in a way that didn't match the tight hold on his arms.

"Where is the harbor below?" he asked bluntly, using his first opportunity to take advantage of his blessings. "The captain said I went to the wrong harbor, but this is the only one on Daemonus. The rest of the island is too dangerous."

They started on the uphill path, semi-hidden from the harbor and entrance by the woods.

"You've never been there?"

"Quiet," Tia snapped, leaning across Boyd to scowl at her brother. "I don't think he's supposed to know."

"How could he have arrived there if he didn't know? Also, why keep anything from him? It's his destiny."

Boyd nodded.

"Not like he has a choice," Zuo continued. "What the Lord wishes always comes true. That's the way of the Spirit. You either submit, or it makes you submit."

Boyd slowed his pace. "You were students once. Don't you wish the Lord told you more?"

The Zealots slowed in imitation.

Zuo leaned to look at his sister, stealing a glance at Boyd. "I know I do," he said, and Boyd heard in his voice just how much he wished he'd been blessed.

Tia searched the forest around them. "He will know," she said. The dead branches and darkness of Tempus seemed to make her anxious. Something howled and she jumped. Seemingly embarrassed, she straightened her posture. "If he figures out because you tell him, I suppose that's technically according to the Lord's design. But you have to tell him yourself. " She dragged them on.

Zuo tugged at Boyd's arm. "The equinox," he whispered. "Our Lord is planning something special for today."

"How am I involved?" They were closer to the drawbridge. He could hear the conversations of the guards. It wouldn't be long until they heard them coming up the path, too. Boyd planted his foot in the ground and refused to move forward, testing their level of respect. "I deserve to know. Tell me how I'm involved with the sacrifice."

Instead of pulling him forward, the Zealots stopped. They looked at each other, and back at him. Tia seemed unable to decide, but the longing in the boy's eyes was undeniable, exaggerated by fear.

"Come on," Zuo begged his sister. "You remember the things they kept from us as students? It's like he said. We didn't even find out about the harbor below before we were Zealots."

"Yes, what is that?" At the entrance of the castle, the gate rattled open. He'd have to run into Tempus. *My old, terrible friend.* At least he was quick. It wouldn't be hard. He'd made it through the forest once already.

The boy shifted around in his tan Zealot garb, on the verge of spilling the truth.

Boyd nodded in encouragement.

He blurted, "You're to meet a grown dragon. A Chrysos."

Boyd looked to Tia for confirmation, but she didn't look as annoyed as he expected, probably because the claim was so ridiculous. If anything, Jericho wanted to avoid letting any dragons become full-grown; the risk was too great, even when they lacked wings and did nothing but breed. Jericho would kill them all if he didn't need their Spirit to shape the world.

"You're to *become* a dragon," the girl said, correcting her brother.

Before he could respond, the boy turned pale. He began gasping, choking.

At the same instant the girl's face grew ashen. Her body twitched.

Both struggled, seeming to choke on words they couldn't speak. Their hands, which had been grasping Boyd's wrists, relaxed until their arms dropped altogether, freeing him. A ruby mist filled their eyes.

Boyd retreated to the forest edge, never risking to look away. The air grew thick as he entered the Tempus fog and it was suddenly hard to breathe.

Their eyes settled soullessly on Boyd, unmoving, despite the camouflage the forest provided.

"After the sacrifice," they said in unison, voices twanged and high-pitched.

The sounds faded as Boyd forced himself to run deeper into Tempus.

It was too much, impossible to piece together. Jericho's ultimate plan wasn't as awful as Boyd thought—offering dragons, small or grown, in exchange for use of their Spirit—but much worse. Jericho wanted to fuse humans with dragons, to create a new design.

CHAPTER 7

SECOND ERA, 113, UAIR FOUR OF RISING GOLD

Rebekah

From her tier of the mossy green temple, Rebekah wished she could at least bless Isaac with the acuity of her senses, if not the red eyes and white hair of the blessed—sparing him the humiliation.

She didn't want to embarrass him by already being a better fighter, but nobody in their year had ever been able to defeat Rebekah. Under the eyes of pastor Zuriel, she wouldn't risk her role as an apostle just to save the dragon-lover the shame.

A pressure loomed over her, the stares of her classmates. Everyone watched except for working pastors and Zealots, busy fortifying the tent with its dragon scale decor. The calm blue river of Yehwa flowed up the lush temple into the black curtain entrance.

Isaac struggled onto the fifth and highest terrace and took his place across from Rebekah. Snickers arose from the students.

She remembered him clearer now, how every morning he would

scurry around the backside of the temple where those who wished to train unseen by Zuriel's accusing eye found solace. Come to think, those were the same students who didn't show up for training today.

"Be careful, young one," pastor Zuriel said from the topmost plateau of the step pyramid. "His lack of blessings may prove contagious." A knowing grin crept along the pastor's face, fading as he glanced out over the class.

Rebekah's stomach turned. Zuriel would know if she went easy on Isaac.

Why should I care? He is unblessed.

"I understand there are many nerves today." The pastor said, pacing along the grassy plateau. The tent reflected the equinox sun above him; rays of light transformed into an array of colors she'd never seen.

He stopped next to a gong hanging on twine rope amidst remnants of dragon bone. "We are at a time of division in the church. A new reign has dawned, revealing the ultimate knowledge of the Spirit to us humans. Knowledge that told us the Spirit is ours to keep. This discovery was expanded upon by your Lord and Savior, Jericho."

"Long may He reign," Rebekah said in unison with the class. She noticed Isaac had only muttered the words. *No wonder he isn't blessed.*

"Soon, the Lord's reign will complete its greatest project yet. A project the Spirit began all those years ago, imagined well before the Lord had come to fulfill his destiny. Since he was birthed and began to walk the seven isles of Indus, our Lord has worked tirelessly to provide us with new methods to live through His light."

Zuriel focused on Rebekah.

She didn't dare look afraid under his gaze.

"Today, a new light dawns for His followers. You may reap what we have sowed, a new realm, where the Spirit will reward its followers justly. To those who stay on the path, I give you this." Zuriel looked out over the class, to Tempus and the sea.

"There is one core principle that makes Jericho's authority more effective than the failure that was the first reign. At all costs, we must preserve this principle. You must be a martyr for the Spirit if you want to be a member of this church. Forget your desires and selfish cravings, rid yourself of material possessions and be willing to sacrifice your soul.

"We do not train in the ways of combat because we fight often. The days of dueling with dragons, watching as your companions are incinerated on the field next to you, knowing your fate is next, their stench lingering in your dreams..." The composed nature of Zuriel's anger made him seem dangerous, unpredictable. "Those days are over. Jericho has created a peaceful world, free of terrible monsters. The Lord banned the unblessed use of the Spirit, and allowed for the chosen to rise, creating a better world in his vision.

"In position," he called.

On the other side of the tier, Isaac took a dueling stance. The class laughed, some mocking his movements as their own pose. The boy seemed unphased, but Rebekah felt sorry for him. Unfortunately, he was going to give his best effort.

With a deep breath, she entered her posture. But something was different today. Never had her movements felt so swift. Her body maneuvered precisely to her command.

She couldn't help but smile.

"This is the way of the spirit." Zuriel's voice echoed through the brisk morning air. He raised the mallet above the gong and dragon bone. "Keep our values in mind, teach them to your sons and daughters until we reach our ultimate state of perfection, of pure Spirit. This is the principle of the second reign."

Zuriel swung the wool mallet with force.

Isaac rushed her, catching her off guard with a high, sideways kick.

His attack lacked execution, and his foot soared overhead.

She ducked underneath and circled behind him.

He swiveled around, searching.

Other students began fighting, settling into their sparring

sessions. With their eyes focused elsewhere, Rebekah had a chance to relax.

Isaac found a second attack posture and ran at her, shuffling to a stop paces away. Wooden dagger drawn, he attacked with a flurry of slices and punches.

She managed to block or dodge every attack, rolling out of the way on his last jab.

Isaac's chest rose and fell.

Her breath was steady.

Not quick enough.

"Boring and unemotional," Zuriel declared from the terrace. "We are not here to practice dodging, young one. Fight the boy."

She cursed Zuriel under her breath.

Isaac grunted and ran toward her with a new burst of energy.

His next strike, a long swinging hook from the right, met her raised forearm. She swept his legs, sending him flat onto his stomach.

Zuriel erupted. "Ha! She is much faster. Switch up your movements, young one."

Isaac groaned as he rolled onto his back.

She reached out her hand, taking the opportunity to whisper under Zuriel's jeering. "Don't attack so hard. Have control."

There was something like gratitude in his face, a shimmer of hope.

She helped him up. "We have to make it seem real."

Isaac pushed her far away, given her lack of strength.

In two leaps, Rebekah was around his side, undetected. *This is too fun.* She threw an instinctive kick at his exposed side, checking the blow at the last moment. She hardly connected but with a tap.

Isaac caught her foot in his arm, then twisted.

Rebekah couldn't help but give, falling to the ground. She landed on her palms and the tips of her toes.

Zuriel was silent. The students' fights stopped around her.

Soon Isaac stood over her, his hand outstretched. "Who said you needed to go easy?"

Rebekah flipped to her feet. *He took advantage of my sympathy. He knocked me down when I wanted to help.*

She bounded across the training section to where he stood next to the river. His defensive posture exposed thousands of potential attacks. Any series of strikes against the dragon-lover would render him helpless.

A few momentary fakes, and she landed a forward kick to the his sternum.

He stumbled back, almost falling off the tier—unprepared for the pure technique she possessed.

Rebekah huffed, stepped back, and pushed aside a strand of white hair.

At the edge of the river, Isaac gave her a curious look. It quickly faded into clear resentment, and he attacked.

She blocked his arm at the last moment, his heavy strike disorienting.

They entered into a grapple, the exact place she wanted to avoid.

He tried to sweep her leg.

She dodged in time.

"Why did you show up today?" she asked through clenched teeth.

He wrapped his hands around her arms and, in a snapping motion, threw her to the ground.

She recovered swiftly, sliding around him to land a heel kick to the middle of his back.

Stumbling a few steps forward, Isaac planted a foot and turned back. With a glance to pastor Zuriel, they circled each other, close.

"I want to be a pastor," he said under his breath.

The honesty moved her. How could he be so ignorant of his chances? Knowing herself a fool, she considered reasoning with him once more. She felt bad for giving up on Priska and storming off. *An apostle must encourage followers of the Spirit.*

"You want to be a pastor," she said. "Yet you show no signs of change. Some would call that idiotic. Some would say—"

Before she could finish, Isaac delivered a series of kicks and punches in a perfect approach, one she recognized, though there were slight variances in the rhythm and placements. The patterns became predictable.

Just listen to me.

They struck at each other back and forth, Rebekah keeping a steady push, making no significant attacks. She could feel Zuriel's eyes watching her, judging, and she performed worse because of the watchful eyes. Isaac's kicks were slow and obvious, but they remained powerful. Her forearms bruised, stinging from her blocks.

Zuriel struck the gong again. Their fight paused and Rebekah risked a glance around the temple. Students on the lower tier abandoned their training and gathered in small groups. Fifth years pointed and whispered. She saw Ezer forming a group.

The fight was a show for them.

Zuriel continued striking the tone, a soft beating rhythm in the gong's low frequency. She could feel the air warping around her, a whirlpool of clashing sound.

Isaac approached, wielding his dagger.

She drew a deep breath and reminded herself to let go. Give in to the fight.

Her hands tingled with a strange warmth.

The continuous drum of the gong made it easier and easier to give in.

If they want a show, so be it.

Rebekah pressed Isaac back, approaching him directly.

If he wants a fight, so be it.

His strong stance didn't falter.

Zuriel picked up the pace of the gong, the volume.

In a steady progression, she attacked. Isaac met each strike with an equal block. She increased the complexity of her strikes. Expert maneuvers, impossible to her yesterday, came as natural as drawing the church sigil.

Isaac retreated with his arms raised. Defensive moves sturdy, he played to his strength as an unblessed.

Students called out, told her to end it and crush the dragon lover without mercy.

She backed Isaac into the corner near the river and terrace edge. Muscles aching, she could see in his pained expression he couldn't take much more.

"Stop," he said between strikes. "Please."

She grimaced, attacking harder. *He wants to quit when it is clear I'll win.*

This is what you get for challenging me openly.

His arms slackened with every strike she delivered. The back portion of his cloak soaked into the river. His left foot stood sideways, halfway off the terrace.

She paused, the gong's tone coursing through her like a second heartbeat. Isaac took the opportunity to raise himself, and in that instant, she landed a punch to his exposed chest.

The remainder of his defense broke, and he stumbled off the terrace edge. Students on the tier below jumped away. An audible huff left Isaac as he slammed against the ground.

The gong stopped, ending on one loud, solitary note.

Smiling, Rebekah was surprised to feel out of breath. She dropped to her knees.

Her classmates backed away with wide eyes.

"This is the way of the spirit," Zuriel said.

She could still hear the low hum, the gong, so sweet she could fall into the sound.

"End of sparring," Zuriel declared.

Isaac had picked himself up and left before Zuriel could give his end-of-the-session speech. Nobody watched him walk away; they were too obsessed with Rebekah—but she watched the poor boy, noticing a distinct sorrow and defeat that hadn't been present before.

That didn't sit well with her, but she'd have to get used to doing whatever the Spirit requested, even if it meant defeating others. *There will always be those who are blessed and those who are not.*

Zuriel told them to go to the dining hall. Afterward, the fifth-years were to meet back at the temple come High Gold for their equinox test, while younger years occupied themselves in their respective rooms for the afternoon and evening.

As Rebekah descended from the highest tier, it felt as if she was coming down from a mountain, a peak where few had gone.

"You did nothing wrong," Azarias said, catching up to her.

Was it so obvious she'd been discouraged? It seemed useless to pretend to be happy. "I humiliated him."

"Not much more than he's used to."

Rebekah looked at him with a side glance. "Do you think there's a chance he could become blessed when he takes the test?"

Azarias was quiet. "I'm not sure. It hasn't happened in ages. Most people don't risk the embarrassment."

He was being polite.

Ezer greeted them at the temple's base. "Struggled a bit?" He smiled at Rebekah. "You did right, though. One less failure we'll have to deal with. You know what I always say? Better not to show your face than be deemed a disgrace." Some laughed. "Hopefully, he's learned by now."

"He just wants to serve the best way he can," she said.

"That's not his choice," Ezer said.

Rebekah couldn't deny the truth of the statement. *What matters is what the Spirit needs. It is all so much bigger than us.*

She entered the lunch hall while recalling the despair in Priska's cry earlier that morning. Her friend's cold, shaking fingers stung as they brushed through her white hair. Priska had cursed the Lord and Spirit for being so unjust. Such a curse would be punishable by expulsion if Zuriel or any other pastor overheard.

CHAPTER 8
SECOND ERA, 113, HIGH GOLD

Isaac

Rather than sit in the refectory to eat his meal, Isaac gulped down his chowder in the gem-studded halls and walked amongst lonely halls for the rest of the lunch period, waiting to hear the tone striking at High Gold, signaling fifth-years to report to the training temple for the equinox test.

They might be right about him. He didn't know enough to deserve to be blessed. Yet he'd deal with the failure as it came. If it came.

If only he hadn't buried himself in his father's notebook the past five years, mind lost in the world of dragon riders and creatures that could feel human emotions. The different realms and creatures of his father's notebook were a thousand times more interesting than the intricacies of draconic body structure and what Boyd rightly called "conformity training," taught by strict second-era pastors.

But the more he thought about it, his knowledge of the first-era

60

seemed like an advantage. His roots were steeped in writings about dragon behavior. There could be many uses for someone who knew how a dragon would act in different scenarios. If he attained a position of authority, he might be able to convince the others that dragons weren't their enemies. *What would the Spirit think of that?*

Perhaps Isaac would get used to the idea of worshipping something bigger than himself. His father spoke of the concept, be it in some underdeveloped, first-era way. *Embrace where you are led,* he wrote.

As Isaac passed the library, his confidence grew. The Acocia gem's story used to be his favorite, how the breath of a thousand dragons forged the oldest stone in Indus, refining it throughout millennia deep within the highest mountain, the Snow Tower. The peak, also known as the Breath of the World, stood shrouded in clouds on Isaac's home island of Windhaven. Today would be his first step toward making things right in the church. He'd forge a destiny of his own.

The tone sounded for High Gold.

—

Isaac paused in the middle of the training yard once he realized everyone had been waiting for him. The others stared down from the top plateau, only half of the twenty students from his fifth-year class—those who showed signs of becoming blessed. Zuriel, cloaked in all white, stood in their midst. Behind them, the sacrificial tent reflected the rays of High Gold like a misshapen gem. The shadow cast by the sun moved like a serpent wriggling its way up the tiers. Legend said that at High Silver, it would slither back down.

The rising Spirit. A surge of excitement rushed through him. *Father never mentioned its details.*

"Young one," Zuriel shouted. "Do you expect us to wait for an unblessed?" Next to the tent, Zuriel and the soon-to-be blessed fifth-years looked like they were from another world, with their shadowy spectral figures.

"No, pastor." Isaac plodded up the tiers, right beside the snake shadow. The river running through the Temple's center was no more than a dry strip of mud.

At the plateau, Ezer shook his head in exaggerated amazement, nudging his friends. The white tips of his hair boasted of inherent blessedness. The only one who didn't seem astonished by Isaac's appearance was Rebekah. When he caught sight of her, she looked away, her eyes sorry, as if she was sure he'd fail.

"I believe you're the last to arrive," Zuriel said.

Isaac wiped sweaty hands on his cloak. All eyes were on him. It was his first time on the highest plateau. The wind was free. It had been years since he'd seen the sea and smelled the bitter salt. He couldn't believe the time had come, wondering if he was dreaming.

"I'm speaking to you." Zuriel placed a hand on his whipping stick.

"Sorry, pastor. I got distracted."

"This tends to happen when you dine alone, head in the clouds. This is your judgment day, not mine. Don't apologize to me. From this moment on, your own actions will define you."

Zuriel walked to the entrance of the egg-shaped tent where a heavy black curtain hung. "You are the only student who shows no sign of receiving blessings. Tradition states those who show no signs of natural connection must be the first to demonstrate loyalty, for fear of compromising the faith."

"Yes, pastor." The wind blew harshly for how pleasant the day was. Isaac felt naked as the class stared at him. He'd rather have a suit of armor than the thin cloak he wore now; every eye was a dagger.

Zuriel peeled the curtain back, barely far enough for Isaac to enter.

Unfathomable darkness stretched in every direction of the tent's interior. The faint odor of burned wood lingered. Parallel torches stood as stilts twice his height, lining a single path forward. A sole purple flame hovered atop each one.

The path led to an enormous rock at the center of the void, the path of the dry river running around its left side. Smooth and black-ish-green, the slab had to be obsidian. The flat surface titled on one-half into a downward ramp, bathed by shadows.

Over the edge of the slab's tilted end, a deep well expanded into forever, swallowing the dry river's end.

Zuriel suddenly emerged from the darkness and slammed a cage onto the level portion of the stone. Cries from a scared, desperate animal responded.

Isaac dug his nails into his palms, bit his tongue, anything to keep his eyes away from the creature.

Impersonal, he reminded himself. He looked at Zuriel.

That wasn't any better. The pastor's face wrinkled at the nose, sneering, probably aware of how scared Isaac was. With a detached sigh, Zuriel stared up to the top of the tent.

Isaac followed, noticing a circular hole—a portion of the clear blue sky. It provided the sole light in the room aside from the torches, warmer near the slab.

"Great spirit of the seasons, purveyor of souls, will you bless this young one with a higher calling?" Zuriel spoke matter-of-factly. He struck a match, but dropped it onto the slab and struggled to pick it up.

The second strike worked and he lit a bundle of twigs and leaves, wafting the mini-torch over the slab. Soot smoke carried up through the hole.

"Great Spirit of the Land, will you accept this soul's offering from Isaac of Windhaven, and use such power to bestow energy upon him, so he may see the world in its purest form? Judge him in your light and in the dark. Is this one a servant of yours?"

Am I?

The dragon crashed against the side of the cage. Zuriel slammed on the metal with his free hand. He reached into his cloak and presented a stick of white chalk. "Draw our sigil."

Isaac's hands were freezing, shaking. The odd interior threw off his perceptions. Light from the torches and sky exposed him in the center of a vast black void. His attention swam from stone to chalk to slab—not the dragon—to Zuriel, and he fumbled for the chalk.

His sketch of the outer edge of St. Daemonus's eye came out looking more like an uneven fish on the dark stone. Isaac depicted the pupil in the center, stepped back to make sure it was correct: two curved lines drawn horizontally, an oval in the upper middle. He added the lines of detail unique to the church of Daemonus and set the chalk down. Zuriel was right. As he stepped back and contemplated the chalk marks against the stone surface, it felt like the eye was judging him with the knowledge of thousands of sacrifices.

The blessed pastor fiddled with the cage lock. The door swung open with a creak.

Isaac worked up the courage to glance at the creature, careful not to look into the eyes. Zuriel's hand groped at the corner of the cage. Isaac caught glimpses of a silvery, terrified thing covered in its own feces, immobilized by pain.

The cage shook, a tiny squeal emitted from Zuriel's cupped hands. He smacked the creature on its head so it went dumb and dropped it onto the stone, smudging the chalk with its filth. Head swiveling, the creature shivered as it tried to stand. The dragon fell to its stomach, too weak. Isaac couldn't determine the species because it was so malnourished. The wings were sharp and refined like a blade.

He determined he didn't want to know. *Impersonal.*

"Conduct the sacrifice," Zuriel said as he returned to the shadows. "Dragon-lover."

Isaac grabbed the creature off the stone. He had waited to hold a dragon all his life, but never like this. The bones were spaced far apart, which made it frail and difficult to hold.

From his waist, he removed his dagger, the sound of his leather sheath a whisper over the subtle tone of the gong, striking beat by beat.

Thum.

Thum.

Thum.

Deep voices singing in harmony joined the underlying sound, seeming to move closer. Isaac's eyes had adjusted enough to see another pastor sitting across from him and the stone. A wooden board was positioned over his legs, and he plucked at what appeared to be glowing purple strings, the same substance as the flames, woven between extravagant motions of his hands and fingers.

The dragon wiggled, almost escaping Isaac's grip.

He focused on the silver form in his hand. A lump formed in his throat.

"Are you going to take the test or not, young one?" Zuriel spoke from the shadows.

The gong pounded on. The other instrument, sounding like voices, grew louder, singing wordless hymns.

"Yes, pastor."

Isaac felt dazed. Shapes and figures seemed to move within the dark, dancing with the music, laughing at him.

"Take the test," Zuriel said. "Take the test or walk out knowing you've disappointed the Great Spirit."

Isaac looked down. The dragon was barely alive. He'd be doing it a favor.

Those tempting, ritualistic voices dug into him, tearing out his truth. He was scared. That's why he'd loved the dragons. It was just a way to run from responsibility.

Not anymore.

Isaac shook as he placed the creature toward the end of the stone. Its head hung over the descending edge. He brought the quivering dagger to the exposed skin under its throat, where scales did not grow.

The dragon gave one last squeal and a mediocre push for escape.

Isaac closed his eyes and pictured wisps rising around him. He saw himself with white hair and red eyes.

Blessed.

He punctured the dragon's neck, sliding the blade through, but it caught halfway.

The instruments and singing ceased.

He tugged.

Under his hand the animal twitched, giving a final whimper. A gush of red burst forth from its mouth. Dribbles of the hot blood seeped over his hand and he shrank back. The dragon's body fell limp.

Isaac dropped the body and dagger onto the stone. The blood trickled down the narrow drain carved within the obsidian surface, into the dry river's well.

Silver wisps, locked within the dragon's scales, rose like steam. Trails of the ghostly air danced around Isaac's body in ethereal bands, circling him, though he felt nothing. Some of the wisps faded as they formed a crown atop his head, others followed the trail of blood.

Isaac peered over the stone and into the abyss. To his surprise, he could see farther than before, though he didn't know whether to accredit the sight to blessings or the wisps. At the bottom of the well, a spring was hidden inside a cavern. Droplets of the red blood created even waves in the water.

It was so quiet, Isaac could hear the fifth-years busying themselves outside. He also listened to his heart beating, the slow trickle of dragon blood down the slab. It smelled sweet.

Everything was so clear. Maybe he was blessed.

Zuriel removed the creature's body from the stone and vanished back into the shadows. Isaac focused on the blood instead. He could almost see himself in the reflection, thin and muddled.

He couldn't believe he killed a dragon. It didn't seem real, or near as hard as he expected. He hardly believed the sacrifice happened.

The ground beneath him rumbled, vibration tickling his feet. For a moment, he doubted what he'd done, that some force of the Spirit might be angry with him for his lack of blessings, then he heard the sound of flowing water outside the tent. Students laughed and shouted.

"He actually did it."

The sacred river flowed in subtly from under the black curtain at the entrance, having resumed its backward motion up the temple. The water rushed by Isaac's feet, clear and fresh, crashing against the slab to split around the side and restart its cycle back into the well.

Zuriel returned from the shadows. His eyebrows bent when he saw Isaac.

"Am I blessed?" Isaac believed he'd done everything right. He'd even started the river.

"Your test is complete," Zuriel said, with a curt nod. "Send in the next student."

He had to be changed. Zuriel would've wanted the luxury of crushing his hopes if he wasn't. Still, he'd have to see the reaction of the others to be sure.

He walked alongside the river, flowing as strong as ever, a hint of red in the crystal blue water.

There were no more dancing forms in the torches. The voices of the odd instrument were as quiet as the gong. A glance over Isaac's shoulder proved the musician pastor was gone. Just the glowing purple lights, Zuriel, and darkness.

His classmates' murmurs grew louder near the black curtain. The blinding light of the High Gold equinox sun leaked through. Isaac reached out, drew the curtain aside, and couldn't help but look for the expressions of his fellow fifth-years.

CHAPTER 9

SECOND ERA, 113, HIGH GOLD

Rebekah

T he black curtain of the tent folded open, and the dragon-lover walked out looking the same as when he entered. Hopeful eyes scanned the crowd. It seemed he thought he'd be blessed.

"My new favorite Zealot," Ezer said. "I'll see you at the harbor, then. Have fun loading my things. I pack heavy."

The laughter began, and Isaac's eyes fell to the running river of the Temple.

Rebekah kept silent. *I can't be around this immaturity a moment longer.*

It looked like the failed student would charge Ezer, but he ran down the temple steps, tripping on the last tier to cause more laughter.

Rebekah sighed, and walked toward the tent.

Zuriel emerged as she reached the curtain. "Quiet, quiet. That could be any of you. As far as I can tell, there are no pastors here." That managed to quiet the class. He glanced down at Rebekah. "Except for you. What makes one so eager to receive judgment?"

"I have waited for years," she said. "It's my time."

Zuriel gave her a proud nod and pulled the curtain aside to let her pass.

Darkness inside the tent felt oppressive. Her eyes took a moment to adjust. Thick, musky smoke tickled her nostrils, itching her throat. The walls of the tent seemed to expand, a blank field of purple and black mist stretching to infinity.

I am in the presence of the Great Spirit. Amazement replaced her anxiety. She knew what to do. *I am more prepared than anyone in my year. I will pass.* Zuriel basically as much at training.

The pastor entered and brushed past her. He made his way to an immense obsidian slab, illuminated by the sun shining through an oculus in the spiral ceiling. When she approached the rock, she felt chosen—free to fulfill her purpose.

"I know you are prepared," Zuriel said. Purple flames dancing in the torchlight cast moving shadows on his face.

"Yes, pastor." She placed her hand on the cool stone and felt a connection. Obsidian symbolized strength and darkness, honor and death, its use limited to prestigious rituals. Rebekah had always loved the stone's glow, but with her newly acquired blessings, the darker swirls hypnotized her. The rock seemed crafted and wise— old, older than she could fathom.

"I didn't expect you to volunteer so early." Zuriel bent and cupped water from the river, rinsing dry blood off the stone's surface. "I thought you might take a wiser approach. Wouldn't you prefer to watch for capable souls who might serve beneath you? Every shepherd needs their flock." He rested his hand on top of an iron-barred cage and looked at her as if they shared some intimate knowledge.

Rebekah couldn't think of what to say. She used to be sure Priska would be her first-hand, but that became a lost hope this morning.

She regarded the miniature creature the size of her hand harbored inside the metal cage. Its eyes were closed. Only two legs protruded from its torso.

Zuriel cleared his throat. "I know," he said. "Birth defects have been an issue with the latest batches. Some say it's the age of the dragons we breed, how we care for them, or the fact we breed siblings. I say we've never been able to rely on the creatures. But such a need will be over soon enough. Besides, you already display blessings possessed by the most experienced apostles. You do not need a high-quality sacrifice. This is a mere formality, young one. You must take the same vow as every other student. The Great Spirit makes no exceptions."

"What if I don't want to work with any of the others?" Rebekah asked, sure she didn't speak out of turn. "That's why I chose to commit the sacrifice so early. I couldn't be around them another second. None of them are like me, pastor. Or, I'm not like them." She thought it best not to mention how she hadn't cared about her friend's lack of blessings either. At this point, she just wanted to be the greatest and nothing else. "They're all just so... I don't know—"

"Immature," Zuriel finished.

"Yes. And incapable."

The pastor nodded, seeming to understand. "Do not be troubled by feeling this way. It is the truth. You may say you don't feel superior to the other students, but my records indicate something different. You are humbling yourself. You are the very thing our church needs."

"What about the Spirit? What does the Spirit need?"

"The church *is* the Spirit, and the Spirit is the church. Each is part of a greater whole, and thus the whole itself. Think of waves in the ocean. A single wave is at the same time the ocean, and something of its own."

A choir's soft hum picked up. Rebekah asked, "Is anyone else here?"

"Does it matter? You are not here to gaze upon others." Zuriel flattened wrinkles on his cloak with his hand. "We shall discuss these matters after your initiation." Zuriel unlocked the cage door. "On with it."

The thought of someone watching her made the butterflies return. *There is nothing to worry about. It is my time.*

Hundreds of voices sang the same note at once. As Zuriel fumbled with the lock, Rebekah scanned the open space, trying to locate the singing. Across from her, a man sat on a stool in the dark fog. A brown board lay balanced on his knees, and his arms moved expertly as he wove intricate threads of purple-hued, ghostly strings in rhythm with the changing pitch and volume of the choir. Robes of pearl white hid his figure, gold-trimmed edges lining the hood and sleeves.

"Got you." Zuriel threw the dragon from the cage and it rolled onto the slab.

She wasn't expecting the creature to be so revolting. The dragon limped about on two front legs, lower body slinking behind, where hind legs should be. *And it would grow to be a dumb savage.*

Zuriel handed her a piece of chalk and she drew the sigil of St. Daemonus next to where the dragon tried to stand. Its front legs couldn't hold long enough. Something about the dark rock seemed to keep it there. Under the watchful eye of the Spirit, she withdrew her dagger. The blade was a gift from her unblessed parents, given to her when they sent her away to Daemonus. *They would be proud.*

The singing of the choir in the distance grew in volume, and the gong repeatedly struck a low note somewhere close.

Rebekah picked up the dragon, feeling its faint heartbeat against her palm. It breathed in quick gasps, each audible because of her ever-growing blessings. A slippery coat covered the beaten scales, faintly resembling their original pale color. *More unique, more potent than the finest of gems,* she remembered from class.

At the far end of the room, the musician spun and wove the ghostly strings faster as the countless voices maintained perfect harmony. Mesmerized, Rebekah felt cold as the obsidian as she held the dragon out over the church insignia, where the stone slanted off toward the sacred well.

Zuriel recited a series of prayers to the Spirit.

The eye she'd drawn seemed to watch as she placed the blade beneath the dragon's neck, needle-like scales pricking at her wrist. As Zuriel's prayer ended, her excitement grew.

She sliced the soft skin.

Blood leaked. The music stopped in a gasp of silence. The dragon squirmed, gradually losing life in her hand. She watched as thick red fluid spurted, accompanied by a sweet, pleasant smell like candy roses. Light pink wisps rose from the dragon's scales, enveloping Rebekah in a wondrous cloud before evaporating.

From what she knew of the textbooks and rumors, being wrapped in the dragonic soul's remnants meant she was blessed. If her hair and eyes changed entirely white and red, leaving no sign of her unblessed self, the transformation would be confirmed. A wave of serenity rushed through her. Her muscles relaxed.

Zuriel took the limp dragon from her hand. "Well done."

She forced a smile as he disappeared into the dark.

Closing her fingers in and out, she didn't feel much different. When she looked up, the musician stood before her, on the other side of the stone.

"Have I passed?" she asked.

No reply.

Zuriel returned, holding another cage, a white dragon inside. "Your test was complete before you made the sacrifice. As I said, it was a formality."

She still needed to prove herself. "Right. I'm blessed then. Thank you, pastor Zuriel. And?" She gestured to the musician, trying to get his name.

After the silence, she looked back to Zuriel, whose face had gone expressionless.

"You don't seem to understand, young one. Nobody has ever been as blessed at your age, not even our Lord. You are capable of so much, and so much you will learn in time." The pastor looked around him. "Doesn't it feel great to illuminate the darkness? Inside this tent, an unblessed would see no further than the torchlights."

"How?"

"Young one, there are other realms around you. The Spirit operates in a thousand ways at once, most of them imperceptible to the bare human eye. With your new blessings, you are only beginning to discover these realms and their influence on the world around you. Those who lack blessings find themselves limited, subdued to the middle realm."

Rebekah tried to understand, searching about the tent. "So, is this...?"

"When you stepped inside this tent, you entered the realm you will come to know most dearly. It serves the essential purpose of alignment. This is the Spirit's will, the same as the churches' and the Lord's, mine and yours. Every time you feel something harmful, wrong, or unjust, this means there is a misalignment of the most important realm with our own. It is up to our church to end this unnecessary suffering.

"Who else do so so, but our Lord Jericho? He has spent his entire life discovering the best ways to align the realms, something the dragons kept secret in ages past, trying to keep us weak and suffering. They wanted to rule over us with the power of the realms, as if they were the Great Spirit themselves."

Zuriel seemed to want Rebekah to say something. She struggled for words. "It's amazing, but I'm not sure if I understand."

"You don't. Not truly."

"Is that why you never told us these things as students? Younger students wouldn't have the mind to grasp the greater will of the Spirit?"

"Few of us ever do. You will always find in the world those who are blessed, and those who are not. Sometimes you will know just by looking at the person, even before they've taken their vows and dedicated themselves to the Spirit. The Spirit is strong with few and neglects many. You must worry only about yourself. You are meant to be an apostle, to enforce the divine will. The Great Spirit put you here, now, though we may not know why. We hardly ever do. The Spirit works in mysterious ways. This you'll come to know as well.

"It was an honor to have you as my student. But now, you are an apostle and must act like one. You would do well not to take the power of the realms lightly. The second era has discovered nothing ordinary. It is true power, and it resides in you. You only need to surrender. Look."

The musician pointed a finger out of the cream-colored cloak toward the pool of blood on the slab.

"See your true form," Zuriel said.

Rebekah peered into the red pond. Her reflection swirled for a moment, then became clear. An image of herself stared back.

Instead of olive skin, peach scales overlapped her old face. No, it wasn't her. Two horn-like spikes took the place of hair, and her eyes shone a blinding red.

She jumped back and reached to her face, grateful to feel skin and soft hair. "What was that?"

"The Spirit you've awakened inside of you," Zuriel said. "Most blessed students would now undergo a few lessons regarding the various realms and their relation to the Spirit, but you are not most students." Zuriel gave a knowing glance to the musician beside him. "We feel you have a much greater purpose."

The man dropped the calm, resting hold at the center of his stomach and lowered his hood. As the sleeves lowered, they revealed solid, rough knuckles adorned with gem-filled rings.

Her heart stopped when she realized Lord Jericho stood next to her. It took everything she had not to yelp. She fell to her knees and lowered her head in praise. "An honor, my Lord."

"Stand," Jericho said, his voice a dreary note.

She dared to look upon his face. It felt just like the eye of the Spirit, watching her movements, knowing her thoughts. She wouldn't disappoint. "My Lord. I apologize for not showing my respects. I didn't know."

The Lord bowed in return. "It was an honor to watch your transition. You are certainly gifted. We've waited years for this day to come, and now, here you are—one of our own. I wanted to thank you personally, and take the time to ask something of you myself. I feel as if even the smallest orders must be understood on both ends, if one expects a predictable outcome."

Rebekah looked between Zuriel and the Lord, struggling to believe this was real. She noticed her mouth was open, and closed it. All she ever wanted was to serve directly under Jericho. "Anything, my Lord."

"You are a loyal servant." He walked around the stone, closer to Rebekah. He smelled fresh. "The church is my passion. My greatest love. We all have one. It's what keeps us going as humans in this forsaken realm.

"You are my most promising student, my hope for the future. I can give you the realms," he said. "All of them. You would be my most trusted follower, performing crucial duties of realignment, allowing the Spirit to flow through all as one. No soul needs to suffer under my reign, and I will not allow it. I only ask one thing before trusting you entirely. One may say this is your real test.

"Is the church your true passion?"

The space was silent, unemotional, and hypnotic. The void pressed into her with a pressure all too great. "I will serve the church with my life," she said.

Jericho inhaled deeply. "I see it in you. A blessed apostle. You are destined for greatness." He donned his hood. "The Spirit hides its answers just beyond your grasp. One may never know the meaning of their life until it is over. The soul goes on many journeys, these we will teach you.

"As pastor Zuriel stated, our teaching methods mimic those of the Spirit. Listen closely to what I say, and it will guide you." Jericho's hands met again at his waist, and it almost looked like there was nobody inside the cloak. Just two floating eyes and golden chains.

"When the equinox occurs, access between realms is more natural than otherwise. It is our best opportunity to try to unite all realms as one. You will play a crucial part in this operation. Do you hear me when I say there is more than one harbor at St. Daemonus?"

"Yes," she responded, trying to remember every little word. "I hear you."

"You are to reach this harbor the same way every other member of the church does. I will not have my pastors complaining of favored treatment. Speak with the library pastor, Nim. He will show you the way."

Before she could say anything, Jericho faded back into the shadows.

Speak to the library pastor. That was simple enough, but everything else happened so fast. Within moments, she was a high-ranking pastor. She needed to pause for a breath. "Can I gather my things?" she asked Zuriel. "Say goodbye to my friends?"

His face bent in anger; she made a mistake. "Know your place, young one. When the Lord gives you a command, it is your duty to act without—"

"Allow it," the voice of Jericho interrupted. "The Spirit encourages relationships. You would do well to learn this yourself, Zuriel."

The pastor's head fell.

"Say goodbye to your friends," Jericho said. "But make haste to visit the harbor below before the end of High Gold."

That was hardly any time. She had to move quickly. "Thank you, my Lord."

Leaving the tent, Rebekah couldn't believe her luck. The other students ran up to her, adoration and jealousy in their voices. She tried her best not to let it go to her head, but the Spirit chose her.

Uri and Azarias caught her eye. They complimented her but were distracted when Zuriel called Uri to be next.

Rebekah's trek through the empty halls was surreal. Everything seemed more vivid. The stone steps had a sort of inanimate life, the gems telling stories of a thousand years ago. *If I had time, I'd stop to listen to them all.*

When she returned to her room, Priska was gone. *So much for saying goodbye.* With her new blessings and Priska's lack thereof, it wouldn't have been the same.

She went to sharpen her dagger while Uri finished her test, stopping at the sight of a glossy black cloak folded on her bed.

It fit perfectly.

She transitioned her dagger into the new sheath of her pastor's cloak and went to look at her blessings in the mirror. Glass shards reminded her that Priska had punched it to pieces.

CHAPTER 10

SECOND ERA, 113, UAIR ONE OF FALLING GOLD

Boyd

C old wind tore through Boyd's cloak. He shouted for help, once, preferring to escape from the clutches of the pastors at St. Daemonus rather than suffer the hell of Tempus, but nobody came to his aid. After all, the forest was forbidden.

The empty silence that returned his call had confirmed the fact. Though, in the distance, Boyd thought he heard children's laughter, and the soft clinging of bells.

Stumbling back the way he came, Boyd had the idea to track his route with marks on the trees. He found a sharp rock and made a tally mark on one of the larger trees that had taken its roots before a bog—a single tan slit on the dead white bark.

Set on going *straight* so he could at least reach the island's edge, Boyd walked another few hundred paces and found himself back at the bog, standing before the tall, marked tree. Somehow, without taking a single turn, he had arrived at the same place in the center of Daemonus.

He carved a second slash in the tree and continued. No luck. The fog grew thicker and the ground softer, like stepping through patches of quicksand. His sandal caught in the mud and he tugged it away with a pop and gargled bubbling as the slime settled.

He stumbled upon the bog a sixth time. Looking up through the all-consuming trees at the sky, day had fallen to night. *I've only been walking a few hours?*

High-pitched laughter returned to accompany his sixth departure—terrifying whines of merriment, giddy.

When he arrived in front of the bog a seventh time, and the towering dead tree stared down at him with its marks, Boyd knew he wouldn't take another lap. He feared sinking waist-deep into Tempus to be buried in the soil forever; the volume of the twisted, youthful laughter would make his ears bleed. Even if he managed to make it through the mud, water, and shadows, he'd just end up here again, in front of the bog.

He dropped to his knees before the tall gray tree.

He couldn't tell how long he'd spent in the Tempus forest. Normal logic didn't seem to apply. Boyd hadn't taken a single turn on those trips around the bog. He should've ended up at the island's edge. Tempus hadn't given him these issues when he visited the harbor. He didn't believe the forest was dangerous then.

I'm not like the pastors and apostles, he thought. *I won't let the forest scare me.*

Tempus had grown incredibly dark in a matter of what felt like moments, a warmth radiating from the plants, leaving no hint of the sky or any outer existence. Most of the trees except those a few paces away fell prey to the darkness, enclosing him as if he were in the dungeon of some castle. *There are no creatures here, nothing that can hurt me.*

Longer moments went by, and the cackling laughter picked up, so close it shook his bones. "Come on," he shouted, standing.

The snickers of laughter grew louder.

"Show yourselves." He reached into his cloak and took out the slingshot, his last form of defense since every dagger he once owned had been stolen away. The sharp, flat rock in place, he aimed into the foggy depths. "I'm not scared of you."

He backed up, halting against the long-standing tree. The voices were a few feet away, just beyond the cusp of the fog. With his blessings, he could hear them. Next to a tree on his left, shrubs moved and bristled. "Come on," he said. "I'm not scared."

The shrubs shook again, and a creature not tall enough to reach Boyd's waist hopped out like a rabbit, though it looked much more like a dwarf. Enormous eyes, half the size of the creature's head, blinked and stared. Fist-sized, soulless pupils floated at their center. The harmless face consisted of little else than a button nose and thin-lipped mouth, a scruffy beard strapped along the roundly defined jaw. The creature dressed in a brown gown with an enormous belt around its bulging stomach.

"I don't know what you want," Boyd said as he stepped back. It felt ridiculous to be wary of something so tiny.

The creature bounced forward again—a singular hop, seeming effortless. As if curious, it bounced again.

Another jumped out from the dead Tempus shrubs, and yet another from behind the trunk of a tree. Soon there were ten, eleven, until a group huddled together.

The horde left him no direction to run. With the rock holstered and slingshot raised, Boyd retreated into the bog. *The only place I haven't explored.* Water filled his moccasins, rising to his shins.

The laughter continued, flipping his insides from the hysteria. Gnomes bounced into the water after him—their gigantic eyes, button noses, and mouths held above the surface. Boyd tried to grab his dagger out of instinct and found an empty sheath.

Then the laughter stopped.

A single creature picked up their chuckle.

Boyd released the rock held inside the slingshot.

The string rang like a beautiful harp and the stone whizzed through the air surrounded by a golden glow.

The stone connected with a row of gnomes. They evaporated, the rock tearing through laughing mouths and Boyd's hope returned.

The rock he launched slowed in mid-air, disappearing into the mist. He waited a moment, and heard a whizzing sound approaching. Instinctively, Boyd stuck his hand out and the rock appeared as if slung in his direction, soaring into his palm with a sharp sting. He shook his hand to rid the pain, staring in wonder between the rock and the multicolored slingshot in his hand.

Brief, snorting laughs called his attention to where the piece had struck the creatures. Twice as many gnomes filled the spots of those fallen.

They hopped toward him.

Boyd stepped backward, feet heavy from the mud, and faced the tiny beings while firing the slingshot as he moved. Each time the creatures dissipated, more would hop out from the bushes and trees to take their place. They appeared faster than Boyd could shoot. The beauty of the slingshot's whip soon drowned under the cackles. His fingers ached from releasing shot after shot, and the continuous pounding of the jagged rock cut deeply into his palm. His shoulder grew sore, legs aching, but the creatures never stopped, and neither did the bog. Boyd found himself crossing the great tree three more times and when he spotted it a fourth, he lost hope. *How much longer should I go?*

Mouths open, some of them caught onto the trees—they'd latch like leeches and hang there.

Maybe it was fatigue, but Boyd gave in and tucked the slingshot away. *I will die here.* He stepped back, letting the creatures approach. Two hopped at him and he punched them into a green mist.

One caught on his shoulder. The mouth felt like a giant sucker, clenching down on his arm as the weight dragged him into the bog. Boyd punched with his free hand, and the creature evaporated.

A mass jumped at his legs. Those that didn't attack with their mouths pawed at his cloak with tiny hands and fingers. He couldn't hear his screams over the jeering laughter.

Boyd collapsed into the swamp, every punch earning him a moment of freedom. The suction made his body weak and numb, and the creatures brought with them an awful green slime that smelled of the foul bog. Open air slipped away as Boyd fell under the piling creatures, choking on murky water, suffocated by the gnomes.

He struggled through the weeds with a second wind, and a pocket of air granted him a final look around, out over the green bog.

A glimpse of midday light shone back. Within the fog and mist, the distorted golden beams looked heavenly. They weren't very far.

I could make it and tell Isaac about the human sacrifice.

I could.

CHAPTER II

SECOND ERA, 113, UAIR
TWO OF FALLING GOLD

Isaac

Isaac's heart pounded as he ran through the gem-studded halls toward the outer wall and the rose garden he'd thrown his father's notebook over. What was he worth, now that he had murdered something so sacred?

Nothing. I am not blessed.

I always loved the dragons. I just wanted to fit in.

Sundials on the wall depicted Falling Gold's first few marks—a pair of dashes descending the mid-right portion of the dials. Come Rising Silver, he'd be forced to become a Zealot of the church or... *only the Lord knows.* He'd heard it said the unblessed have their own island. Yet he had seen the pastors making slaves out of Zealots. He could only imagine how they treated the unworthy.

Isaac slowed to a walk at the consecutive archways enclosing the southern path, yearning for a way out of this mess he created.

The Spirit had deemed him unworthy. His appreciation for the dragons need not be hidden any longer. His father's notebook, once he gathered the loose pages from over the wall, would tell him that the dragons must be worshipped, that they weren't betrayers. He knew these writings, this history of the world. But how could his father have known the truth of the draconic nature when he'd never seen one of the creatures before? How could anyone be so sure the dragons were safe?

There had to be some way to discover the truth, leaving no questions. He had tried pursuing Jericho's way of the Spirit wholeheartedly and was rewarded with humiliation. Perhaps he'd missed a hint in the notebook all these years, and one last look would spark a hidden connection he failed to make, some hope or way to save the dragons and himself.

I must try, one last time.

The rose garden on either side of the southern path appeared plush in the soft equinox light. Few pastors ever ventured out to this path, situated as it was near the back half of the school, and closer to Tempus. There was an air of death people tended to avoid.

But Isaac had come to enjoy the silence. He found this side of the church familiar, comforting at times. It was the only place where no one would bother him. Five years ago, they had placed Isaac and Boyd, with other students they didn't favor, in these back dormitories.

We were written off from the start.

Isaac scanned the cresting and falling roses for the papers that dropped out of the notebook when he threw it over the wall. He spotted a few browned pages resting atop the red petals.

Unsure of where to step, Isaac tested the strength of the rose bed. They weren't ordinary flowers, standing a few feet tall with a shine like red flames. The brighter, more robust roses near the path supported him, growing softer with a slight give the further he walked from the path. *The roses are weaker where the bodies of dragons aren't disposed.*

His foot sank into the dying flowers. Something popped and

squashed beneath. A wet feeling came over his ankle, moved and tickled. Isaac lifted his foot from the roots and gagged at flesh-white maggots swarming his moccasin. Trying not to scream, he shook them off and summoned up the strength to run through the rest of the garden and snatch the three papers.

Isaac hopped onto the wall and batted the parasites off his legs. He never admitted it to Boyd, but he hated maggots. For a few minutes, he sat there, swallowing spit while trying to keep everything else down. Beneath the rose bed near the wall, he saw decayed dragon bodies, faces missing whole sections, gashes filled with gnats and the quivering flesh-eaters.

This is the fate of the Anthros I killed. Will it know, even after death? Will it feel the maggots feeding? Will it become a rose?

Isaac turned and looked at the field outside the wall, seeming to call to him with a free wind like that of the temple's peak. He always wondered what it'd be like to run through that expanse of nature. It was even more amazing up close than he'd expected.

His father's notebook lay in a puddle.

Isaac dropped over the wall into a cushion of plush grass, thicker and more untrimmed than any blade of grass in St. Daemonus, and picked up the damp and stained notebook.

A bird's shriek startled him and Isaac looked up, struck by the scene.

The sprawling field of sand-colored grass grew in an uneven square between St. Daemonus and the dead white trees of Tempus. Black sheep grazed and roamed, though now that he was further out, he could see the field was also littered with rabbits and mice, field animals of all kinds, but none from the other realms as his father described in the notebook. *If only we could sacrifice the sheep instead.*

It hurt to think about that innocent silver creature's life he ended. He wanted to make things right, take down Jericho and this entire second-era way, but one person could not take down an entire church.

Out in Tempus, the dense fog gave him a feeling of emptiness and an absence of hope for Boyd. *Give up,* the trees seemed to say with their menacing height. No matter how many daggers Boyd carried, there was no chance his friend made it to the harbor.

He supposed he wouldn't mind if something emerged from Tempus and came all the way to the St. Daemonus wall to devour him. It would take away whatever suffering he must undergo in the future. If he were lucky, maybe the creature would still be hungry enough to climb over the church wall and eat everyone else on this wretched island, so the dragons could be free again.

Isaac sat on the cool grass, fighting back the tears, feeling them come back twice over. *I'm glad I'm not blessed,* he thought. *I wouldn't change a thing since the moment I arrived here.*

What about his father, who came with him and dropped him off after seeing the church? Did he not know the church preached everything the notebook was against? His father loved dragons enough to study and dedicate a considerable portion of his life to them. Why send Isaac to a church that killed the innocent creatures in droves? It was as if he didn't know. He'd spoken of the church many times in the notebook, about how Isaac would thrive, telling stories of old apostles, referring to them as heroes. What would Isaac's father think now that he was a murderer?

Isaac often wondered what happened to the past texts referred to in his father's notebook, why none of them were included in the library here. That meant none of the other students had ever been exposed to the ideas of the first-era. If they had been, it might have been enough to change them.

Isaac sat on the rough grass and opened the notebook. He felt a pang of regret at its condition. The pages were torn at the edges, the leather cover soggy from the mud and morning dew. He brushed it off with the back of his hand.

He the notebook out in front of him. As he drew his hand away, a breeze flipped the pages, coming to a stop on a page with a drawing Isaac recognized. The top of the page read *Anthros—the Silver Striker.*

Isaac shivered, unsure if he was ready to read about the dragon he killed. He couldn't stop his eyes from drifting to the middle portion of the page, where it stated facts about the species.

The Anthros are recognizable by their shining silver scales, rivaling the most impressive metals, as well as their superb sight. An Anthros in the light of the equinox will blind their prey after hunting it down from a few thousand paces. For this reason, the breed hunts in broad daylight, when there are few clouds, and in places such as open fields and deserts, areas with few obstructions, so their reflection casts wide. On occasions, they'll hunt in groups of three... Imagine such fury... No matter what strength the Spirit may have blessed you with, the wrath of three dragons is unrivaled. The Anthros subspecies is one of few that often show themselves around humans, referred to as "The Proud Kind." They eat a healthy diet of sheep and anything else that may satisfy their cravings.

Isaac sighed. He couldn't read any more. The dragons were so obviously meant to be free. If there was nothing he could do, at least he could honor the species by dedicating himself to its redemption. *What does it matter if they betrayed us? Dragons should be able to live free.*

I should be able to live free.

He flipped through the rest of the frail pages containing myths and legends, finding little more than speculation about the island of Daemonus. *Forged by the will of dragons,* the notebook said. *And the promise of man to walk the holy path.*

A promise that was broken.

Isaac always wondered what decisions his father would make if he were in his position. He never had the luxury to ask. Would his father have stayed at St. Daemonus and served the Spirit as a Zealot, or would he have chosen to board the ship, sent to live on the unblessed island? Which way would he think safest, and which the most brave?

Isaac looked out to Tempus, eyes burning, trying to fight the rising emotions. A soft wind blew out from the forest. *The trees know the answer,* he thought. *What is left of them. They've had hundreds and thousands of years to watch. They know the truth about the dragons and the Spirit. If only there was a way to speak with them.*

Entertaining the thought, he remembered a short lullaby his father used to sing. He started to imagine the melody, actually hearing it, as if sung by a group of angels from the forest.

The voices executed every note flawlessly, drawn out like the holiest of bells. Tears made his sight blurry. He thought he saw bright lights, even more than the equinox sun, moving throughout the trees. Every sense seemed to magnify. His father last sang the lullaby on a cold night by the fire of their home, and he could almost see the moment again.

The dragon fights fierce in the moonlight,
The dragon,
The dragon,
The dragon,
Fights fierce.
The warrior strides true in the daylight,
The warrior,
The warrior,
The warrior,
Strides true.

The voices faded into the wind and Isaac hung on the last note, wondering where it came from, who sang it and how he could hear it again. He remembered his father explaining the lyrics to him.

"The choice between night and day, darkness and light, is something we must always acknowledge, otherwise the choice is no longer ours. It requires constant work to keep our eyes open to the truth. Every young boy always prefers the darkness, at first. It is our nature to be drawn to that which is most comfortable. But each of us must make the decision one day to choose the light, and when you do that, the darkness will fade, and we will find our souls balanced, exactly where we are supposed to be."

The truth.

Isaac felt an odd, tingling sensation in his legs and feet. He looked down at the notebook. It was shaking—slivers of golden light leaked from the side.

The bottom of the book went red hot, and he had no other choice but to watch the grass around it turn to embers. The notebook shook and flipped open with a flash of golden light, forcing Isaac to bury his face in his arms.

The next second, all was done. Isaac searched around him. The sheep seemed unphased. The only sound was the whispering wind.

There the notebook laid, a patch of burned grass around it. Isaac bent forward and touched the leather, a normal temperature. He picked up the notebook and turned the pages—excited, scared, wanting to stride true. He had to figure out what was happening before pastors forced him to leave and he never saw Daemonus again.

Toward the back of the notebook he noticed a lingering glow. Isaac flipped to the last page, and saw a new entry.

On clear, fresh paper, dark ink swirled vigorously halfway down, writing in real-time. The handwriting was clearly his father's—the words scribbled on the page, crossed off, and written on the sides. Isaac looked to the top of the page at the drawing of a dragon he'd never seen. The wings were pointed like scythes, and its narrow head bore two slanted horns The word GOLD was written above dozens of arrows pointing at the dragon's scales.

CHAPTER 12

SECOND ERA, 108, UAIR ONE OF RISING GRAY

To settle my soul's unrest, I must inscribe my terrible mistake.

My ship is departing from Daemonus, and I'm leaving my son, but it is not the distress of leaving Isaac that brings ink to this letter.

The tour of the St. Daemonus church that other parents and I received was far different than my expectations.

If I stood from this desk within the tiny ship's hull and looked outside, I would likely still see the magnificent church of St. Daemonus in the distance. Until my visit today, I thought St. Daemonus continued to worship dragons for everything their blessings bestowed upon us. Yet, as the day continued, I couldn't help but notice distinct changes in the formal rituals of the past.

As we docked on the white-sanded beach after several days at sea, I had the odd feeling of taking part in a joke everyone knew of but me. A few select pastors greeted us with a practiced welcome and anxious hand-waves. The only other ships occupying the dock, from what I remember, were those harboring the vast array of imports St. Daemonus acquires in trade for its most precious gems. I couldn't help but notice the famed gems were relatively absent on the beach, and how forced the smiles on the welcoming pastors' faces appeared. There was a nervous fear in their movements. These same pastors were the only ones who stayed with us for the entire day. When Lord Jericho gave orders, the pastors acted with canine obedience.

"I am the Lord of St. Daemonus," he declared, as if we couldn't tell by the wealth of chains around his neck, enough to feed every starving fisherman on the coasts of Windhaven. When had the role of the Lord become so flamboyant? "My name is Jericho," he said. "I hail from the great land of Dola Vira, of the Obsidian gem."

I knew little about the new Lord, as not much news reached our remote northern island. Windhaven is a Lesser Island, and as such, it doesn't receive much information except on the trading harbors and inns, which I try to avoid as much as possible. I figured the Lord would act according to traditional praise, as had every past Lord in service of the Spirit. Yet, as we entered through the towering arch of the church entrance, it seemed as if the carvings on the walls intentionally explored the human aspect of draconic worship. Obsidian statues were carved in the likeness of great apostles of recent times, whose names I do not know and refuse to rememb. The corridors loomed tall and intimidating as the rest of the church, illuminated by natural sunlight seeping through the arches, absorbed by the gems built into the stone path.

Most churches I've studied look like golden palaces, bright shining structures that encouraged hope, not this continuous building without any real difference from room to room or hall to hall. This structure induced fear or exhaustion, not the inquisitiveness necessary for learning. Where were the usual sculptures of the Great Qaoudron, who saved the Westmost lands from the wrath of the Deacons? What about paintings that depicted the holy realms? How were students supposed to learn with passion if they did not have inspiration of their own, or a firm understanding of the world?

I suppose now is as good a time as any to mention the pastors' cultish initiation ritual, where church followers dyed their hair white and changed their pupils red through some method of the Spirit unbeknownst to me. I'm beginning to think they are bored here.

Moreover, as I have now had the opportunity to contemplate what my ignorant eyes witnessed (if only my mind worked faster), these practices are reminiscent of the ancient death cults on Dola Vira. It used to be common amongst occult sects to worship deities that were part human and part animal, specifically of draconic variation, believing them to be manifestations of the highest Spirit here in the human realm of Indus.

In the moment, however, I dismissed the alterations of the Lord, pastors, and even some of the more developed students as a form of expression, or at its worst, a sort of pastoral elitism. This also accounted for the strange looks of confusion and distaste.

We followed the Lord and his billowing red cloak through a maze of dark stone hallways. Within carved niches of the wall, more marble statues stood that took the form of the seven dragon types. The last two Chrysos at the end reached up to the steepled ceiling, where their heads writhed in a scream, pointed wings spread wide, filling me with a loving excitement that I admit, quieted all else.

The halls gradually became more broken and deteriorated with missing gaps, as if blown apart by a warring force. We finally entered upon the sacred training field of St. Daemonus. I lingered to bask in the view of the structure that was the sacred temple, and the miracle flow of water traveling up to its peak.

"The pride and joy of St. Daemonus," the Lord said. "The temple was deemed so essential by pioneers, they built our entire church around the divine artifact."

Students trained amongst the tiers, fighting one another. A child on the lower tier struck another to the grass and walked away carelessly in preparation for the next bout.

"We have yet to unlock the true meaning of this structure," Jericho said. "But until my reign, this river was no more than a strip of dirt. Today, we have the miracle of its upward motion. A sign of my divine touch."

Parents and young students clapped, gathering close to gaze at the grassy artifact.

"Where else would someone want to become blessed?" The Lord waved his hand out over the temple. A black-cloaked pastor with the same cultish indications stood on the top platform watching students fight below. In his hand, he held a mallet. He raised the brown wooden hammer ceremoniously.

The pastor struck a gong next to him. It made one of the most pleasant sounds I ever heard. It was as if the church put a spell on me since we arrived, and this was the moment I became hooked. Only now, aboard this wretched ship, am I able to recollect what happened with total clarity. I forgot about the issue I felt with the Lord showing us the temple, how it was so obviously a cheap way to make up for the lack of dragons we've yet to see here on the island, where the Spirit was supposed to roam free. Forgive me, whoever reads this now, for I was too blind in the moment to see what I now believe to be a clear form of manipulation.

The tour of St. Daemonus ended abruptly, and the fact that I hadn't seen a dragon became a last-second worry. Before I knew it, we said goodbye to our children, and after seeing Isaac's sad but brave face, my emotions overcame me. I dwelled on all I hadn't done with my child, the fact that we hadn't seen a dragon together. My boy and I did many things together and he had a great childhood growing into a man under my direction, but even as I write this now, I can't help but feel a significant loss at all the things we will never do together, and all that he must endure alone.

When I reached the harbor with the other parents, and the Lord asked if there were any final matters to discuss, I couldn't contain myself.

"There is one thing." Everyone's eyes turned to me, and I emerged from my sulking posture. I didn't know what I was going to say. My throat tightened, and the words came all at once. "Is there any chance you can expand upon the dragons? I do enjoy seeing the quarters where my son will stay, and your renovated library is glorious, but, if it would please you, my Lord, tell us about the sacred ones."

The Lord quieted mumbles from nearby parents with a stern look. The Lord had most likely read the letter of correspondence I sent to the church, asking them to accept Isaac into their pastor's academy. He had to know about my genuine love for the creatures, despite lacking any real education.

He approached me in front of the group, rested a warm hand on my shoulder, and pinched to a pain. "Abraham of Windhaven, it would be my pleasure to please your appetite for the creatures. We won't be long," he said, turning to the other parents. "See the fine designs aboard our ship, explore the crystal beach. We have Rikouwa for the taking, though we ask you only take one stalk on your departure, less you'd care to purchase more."

I followed the Lord and his carpet of a pearlish cloak back to St. Daemonus. "The draconic species have always cared for us," he said. "Nurtured us, showed us the way." We turned into a seemingly random brown doorway built into the outskirts of the halls and made a sharp descent into unlit corridors. Nobody was present except for a guard standing before another door further inside. The pale-faced watchman stared through red eyes without expression. He wore a dozen coats. His face appeared severely malnourished.

"The dragons have helped us and helped us." Jericho approached the door, and the guard stepped aside. "It is time we help them for a change."

"Has that not been the church's goal all along? To aid the creatures and establish mutual profit through our worship?"

"That is what we are taught, yes." Jericho released a series of latches spanning the length of the door. Lastly, he lifted a sliding bolt made of some sparkling silver metal.

"I'm about to show you a new way to help them, known by only the highest pastors and apostles of our church.

"It is soon to be set free, but for now, requires no less than the very soul of this church and island... Indeed, the type of dedication that consumes redirects the influence of time. That is precisely what this creature will do."

"Why show me?" I asked. "I'm just a shepherd."

"Never just a shepherd," Jericho said. "I believe anyone can be blessed with the Spirit. Do you? You must, for you sent me that letter, and by doing so, showed me a new form of worship. Yes, Abraham, I thank you for opening my eyes to a new way to lead. In truth, I owe you this." The Lord donned his white hood and gestured to my coat. "You might need that."

I draped the fur over my shoulders.

"Before we enter and I show you this glory, I have to ask one promise."

"What is it?"

Jericho's voice grew louder in the space beneath the church. "Do you swear not to speak of what you see here, to those on the return boat and on your island of Windhaven?

"Abraham, can you hold this secret for all of eternity, if need be, or at least until your son fully grasps the way of the Spirit?"

"Yes," I lied. "I'm never by the harbor or the inn. Besides my wife, the only person I see is the courier, who comes once a month, and I would rather talk to the sheep."

"No small task it is to talk to sheep."

The door swung open to a snowy tundra. I followed the Lord inside to what didn't seem to be a room but another island entirely. In the distance, I recognized a steep peak jutting out amidst a range of jagged mountains. I would've recognized it anywhere—the Breath of the World.

"Windhaven?" I heard the door slam behind us, but when I looked back, it was gone.

"A recreation," Jericho said. He'd started toward the mountain, trudging through the gathered and falling snow.

I ran to catch up. "How do we get back?"

"The door is still there. This place looks like Windhaven, feels like it as well. But it is a mere creation. If you were to try to walk to that mountain, you'd hit a transparent wall about halfway, and no, it would not be pleasant. "

As I paid more attention, I noticed flaws like the absence of mountains surrounding the Breath of the World, and the lack of the essential pine-needled fauna of Windhaven. The snowy hills descended and ascended without end in a dizzying, colorless emptiness. The Lord held out his hand, motioning for me to stop upon a slope that dropped into a valley.

"There." He pointed to a tree in the center, a few pink leaves lingered on the branches. The rest had fallen around the base.

A golden creature crept out from underneath the empty branches.

"The dragon seems satisfied in this habitat," Jericho said. "I suppose it's what the creature is used to."

The dragon looked up, stretching to take the arched shape of a bridge. It gave a yawning, clicking screech, more beautiful than the song of a thousand birds. The creature's youthful stature suggested the age of near a hundred years. Young.

"Is this a creation?" I muttered.

"Not her. She is real."

It's hard to think of it as possible, even when I look back now—this world inside the church, the dragon kept inside of it like a caged animal. I tried to find a way to tell the Lord my doubts, but it was impossible with the proof right before me. "What breed?" I asked, even though I could quickly tell through the blizzarding haze. Above this entry, I've sketched how I believe the animal would appear in clear daylight.

"A breed not even you have much knowledge about. It is a Chrysos."

"A promised one?"

The last golden-scaled dragon revealed the location of Daemonus to the prophet Alyosha, and the other golden-scales had revealed prophecies before it, bringing such monumental change they altered the course of history—all with a look into a trained pastor's gaze. The golden dragons indicated a significant shift in worship, unknown until someone skilled enough to speak to it without going mad had the brave gall to attempt such a feat as understanding the dragon.

"When we arrived at the sacred island of Daemonus, there was much splendor for us, as was foretold, though the island also brought danger. With new discoveries come new responsibilities. We rescued this Chrysos from the forest. Look closely, at the wings."

Through the blizzarding snow, I noticed its wings were missing.

"It cannot survive alone. Not yet," Jericho said. "What is a dragon that cannot fly? Instead of leaving us a vision on this island of Daemonus, the dragons left *her* in our care. How are we supposed to interpret this?"

The dragon's beauty was too captivating to focus on anything else; an ethereal, golden aura radiated around it. I dared step closer for a better view, but my foot slipped, and I barely caught myself before plummeting into its lair.

"Careful." The Lord helped me recover.

We walked back, and when he reached for the door, its outline shimmered in brown wooden dots, appearing at the will of his hand, and the other side revealed the cramped underground halls.

"We are still managing these changes, and will be for some time. This Chrysos is a great product of our discovery of the island, but we found it injured and dying."

"What is the church to do about this?" I asked. Perhaps Isaac would receive its vision, I thought. This thought consumed me.

"With our help, we hope the Chrysos will return to its full strength, and show a blessed prophet the next island. But will that be humanity's fate forever? To continue finding new islands? Until when? For what purpose? We must innovate. This is what the dragons are trying to show our kind by leaving their young here.

Still, we need the next great apostle to decipher the message of this Chrysos. I believe that apostle could be your son."

He knew exactly how to appeal to me, I realize now.

"Is it happy?" I asked. "The dragon?"

The Lord hadn't lowered his hood, so I could only see the ruby glow of his eyes. "As happy as something can be that has lost its mother and father, and its wings. Dragons are loyal creatures, but they are not quick to trust. It will take time for the Chrysos to befriend us. Only then will we have made progress in understanding its message."

"So the project isn't going well?"

"The dragon believes we're its captors. When the elders left, we took her in, but it doesn't seem to understand we are trying to help." These were the last words Jericho spoke to me inside of his church.

A golden Chrysos signifies change—to what extent did Jericho use the word change to justify his desires?

St. Daemonus now lies in the distance, and now I must trust Isaac to know right from wrong. I've taught him to love the creatures ever since he was a boy. That respect will never go away.

If he is tasked to free a dragon from its chains in the dark undergrounds of St. Daemonus, I believe he will. If he must do so against the wishes of the Lord, because he knows what is right, I urge him to know his place. The dragons will forever remain much wiser than us. The Great Spirit speaks through them, the holiest of beings, and whoever is strong enough to listen will endure. This is the way of the Spirit, which all things serve.

Isaac will be up to this task, I know. My boy is brave. Nevertheless, may the Spirit guide him along his righteous path, wherever it may lead.

- *Abraham of Windhaven*

CHAPTER 13

SECOND ERA, 113, UAIR
TWO OF FALLING GOLD

Isaac

Isaac knew which path to follow. He looked up from the newly printed words written by his father the day he was left for dead at St. Daemonus.

Except it wasn't like that at all. His father cared. He had no idea about the draconic sacrifices, and he cared.

He hadn't noticed his tears had dripped onto the parchment. It felt like he had a chance to speak with his father again, be it however many years apart. Isaac finally understood that he'd never been abandoned. *When father realized what St. Daemonus was, it was too late. He trusted in the dragons.*

The fact of the new entry made Isaac leap to his feet with excitement. He paced about the grass as his entire life crystallized into one clear picture. Father never sent him here because he thought he should kill dragons. The beliefs of the notebook and its writings were true. The first era was the only true era.

There can be peace between dragons and humans.

There always was.

Isaac tucked the notebook into his cloak pocket next to the dagger he'd used once. Where to begin? How could he expect to take down an entire church before he was shipped away or forced to become a Zealot without access to Daemonus? He'd have to get everyone to realize what Jericho had done—but not everyone could take the time to read his notebook, and nobody would listen to a speech from an unblessed. Even if he could convince the students and pastors to give the dragons a chance, the creatures were so starved and beaten they would have no other desire but to fight for escape and wreak havoc on their captors.

I don't blame them, Isaac thought bitterly.

The sound of footsteps to the right made him freeze. He'd been so caught up in the new entry of his notebook he'd forgotten he was outside of the church wall, where students were forbidden to roam.

The steps drew closer, sporadic running over dry twigs.

Isaac readied himself to jump back over the wall.

Then a white-cloaked, white-haired student tumbled out from the forest onto his hands and knees. Flipping onto his back, he swatted at his body as if covered with hundreds of insects, but the only thing Isaac saw was pure panic in the friend he'd written off as dead.

CHAPTER 14

SECOND ERA, 113, UAIR THREE OF FALLING GOLD

Boyd

"What happened to you?" The amazement in Isaac's voice was apparent. He looked terrified and perplexed. "I thought..."

"You wrote me off as dead as soon as I left the room." Despite his arms and legs being weak from the effort of ridding those sucking monsters, Boyd raised himself to his knees. "I don't have time for your excuses." *I almost didn't make it out.* At the moment, it felt good to give in, like the escape he always wanted. A slimy, clear substance dripped off him onto the dry Daemonus grass. Isaac reached out to help, but Boyd waved him away. He'd made it this far alone.

"Well," he said. "Don't go telling me you were right... But aren't you curious about what I saw in there?"

"Yes," Isaac looked out to Tempus.

Boyd recognized the blank fear in his friend's eyes. He'd seen it often. "Does it scare you? It should. Tempus is a nightmare, but not like Jericho said. Even he couldn't beat this type of evil." Boyd thought back to the laughing minions, thousands of them trudging after him through the bog, figures that would evaporate when struck, then return twice over. Their childish laughter was fresh in his mind and would be forever, he feared. "The first time I went in, the forest it was fine. Nothing attacked me. There was no fog, just the river. I think it's because I was so close to the wall. But after I left the harbor, there were these bloodsucking little dwarves. They jumped at me, laughing and laughing...."

"You made it to the harbor and couldn't escape?"

"I almost died," Boyd said. "The forest isn't what it seems, and neither are the harbor or Zealots. They wanted to gouge me apart as soon as I boarded the ship. The point is, it's all a lie Jericho created."

Isaac walked out to where the grass reached his knees. "I don't see any dwarves, but I have no doubts about how dangerous Tempus is."

After all Boyd had been through and seen, Isaac still hadn't changed. "All right, go ahead. Say something about how right you were. I know it's all you want. You don't care whether I'm alright, or what I learned about Jericho and the sacrifice."

"You were the one who was right," Isaac said. "Not me."

Here he goes, Boyd thought. *On his high horse.* "I was right? I know. I saw the truth with my own eyes." A sheep had grazed nearer to them as if curious. Isaac reached out to pet its plush, night-colored wool, seeming more sure of his actions than Boyd had remembered.

How had he come to grasp Jericho's evil so quickly, when just this morning he was trying to join the pastors? What was he doing out here in Tempus? "Did you take the equinox test?"

Isaac didn't turn back from contemplating the field.

I knew it. Fire rose through Boyd's body. "Murderer. You never really cared about the dragons."

"I did," Isaac said, his voice cracking. "I thought I could get inside of the church and free them that way. I wanted to convince other pastors to see the good."

The words out of Isaac's mouth were meaningless compared to his actions. "By killing an innocent creature? As if the Spirit would bless you, you walking contradiction." Boyd paced the field, pulling his hair. "You never even showed any signs. It was obvious you'd fail. But you still chose to go through with it. Tell me, how did it feel to end the life of an innocent creature?" His tone scared the sheep into the deeper grass, where they could hide.

Isaac was silent for a moment. "Like something I may never recover from."

Boyd hardly had the energy left to argue such a stupid, invalid point, shoving Isaac out into the field. "You're a coward."

Given Boyd's blessings, he was much weaker. Isaac no more than stumbled.

When he turned, he held in his hands his father's old leather notebook.

"This again? I thought we were done being children. There's nothing that can help us inside of there. We've read it a million times."

"There's a new entry," Isaac said.

"What do you mean? I don't want to read something you've written. You don't understand, I saw real things out there, stuff that—"

"I didn't add the entry," he said.

"Then how did it get there?"

"It kind of just appeared."

"Appeared?"

"Out of nowhere. I heard music, a lullaby my father used to sing... Ccome to think of it." Isaac flipped through the notebook himself and stopped on a page. "Everything I experienced matches with the confrontation of a spirit's manifestation in the form of something called a Dyra. It even talks about the singing of children, like I heard."

"The only children in Tempus are those bloodsuckers. This stinks too much of the first-era. Are you sure you aren't having some sort of episode, trying to make up for failing the equinox test?"

"What I have is real too. Here, at the very back."

Boyd snatched the notebook and flipped to the last page. His interest spiked at the new entry with the same handwriting as the rest of the notebook. He scanned the new pages of sideways words and ink trails in astonishment. Too much was happening in their favor for them to leave or become Zealots today.

"My father wrote the entry the day he left me at the church, as the ship was sailing away."

Boyd thought back. He could remember that day. A few weeks prior, he'd packed his own clothes, cleaned out his room, all but sailed to Daemonus himself. He was the only first-year on the tour without a parent.

There was an emptiness in Boyd's chest, something he felt he missed out on, never even had, his mother and father being busy and blessed, no more than vague figures whose existence he often doubted.

"It was like I thought," Isaac said. "My father never believed in Jericho. The first-era was the one true era, and dragons were meant to be worshipped. It's all right there in that last letter. In the notebook. The dragons show us the way to the Spirit, otherwise we're lost." Isaac laughed, despite tears in his eyes. "I'm a murderer, yes, but I held one, I saw how amazing they are. No wonder Jericho needs them."

Boyd doubted his friend's devotion. "But... you still killed it? How is that possible?"

"I'd do anything to take that moment back."

Boyd had trouble forgiving so quickly. He pointed to the new drawing in the notebook. "What about this dragon? It says it has golden scales."

"My father spoke to Jericho for a short time, that's what the entry describes. The Lord brought him to some place underneath the church."

"He hid the dragon beneath the church?" Boyd asked, keeping in mind that this could be fake and led on by a pastor or Jericho himself. "That has to be the harbor below."

"What is the harbor below?"

"You were right about the ships." It was time to reveal discoveries of his own. "There was no way to sneak aboard one at the harbor."

Keeping his distance from the dark vines of Tempus, he told Isaac about the Zealots mistaking him for another student the Lord planned to sacrifice and turn into a dragon; about how he heard of another harbor called the harbor below and its location somewhere beneath the church. "Maybe that's where Jericho took your father."

"It doesn't say anything about a second harbor. He went into some sort of room. They're both below the church, anyway. I still think that's where we need to go."

"We're rogues," Boyd said. "I escaped from the harbor with the knowledge that they're going to use a student as a sacrifice. They must have Haskil and every pastor in the church looking for me by now."

"What other choice do we have?"

None, Boyd thought. "You've read that notebook more than I have... Do you remember it saying anything about human sacrifice?"

Isaac grimaced. "I think there is mention of cults who tried fusing humans with dragons in the early days of the Spirit, when there were only two islands, Dola Vira and Gazi."

"But why with a student? And who? What if we found the student he planned to sacrifice and convinced them not to go? It shouldn't be hard to talk someone out of their own death."

The sheep had returned to Isaac's side to be petted. "It would be near impossible to talk a new pastor out of their service to the Lord. Besides, how could we know who it'd be?"

"It has to be someone like me," Boyd said. "They mistook me for the sacrifice at the harbor, because of my blessings. You were at training today. Is there a fifth-year who is far more blessed than the others?"

Isaac's eyes grew wide. His mouth dropped as he looked at Boyd. "What?"

"I'm not exactly happy, now that I know who it is," Isaac said. "There's no way we'll convince her."

"Who?"

Isaac sighed. "Since you didn't come to training, I had to train with Rebekah."

Boyd was waiting for Isaac to laugh, but he stayed serious. "How was that?"

"Almost as humiliating as the equinox. I've never seen someone move so fast."

"She's always been at the top of the class, but how blessed was she?"

"I don't know... When I saw her before the test, I could hardly tell her apart from Zuriel. Imagine her blessings after the equinox."

"After the sacrifice."

"Yeah, that. Zuriel had her humiliate me. She kicked me off the top tier of the temple."

"Sounds fun." There was no time for pity. "If Rebekah is as blessed as you say, then she's the sacrifice."

Isaac walked up to the wall and placed his hand on a gem. "We have to find her before it's too late. It will be near impossible to convince her of the Lord's plans. She was the most dedicated student out of all of us, the top of our class. Why would she believe an unblessed and a rogue?"

The thought of speaking to Rebekah made Boyd's palms sweat. He had to admit, it wasn't the most pleasant idea. "We'll follow her to the harbor below, then."

"And try to fight against Jericho, pastors, *and* the student Zuriel said was the most blessed in history? We need her on our side to stand a chance."

"I have trouble believing she won't be on our side once she finds out she's going to be sacrificed."

Isaac huffed. "Let's hope." He peaked over the wall, then pulled himself up with all the clumsiness of an unblessed.

Boyd followed effortlessly.

They crept throughout the inside of St. Daemonus, making sure to stay away from the outer edge, where the sentries were. Nobody saw them as they snuck past the lunch hall, the library, and the temple, on their way to the northern dorms where they suspected Rebekah stayed, like the rest of the promising fifth-years.

"I've never seen the church this empty," Boyd said.

"There weren't very many students at the test."

Boyd led them up the north tower's staircase, his feet light as air, while Isaac was galloping behind him. He never knew how loud the unblessed trampled.

They emerged on the tower's uppermost floor, so much brighter and cleaner than their own, near the school's front entrance. As he turned to tell Isaac they should split up and look for her on separate floors, a door creaked open down the hall.

He pushed Isaac back into the staircase as a girl with a black cloak and ice-white hair locked the door behind her, starting the opposite way down the hall.

"That's her," Isaac said.

"Of course it is." Boyd watched as she walked away. He'd only ever seen Rebekah talking with friends, in class, or after training. Isaac was right. She looked like a pastor.

"Do we really need to sneak around?" Isaac whispered. "It feels wrong."

"Yeah..." Boyd gulped. A nervous lump slid down his throat. "Unless *you* want to talk to her."

CHAPTER 15

SECOND ERA, 113, UAIR FOUR OF FALLING GOLD

Rebekah

Mixed feelings of excitement and loss tore at Rebekah as her friends opened the door, smiling with their hair like fresh fallen snow. Both Uri and Azarias had passed the equinox test and appeared nearly as blessed as her. At first, she mistook them for pastors.

"I'm going to miss you guys." She forced the goodbye to begin, checking the time on the wall.

Uri ran up and hugged her. "We'll meet up soon."

There was a slight chance they'd ever hear each other's names again. Once blessed, every student was placed into the role of the church that best fit them, regardless of friendships or preferences.

"If only we could stay in touch," Rebekah said to fill the silence. She'd never been good with goodbyes. Especially when they involved people she cared about—they required too much feeling, and it disrupted her praise.

Uri reached into her cloak and presented Rebekah with a leather sheath, a light green emergent hilt. "Take it," she said. "To remember me by."

"I can't."

Uri removed the sheath to uncover a sharpened emerald blade, pleasing to the eye. "Please." She urged it forth. "We have hundreds like it back home. I'll get one when I return."

How could you be so sure of your destination? Rebekah thanked her, the blade airy in her hand, as if hollow. *No wonder they have so many. The cheap stone doesn't require much effort to craft.* "I've never seen you use this in training. What is it?"

"It was made on my home island of—"

"Lux," said Azarias. "We know."

Uri shoved him. "The blade was infused with emerald, our island's gem. It's everywhere in the caves, and of course, the caves are everywhere." Uri studied her, tilting her head. "I know you're sad, but we'll be okay. Do you think you can remember me by it until you come and visit?"

"I will." The study of gemstones had never been of much interest to Rebekah nor any earnest second-era pastor. Lord Jericho disposed of anything used as worship in the first-era the day his reign began. But that didn't mean this blade was any less beautiful. "Thank you."

Azarias stood and opened his arms. "I don't have a blade for you, but get in here." They hugged, and when they separated, he was fighting back tears.

Rebekah hadn't been as close to anyone as she had been with Priska, who had left without saying goodbye. If her best friend could do that, these two didn't care about her either. Nobody did.

She felt as hollow and cold as the emerald blade. After this was over, Uri and Azarias would be sad for a moment, then forget about her and go on with the rest of their lives, like she would. She saw how pastors would speak of their golden days. On her thirtieth, fortieth equinox, she wouldn't be able to remember more than a few good memories about these two.

"I should be off," she said.

They glanced at each other, likely wondering where she had to go, but would never ask.

She shut the door behind them and leaned against the oak, staring at the empty room she'd occupied for the last year. Azarias's low voice carried off down the hall.

Rebekah replaced her old dagger with the one Uri gave her and left it with everything else in what used to be her room. She sighed, shut the door, and started on her way to the library, where pastor Nim would show her the way to the harbor below.

Two distinct voices echoed out from the far stairwell behind her. One of them she recognized was Isaac, the unblessed boy who chewed his words when he spoke, uttering each one carefully. *What is he doing out of his room?* Another sentry or fifth-year would catch them.

She had more important things to worry about.

Acting as if they weren't there, she continued down the opposite stairwell. Once she was out of sight, they followed her, and her indifference turned into defensiveness. One pair of feet was as light as a broom. The other clambered along. *The loud pair is Isaac. And the other...*

A blessed one?

Descending past the main level into the fifth-year basement lounge, she knew how to trap them.

She walked into the basement dead end and her stalkers followed inside, Rebekah walked back, past the shadow clocks cast onto the wall, waiting for them at the top of the stairs—the one entrance and exit to the room.

Muffled brown hair peeked around the stairwell corner, and darted back. She had a moment of eye contact with Isaac, seeing the surprise fill his eyes.

"Isaac," her voice carried through the dusty stone hall. "What are you doing? The Lord could expel you for this. Worse." The unblessed's resilience had started to become annoying. "Stop following me. If you continue, I'll have no other choice but to report you to Jericho myself."

The two boys emerged from the staircase slowly. Isaac looked around while the other stared right at her.

His roommate, Boyd, was extremely blessed for having not taken the test. He stood a fair amount taller than Isaac but likely weighed less. From where she stood, she could see his eyes turned maroon. *Why didn't he take the test?*

"Did you not hear me? I don't want to repeat what happened in training."

"What happened in training?" Boyd turned to Isaac, a grin on his face.

"I told you..." Isaac's face flushed red.

Now Rebekah felt sorry for the weak boy. "A lot has happened since then." She adjusted the hood of her cloak, smooth silk around her neck. *Why should I apologize to a rogue?* "Just go back to your rooms and wait. I won't say anything." She turned to walk away, but Boyd reached out and grabbed her forearm with a quickness of his own.

Looking at his hand there, gripping her wrist, it took everything she had not to let the wrath of her sacrifice end the rogue boy, and it became more challenging when she looked at his pale, pointed face, seeing the fear she struck in his soul painted across it like a first-era statue.

She twisted her wrist outward and broke free.

Boyd stumbled back. To her surprise, he was smiling.

"Do you take me for a joke?" she asked. "Never touch me again."

"Hear us out," Boyd said.

"I don't have to, and I won't."

"We have to show you something," Isaac said. "You specifically. If you don't have anything to say after, we'll go straight back to our rooms. Otherwise you can turn us in yourself."

There was no apparent reason why they'd want to speak with her. Besides, it would look good if she managed to capture two rogues her first day as an apostle. "Anything that's intended for my ear can be heard by the Lord as well." She glanced around at the walls. "He always watches over us."

"Wow," Boyd said. "They really have her, don't they?"

Your opinion means nothing to me, rogue. Touch me again, and I will make the world a better place.

"You have your black cloak," Isaac said. In his hand, he held a rotten notebook. "You're a pastor now?"

"By the Lord's word. If you're going to talk about something dragon-loving and unproductive, I'm not interested in your hoaxes."

"Hoaxes?" Boyd jumped forward. "How can you say our opinion is wrong when you've never given it a chance?"

"I'm not interested in your proof, or your opinion. I'm not even interested in mine. That is something you two have never understood. When you serve the Spirit, you are an instrument of its will. Now, leave. Otherwise, you're blocking me from my path to the Lord, and that means I must take precautions to fulfill his orders."

"Then, you're going to see the Lord now?" Boyd stepped in front of her as she tried to move away.

"That is none of your concern." She balled her fists.

"I wonder... If you're not headed to see the Lord, maybe you're going to a certain harbor?"

She looked at Isaac, who watched her too closely. *He couldn't know what the Lord ordered me to do. They're white cloaks. The secret harbor's existence is hidden from everyone but the highest pastors.*

"The Lord told you to go to a harbor," Boyd asked. "Did he not?"

She searched for an answer, panicked, and found none.

"Some other pastor, then?" Boyd laughed. "*Tsk-tsk.* As such a blessed student, I'm surprised. You should want to read every holy document you come across, yet you want nothing to do with us and this old raggedy notebook."

"It's not that old," said Isaac.

"It's old, but still more valid than anything else at this church."

"It doesn't matter when something was created," she said.

"Anyone can write a passage in a book claiming to know the truth. I need to see something for it to be true. Everything developed in the first-era was built on a dream. They were visions and false ideas that led nowhere. Look around you, Jericho has made real progress with the Spirit. He has almost cleared Tempus of its evil, allowing us to explore it for the first time since the great war."

Boyd yanked forth the torso of his cloak, pointing at dark and blotchy stains. "Jericho's progress is the new lies he comes up with. That's why I climbed over the wall. I went into Tempus to see what kind of progress the Lord made."

Now she knew they played a desperate trick. It was the same conspiracy they always told. Did they think she'd grant them pastordom or something? The forest of time was forbidden. Hundreds of pastors have given their lives trying to rid evil Spirits from Tempus. Most never returned. *And to think I would believe he's stronger than Gerald the Wanton?* "Impossible. The Lord would have known you left church grounds. He knows our thoughts, let alone if a student escapes over the wall."

"That's what he wants you to think." Boyd played with something behind his back. She thought it was a dagger, though he wore no hilt. It still wouldn't hurt to be careful. The blessed rogue was better than Uri and Azarias at hiding his feelings and expressions, likely because he wasn't hiding anything. He believed his claims about the Lord.

"Nobody stopped me when I climbed the wall. C'mon," he turned to Isaac. "Tell her you went too."

"I saw everything," said the dragon-lover. "The grass, the sheep. Tempus."

"But you were at the test," she said.

"Yep, he's a murderer, just like you." Boyd finally showed his hands, holding a slingshot made of a beautiful golden band and twigs though the bark had a luminescent quality.

She reached out to inspect it herself, but he pulled away.

"I went to Tempus and found this slingshot, then I went further, to the harbor. Not the one below, like where you're headed, but the one we first saw when we came here. And, I pretended to be you." He laughed a shrill laugh.

"I don't need to listen to this," she said. *He did mean the harbor below, but how could he know? He couldn't have gone into Tempus.* The peculiar slingshot in his hand taunted her, infused at least to some degree with evil forces, especially if he got it from Tempus.

Now that the thought of temptation had risen and passed, she wanted nothing to do with the weapon. This entire occurrence could be the Lord testing her. "You wouldn't be standing here if you went over the wall. The wall is what keeps us from the evil forces of Tempus. Beings that disobey the Great One, like you two."

"We're telling the truth," Isaac said. "Boyd went to the harbor, and the pastors thought he was a blessed student they planned to sacrifice later, at High Silver. The only other student I could remember being as blessed as him was you. That's why we're here, to save you before it's too late."

"Why would the Lord use a student as a sacrifice?" The accusation sounded twice as crazy once she repeated it.

"Jericho is turning us, the blessed ones, into dragons." It wasn't easy to tell if Boyd was making this up as he went, or if he planned this out beforehand. "It's in our blessings. He wants his students to be servants, and you're their leader. The big dragon in the sky, overlooking all her minions."

The image of herself with a dragon face and shiny scales rushed back. Their theory was crazy, obviously false by how it sounded, but she couldn't deny how well-developed it was. *When you have five years...*

"I don't understand you," she said to Isaac. "If you believe the entire church is a lie, that the Lord is evil, why show up to training? Why sacrifice a dragon and try to join the blessed when you show no signs?"

Isaac looked at the book in his hand. "Every time I lose my way, I always come back here. My father wrote this for a reason, maybe one that he didn't even know about. Please, just look once. Once you see the pictures, you'll know what I mean."

Apostles were supposed to convert others to the Spirit, not bully them. No matter how ridiculous it is, looking at the notebook might help her see the world how they do, and maybe then she could lead them to the light.

Grabbing the notebook from Isaac's hopeful hands, she wiped off the cover. A mischievous rush came over her. The book certainly wouldn't be welcome in the Lord's library given the tearing leather with pages stuffed in random places.

The Lord will know, she thought. But if so, he also knew of her intentions to convert them.

The images inside the notebook were troubling. In its entirety, the book studied dragons: ways to communicate with them, navigate their messages, and find a vision in the Spirit. First-era methods, disproven years ago.

She looked up, met by their stares. "We've come so far," she laughed off-handedly, scanning more. The book showed a few pastors looking into the dragons's eyes as if the act were harmless. Whoever made the drawings took years to correct the tiniest details —the sheen of the scales regarding its surroundings, draconic postures and what they meant depending on the species.

"I could turn you in right now simply for having these," she said. "This is unholy propaganda, first-era nonsense. We know better now. The dragons deceived us."

"We knew better then," Isaac said. "You held a dragon. The second-era texts always make them seem mindless and boring, but this shows the truth. They have personalities, sure, but more than that. They show us how to live, guide us on the way of the Spirit."

"They deceived us through their visions, and led us to what was supposed to be our deaths on this island." She looked down at the notebook, flipped through more pages. "I will admit, this is great drawing. These dragons are..." She paused, went back a few pages.

The curled tail seemed too familiar to pass. Two legs at the midsection confirmed she looked at the dragon of her sacrifice. At the top of the page, it read *Wyvern*. The drawing showed the dragon staring right at her, knowing she'd killed one of its own.

Nausea set in. She could hardly stand. *They are mindless.* "What are you guys trying to do?" She closed the notebook and shoved it back to Isaac, scared of what Jericho might think for her having seen it. *He knows.* "I serve the Lord. My blessings are enough for me."

"What about me?" Isaac asked. "I took the test, killed a dragon for the Spirit. Where are my blessings?"

"Don't for a second think you made the same sacrifices as I did." Her hand drifted to her dagger. "What are you two after?"

'The truth," Boyd said. "You're living a lie."

"I don't care who you would or wouldn't worship. I believe in the Law of Utility. What works is the truest way. The inner workings of it all, you two wouldn't understand the complexity."

"What about a simple way, one that's worked for so many years?" Isaac tucked the notebook in his cloak.

"We tried that already," she said. "And suffered the consequences."

"No," said Isaac. "Some people might have, long ago, but you never did."

These two are beyond saving. "I don't think you know the punishment for what you're saying."

"Trust me, we do," Boyd said.

Isaac walked closer, into beams of the falling sunlight cast down through high, open windows. "My notebook isn't some crazy delusion. Dragons didn't attack us when we arrived at Daemonus. Jericho twisted the story. He made everyone believe they kept the power of the Spirit from us, and drew us into a trap. But why would we still need the dragons if that's the case? Why wouldn't we kill them off? Jericho needs to use them for something."

"He needs their natural power," Boyd said. "Until we become them, and have it for our own."

"The dragons are everything that Jericho hates," she answered.

"The sacrifice is an offering of evil to the Spirit, an effort to restore the natural balance."

"Nothing about these blessings are natural." Boyd ran his hand through his hair.

"I'll worry about myself," she said. "I advise you do the same. Now, I have to go." She turned and made to leave. "Please, don't follow me."

"At least lead us to the harbor below," Isaac said. "You'll believe us when it's too late, but if we're there, we can save you."

"I've been saved," she said.

"Your savior is going to sacrifice you," Boyd said, but he didn't dare reach for her.

As she walked down the hallway, Rebekah's mind filled with images of the dragon she murdered, its blood dripping into the river, the candy scent she couldn't stop herself from enjoying, the reflection, horns, and scales.

She heard footsteps ahead, the gossip and laughter of a group. Around the corner of the hall, graduated black-cloaks walked toward her.

She couldn't help but look back at the two rogues. They had the same sort of helplessness she'd seen when she kicked Isaac off the terrace.

The best shepherd can lead any sheep.

Rebekah went to the unblessed and rogue. "If you're seen, you are going to act like we never had this conversation. Even though the Lord knows."

Isaac's eyes doubled in size.

"What do you mean?" Boyd asked.

"I'm helping you. Follow me to the harbor below, but no further. I want you to see for yourselves. If you get caught, I never knew you." The gossip and footsteps picked up. Rebekah donned her hood, went to the stairwell. "Let's go."

"Why?" Boyd lingered in the hall.

"Seriously?" Isaac asked.

"Fine." Boyd dashed to the stairs. "What does it matter if the Lord turns you into a dragon anyway?"

They ascended the staircase and walked through the hall, escaping from the black-cloaks. Rebekah rapped on the reddened stone next to her tower three times, and the underground halls opened in the dust. She snuck through dirt-covered passageways where fewer pastors roamed, toward the library, checking now and then to see if the boys followed close behind.

"I've never been through these halls," Isaac said.

"Me neither. I don't think we're going to the library at all. She's probably turning us in."

"I'm saving you."

"Yeah, right. 'Saving.'"

"Let's hope you'll become enlightened before we reach the harbor." They entered back into the main halls, a few sentries passing too close for comfort. "But as of now you're rogue, so be quiet unless you want to suffer."

CHAPTER 16
SECOND ERA, 113, UAIR
FIVE OF FALLING GOLD

Isaac

Isaac watched as Rebekah snuck out of the cramped hall and disappeared under the ruby arch of the library's entrance, hoping she wouldn't tell on them. It seemed crazy to trust her, the most blessed follower in the church. But if she truly was the human sacrifice, they had no choice.

He followed with Boyd into the silent, expansive room. The library had a damp dreariness to it. Second-era books filling the various corridors wafted the musk of freshly printed pages throughout the galleries, divided by subject. Isaac crouched behind a row of standing shelves and Boyd stood alongside, staring at the far away oval desk in the chamber's center.

"This place is empty," Boyd said. "Guess the fifth years are too good to study now."

The library had been one of Isaac's favorite places to visit. Illuminated by the light of fluorescent blue and green plants that had grown their roots all over the ground, up the hollow stone walls and bookshelves, the cornered and cushioned seats felt like home. The lamp-like plant vines wrapped the place in ribbons of the dim blue light, perfect for reading and studying into the late night hours. By some way of the Spirit, they only emitted their glow when a student walked or sat near them, set off by motion.

Currently, the library was a gloomy tomb. One spectral light shone in the center right above the round desk, under which the library pastor sat quietly reading. Whoever designed the place according to Jericho's will had planted a garden of the fluorescent greenery before the desk. The garden shone bright enough to illuminate Rebekah as she approached the pastor, a trail of the ghostly hue left behind her.

"Pastor Nim." Her voice echoed a pleasant note in the empty space.

Nim jumped at the sound. "Uah, ah... Rebekah? My, am I jolly to see you." He cleared his throat and entered into a coughing fit.

Despite looking like a relatively young man, pastor Nim appeared to have some sort of disability that made him hunched, overweight, and slow to move, or perhaps it was all the reading. Nim wasn't even blessed. Nobody knew why Jericho chose to keep him in the church and not ship him away or make him a Zealot. Pastor Nim only worked inside of the library. *Quite the way to serve the Spirit.*

Despite reading so many books, Nim seemed an excruciatingly slow thinker. He likely couldn't handle any other tasks besides the monotony of checking books in and out. Yet somehow, with his dark red-brown hair and shaggy beard, he'd been awarded a black cloak, and Isaac watched it almost reach up past his knees as the pastor stood, wheezing and recovering from his cough.

A dopey grin sprouted upon Nim's face. "What, you think you're all fancy in your new cloak? *Get in here.*" The torn excuse he wore for a cloak lifted up and around Rebekah like a tent as Nim gave her a big hug, lifting her off the ground.

"I don't want to imagine how that smelled," Boyd whispered.

"I'm so proud of you. I knew you'd pass, I knew it. When the Lord told me I should be expecting to take you to the harbor. I couldn't wait to congratulate ya. Why, the other day, I even made you a gift." The pastor dug in his cloak and held something out to Rebekah.

"Oh," she sounded off-put. "Thank you. What is it, exactly?"

"Made it myself," Nim said. "Don't you remember when you told me not to give up, that anyone can become blessed if they tried?"

"Yes."

"Well, here ya are now, all grown, and I was telling my son, 'the very next Lord is graduating from St. Daemonus. This very year,' I said. Can you believe, he told me, he wanted to be like you? Oh, the way my heart swelled. My son wants to go to St. Daemonus and become a pastor." Nim made a high-pitched whimper. "I was... I was so proud, I didn't know what to do with myself. Imagine, one of us, from the lowly island of Gloucheshire, becoming a real pastor. Guess anything is possible in Jericho's second-era. Little Roe could come back home, nurture the Spirit there, then we'd have an entire island of pastors, maybe get our own church."

"That sounds amazing," Rebekah said.

"Sounds like another hell," Boyd whispered.

"I told everyone my boy's going to be a pastor. We all got together, made necklaces. I made one for you and my boy, each one the very same. That way, when he becomes a pastor, and you two meet, he'll know it's you."

"I see now. My gratitude is beyond words." Rebekah held out her hands. "But I can't take this, pastor. The Spirit doesn't permit its followers to wear jewelry."

"Ua, oh, I see." Nim took the necklace back. "Bu' what about his Holiness?"

"Lord Jericho is an embodiment of the Spirit. His jewelry serves a purpose, to aid his praise. It doesn't mean I'm ungrateful, pastor. I'll cherish the act forever." Rebekah straightened in her posture. "The Lord sent me here to speak with you. He said you can show me to the harbor below."

"Yes, I-I suppose I understand. Big fancy pastor, gettin' all pushy." Nim let out a mucus-filled laugh. "Right away, right away."

"I'll always be a student of the Spirit," Rebekah said.

Nim groaned and bent beneath the oak desk. "Don't be so slow to grow. Often we're too late to see our faults for what they are, nothing's clear till we move on. Become a pastor, and you'll see."

Nim rose, holding a staff with radiant blue vines over every inch. The garden's light at the center of the library seemed to double at the new presence.

Rebekah pointed. "What is that?"

"Just a curious little key." He walked in front of the desk, the staff thudding as he entered the circular garden. Standing in the midst, pastor Nim raised the staff high into the air and forcibly struck the ground. Instead of a thud, there was a sharp *click*, and a sound like a lowering bridge as gears shifted beneath them.

In a rush, pastor Nim lumbered out of the garden, tip-toeing between plants. When he reached the edge, the garden seemed to collapse, folding into itself, leaving nothing but the outer stone ridge.

In its place descended a series of spiraling stairs.

Isaac couldn't help but lean closer for a better view. His hand slipped, knocking a book off the shelf. It clapped against the floor; a subtle bluish glow pulsated where the book landed.

"Did you hear that?" Nim twisted around moments after the glow faded. "I almost forgot to be sure the place was empty. Let me take a look, won't be more than a second. You get started."

"But... I don't know the way," Rebekah said.

"You'll find it."

Isaac and Boyd were sneaking out of the gem-studded arch, away from Nim's growing voice.

"On second thought," Rebekah said. "Can I have the necklace?"

"Really?" Nim sounded like he'd just become blessed. "Ya mean it?"

"Yes," she said. "It might actually aid me in my worship, since you made it with such sincerity. Here, let me take it. We're in a rush. The Lord needs me."

"You're the one who took a moon's quest to get here."

Isaac watched from their old spot as Rebekah walked down the stairs.

"Erm, wait, wait, you don't want to get lost down there." Nim wobbled after her, the glowing staff in hand. He took one final sweep of the library at the edge of the stairs and slammed the end of his staff into the sidewall. The grinding sound of stone and gears returned and the garden folded in at the edges, beginning to cover the hidden space.

Boyd ran into the open.

"What are you doing?"

"It's closing, we have to follow."

Half the garden had returned by the time they neared. The grass —green, short and sharp, shining blue at the outline of Isaac's feet— differed from the grass beyond the wall. He walked out over the unfolding surface and jumped onto the staircase, met by hard rock that stung his ankles.

The garden's soil, roots, and stretching vines soon formed a roof over them, bringing the fresh, dry scent of earth. Fluorescent vined lined rusty rails, and through the consecutive swirls of stairs Isaac saw Pastor Nim struggling into a tunnel in the wall, devoid of any light.

Rebekah's voice echoed back. "How far does it go?"

"You think I know?" Nim grunted. "It's faster if ya know where you're headed, restricted to pastors and Zealots, given the intricates."

"I thought Zealots weren't allowed in the church?" Her voice was buried in the distance.

"You'll see at the harbor below."

Once Boyd deemed the pastor's footsteps faint but loud enough to track, Isaac followed him down the staircase and into the tunnel, not as dark as it appeared. The passageway reminded Isaac of his log cabin back home, dim and cozy, though at times it grew so confined he had to crawl.

A single torch led the way far ahead, giving light to markings on the wall made from a clayish, sand-like substance that gleamed blue, white, and green like the vines. It seemed like every type of painted dragon, two-legged or serpentine, wingless or many-headed, bared their teeth and descended from the sky, hunting for pastors.

The Lord shows the worst of their kind, claiming it is the creatures themselves. But he needs them. We need them.

They reached a torch on the wall, the images ended, and the tunnel split into four different directions.

Boyd picked a direction, claiming to hear the pastor's voice, and Isaac followed. He'd lost track of Rebekah and the pastor long ago, forced to trust Boyd's blessings. Come to think of it, he didn't have an excellent weapon or particular fighting skill, either. All he had to offer in stopping the sacrifice was a deep knowledge of his father's notebook and first-era ways, and what was that worth? *Hardly anything when it comes time to fight.* Father always said the mind was the most powerful thing we have, but that didn't seem entirely accurate.

They continued ducking in and out of the dizzying tunnels. Isaac didn't care about the pictures on the walls anymore, just escape. "We're lost," he said.

"No. I smell sea-water."

They trekked further, and Isaac was relieved to smell it, too—the bite of salt. It'd been so long he hardly recognized the scent.

"I hear the ocean tide," Boyd said. "Seagulls."

The next turn revealed a long tunnel with daylight at the end. Isaac forced each step forward. Rock scratched at the sides of his arms. His spine felt like it was about to snap, but the fresh, easy to breathe air felt cool on his cheeks, urging him on. He could see the emerald sea, a promising window of crashing waves confined by the exit.

Settling at the tunnel's end, Isaac registered the underground cave with a slow clarity. At the furthest end was the harbor entrance, where the ocean extended out to infinity, the surface shimmering with orange equinox light. Waves lapped over jagged rocks lining the cavern's entrance, some of which still had the legendary assortment of gems.

"Look," Boyd said. "Jericho claimed Daemonus was stripped of every gem except for what's inside the church."

"They're everywhere," Isaac said in amazement, following Boyd's gaze to the ceiling and seeing smooth-coated spikes drip from the dark rock. The stalagmites reached out like straightened tentacles, nearly grazing the sails of the only two ships occupying the harbor—a wooden sore in the middle of the precious cavern. The vessels docked on opposite sides of the cave.

"I've never seen sails that color before." Isaac wasn't sure if he'd not paid enough attention in class, but standard sail colors signified the ship's purpose to others at sea, distinguishing church ships from those of raiders and pirates. Red represented warships, yellow for trading, white for transport, but these sails were black with the second-era sigil, the Spirit's eye stitched in the center.

"It can't be a good thing," Boyd said. "Zealots are aboard those ships."

Isaac could barely see, distinguishing no more than yellow cloaks, some faded and others like gold moving amongst one another. "What are they doing?"

"They have cages, unloading them."

A good amount of the Zealots walked off the rightmost ship carrying silver blocks. Isaac also knew what the cages held. The Zealots moved toward a divot spanning the cavern's length, dug in front of the harbor. Because of their view, Isaac couldn't see the Zealots disappear into the crater, but they emerged with empty hands. "Do you think the black sails mean…"

"Dragons," Boyd said. "Those are the ships that bring them here."

"From where?"

Suddenly Rebekah appeared from behind the divot on the left-most side of the cavern. Boyd went silent, and Isaac squinted to see as best he could. She stood out in her black cloak, along with pastor Nim. The yellow-cloaked Zealots moved aside to let them through. As they climbed up the plank of the ship, the Zealots started cheering, screaming.

"What are they doing?"

"This happened at the other harbor," Boyd said. "The Zealots go crazy at the sight of anyone who is blessed. They'll try to kidnap her, sell parts of her body so people could use it for potions and other things."

On the ship, pastor Nim batted Zealots away. A few tried to grab Rebekah, but Nim's size scared them away. She lingered close to the pastor, face hidden beneath her hood.

"We have to do something," Isaac said. "They're going to kill her."

"Not yet, remember? Jericho said he needs her for the equinox. I think she could defend herself against a few Zealots." Nevertheless, Boyd had that strange slingshot ready in his hands.

"I guess you're right. She wanted us to leave her alone." Isaac drew out his dagger.

Rebekah stood motionless amongst the chaos. Maybe she was okay.

Isaac searched for another place to hide near the harbor in case someone else came from the church. A sliver in the side of the cave looked hidden by shadows, but wide enough to hide a few boxes, some crates, and them.

He nudged Boyd and pointed to the cramped space. "We need a better view."

CHAPTER 17

SECOND ERA, 113, UAIR FIVE OF FALLING GOLD

Rebekah

The Zealots formed a circle around Rebekah, moving closer in droves, overwhelming poor Nim who tried to fend them off.

One Zealot had snatched her cloak as she boarded the ship, and she resisted the urge to fight back, choosing to have mercy for the lost, unblessed soul. *They are merely confused. Stay calm,* she told herself. *Show them a faithful servant of the Lord, so they may follow.*

Nim shouted at them like a guard dog, snapping and lunging, entertaining them more.

What do they want so bad? When she tried to look into their eyes and understand their point of view, like she had with Isaac and Boyd, there wasn't a hint of anything other than pure desire and the terrifying envy that fueled them. They wanted her, needed her, to a point where they could hardly control themselves.

She remembered what Boyd had said about the Zealots wishing to capture and steal her blessings. *The sea has made their mind wander,* she thought, watching as they taunted the library pastor. Nim shoved his staff into the gut of one yellow cloak, and the Zealot keeled over a barrel of Rikouwa. "Which sorry soul wants more?"

Jericho and I will heal them all. She just hoped the Lord would forgive her for allowing the two rogues to follow. He had to understand her intentions, not to let another soul end up like these Zealots. *Does he watch me now, aboard this very deck?*

A door to the captain's quarters, kept separate from the commotion, flung open with a wooden crack. "Pastor Nim, your ogreish qualities will no longer be necessary." A black-cloak with scrawly gray hair and a long, judging face strutted onto the deck of the boat and the Zealots fell silent.

Finally, Rebekah thought. *Some order.*

The pastor's hair was slicked back from a hairline starting behind his ears. When he arrived his porpoise eyes stared down out at her—more of a wine red, lacking the halting glow of the higher blessed.

Pastor Nim, struggling for air, took a few steps back. "Yes, I-I believe my duty is well done here..." In a few moments, he shrunk from her protector back to the librarian. "This one'll take good care of you." With a slight bow, Nim limped off the ship.

"Man the ropes," the new pastor yelled in his bellowing voice. All Zealots except two nearest Rebekah ran off to follow the pastor's command, a frenzy aboard the ship and on the harbor.

Swiping his cloak aside, the pastor crouched to meet her gaze. "No need to be scared," he said in a low, deep hum. "Pastor Solomon." He extended his hand.

As soon as Rebekah reached out, he swiped her closer and pulled down her hood, showing her face and locks of white hair.

She curled into herself, trying to seem normal. *He must inspect me before I board his ship.*

He wrapped his hand around her curls and pulled tight, smelled them. "Yes," he said. "So pure. She is the one." His clutch released, and his hand drifted over her shoulder. "You are the Lord's chosen. What have you to say in thanks?"

"I'm grateful for my blessings," she said. "But I don't know what I'm chosen for."

When the pastor didn't respond, she thought she might have gone too far. The boys had made her too skeptical. *How could I question my undying love for the Lord? That is not the way of a true pastor.*

"The Spirit works in mysterious ways," Solomon said. "What you may not understand today, you will be grateful for on the morrow." He stood and nodded at the two Zealots near her.

They grabbed her by the arms—twisting, pinching her wrists.

"What are you doing?"

They tied her wrists together with rope, too tight. It burned.

"I don't expect you to understand what's about to occur," said pastor Solomon, "or go willingly with your future role. Your disposition toward the Lord's light already seems rather... opaque. All the same, no person as young as you should be expected to perform such a monumental task willingly." His head wavered, loopy, and settled on her. "Or do you have just the right amount of dedication one must show to receive such power? Tell me," he leaned close. "Do I see treason in your gaze?"

"No," she said too quickly. "I'm a loyal servant of the Lord."

Solomon turned to the rest of the Zealots, now ashore. "We shall see." He lifted his arm slowly.

Zealots on the harbor held rope extending up and around the ship's sails, curving over to link with the deck. Every crewmember had evacuated the deck's central portion. As the Zealots on the harbor pulled, a square portion lifted to reveal darkness beneath.

It can't be.

Rebekah analyzed the form; the tail, curling up and around to its snout, scales like an enormous pile of dusty, aged silver. *It's grown, well past the harmless stage.* Jericho had banned any dragons' growth past maturity except for those that breed. Even those destined for procreation had their wings severed to prevent them from escape. This dragon had the same treatment, small nubs on its back like missing arms, yet it was still far too young to take part in the act of birth, still a child in its relative years.

She tugged at the rope around her wrists, to no avail.

"Another beautiful specimen," Solomon said. He twisted to Rebekah. "Come."

The Zealots brought her under the hull. The deck crashed into place above, encasing her with Solomon, two Zealots, and the sleeping dragon, which took up most of the space.

Whatever made it so hot, Rebekah felt her chest seeming to collapse, her throat burning.

Solomon crouched contentedly.

"What are you doing with me?" she asked. "I told you, I serve the Lord." The rock and sway of the ship was making her nauseous. It was so *hot*.

"You are blessed," pastor Solomon said in his monotone voice. "A determined young pastor. But you lack manners. Rude questions are no way to make friends with your fellow pastor. Even if I am beneath you in the hierarchy of the church, I am your elder, and you shall serve me as I please." The pastor turned, studied the gray dragon next to her. "As for your question, you agreed to help the Lord at any cost or measure, did you not?"

"I did, but that was within whatever means I could imagine. Never this." She shrugged her shoulders and tied arms. She thought of the boys, what they'd say about her being in the same situation as the draconic creature a few feet away. "I thought dragons were the sacrifices, not us."

"Oh, but you are smarter than that? I know that you remember your hymns. Verse thirty-six, shall we? 'A good pastor serves the Spirit, however it calls them, regardless of their own way.' You completed your first task of devotion diligently. Now, you must be patient to complete your second, after which you will be free to ask any question you please. Though by then, I'm afraid you'll know much more about this realm than me." Solomon donned his black hood.

The Zealots pushed her closer to the scorching dragon. She kicked and screamed. The Zealots were much, much stronger.

With the dragon there next to her, motionless, Rebekah couldn't help but feel connected in the worst possible way. *Tied up at Jericho's will.*

Shouldn't I have some say with the Spirit? Shouldn't everyone? Jericho was the only one who was supposed to care for everyone unconditionally. *Why would he make me suffer like this?*

Without any way to be sure, she wondered whether the dragon's heavy sigh meant it felt the same despair.

"Whatever this role is," she said. "The Spirit would never allow it."

"Shut up, girl." One of the Zealot's bent close to her.

"She is quite the piece though," said the other, further back. "The things we could do with just a finger."

"Can't you forego even a little bit of your damn pleasure, Larky?" The Zealot turned to her, his breath rotten. "But you are right. Extend your fingers, m'lady."

She didn't.

"Don't make me use the tickly torcher," said the sickly Zealot in the back.

She did as she was told.

The stronger Zealot pulled her down toward the gray scales. "Be brave," he said. "This is good for you."

Her throat was burning, but she tried to scream more, so someone might hear as her hand evaporated against the scale.

The world went mute, her palm and fingers turned to a charred statue, and the burning spread through her arm over the rest of her body. No matter what she did, the Zealot kept her hand pinned hard to the scale. The heat turned blood in her veins to stone. A hazy dark fog settled over her eyes, blocking all sight of the world, and she entered into a melted slumber.

~

REBEKAH WOKE to a cooling in her chest. The stony shield that lay over her eyes gradually cooled, broke, and dissipated. An icy wind came over her, its source the pocket of her cloak.

Pastor Nim's amulet.

The cold spread over her arms, fingertips. The underground hull didn't smell of the natural, motherly scent of the dragon, but of pungent Rikouwa. The raised deck showed the empty harbor. *They must have left with the sleeping dragon and pastor Solomon.*

Two voices drew closer, louder than the lapping waves. The Zealots that subdued her walked around the corner, and she watched through slits in her eyelids, snoring, as they continued without so much as a glance in her direction.

How long have I been here?

She couldn't go through with whatever the Lord had planned for her, not after seeing how Solomon treated her.

He said she would know much more than him, that she would understand and be thankful for this one day. But what was she to think today, trapped and tied underneath the ship, put to sleep like a dragon?

I don't want to be a sacrifice.

She tugged and twisted the rope around her wrist, but it wouldn't loosen.

Zealots paced up to the opening, and she feigned sleep.

"I'm just sayin', I never seen Nim commit a sacrifice. I don't think he deserves the robes is all."

"Do you think he'll bless us like that?"

"Doubt he'll bless us at all," said the other. "We're just the lads who carried the beast."

"But it's judgment day." He sounded disappointed. "You know

the scripture, 'Every soul who serves the Lord is promised to be blessed.'"

The Zealots' footsteps hit the creaky wood inside the hull, a few paces away.

"To serve the Lord means being blessed. Only the blessed ones'll rise. Did you forget your lessons already?"

"No I just, I think it's that being blessed means serving the Lord. We're keeping watch over the girl, isn't that enough?"

"Why don't you ask me," Rebekah said.

The two Zealots jumped back, looking at each other with pale faces.

"I'm just saying, I'm the most blessed after him. They say I'm destined to be the next Lord. You saw how the library pastor followed me around?"

They looked at each other again.

"Well then," said the burly one. "Go on and tell us. You think we'll be blessed?"

"Of course. By most means you will be the most blessed of your Zealots, for here we are, speaking now."

Their faces lit up. The dopey one laughed giddily.

"But there is one condition."

"Huh?"

"Well. Go on."

"I need you to undo this rope. I'll get to my next task on my own. Go to the Lord, and tell him of my success"

The wimpy Zealot scoffed.

The burly Zealot took but a mere glance back. "I'll go have a word with the Lord, on account of his most blessed heir."

"Okay, alright, fine."

The Zealots cut the rope on her wrists and the cool feeling rushed to aid the burns. As if they were her sworn followers, she led them out of the ship and up the harbor, stopping at the tunnel's edge, where she emerged from earlier with pastor Nim.

"Okay," she said in the bright equinox sun. "Listen carefully, because it is easy to get lost in these tunnels. To reach the Lord, you must go straight, and take the first stairs you see all the way down. Keep going until you reach the Lord, for his room is the deepest in the church."

"All the way to the bottom."

"We got it." The Zealot bowed.

"Good, now hurry. The Lord must be awaiting word of my success."

The two Zealots bowed in angst and scurried off.

Rebekah lingered as a shadow, listening to them descend the first set of stairs. *I don't know how long they'll go, but they seemed devoted.*

She snuck over to a nearby rock, overlooking the divot carved across the center of the cave. She had meant to look inside when passing with Nim.

The horrific sight made her gag.

Hundreds of infant dragons appeared on the verge of death—bathed in tons of their own filth. Most looked exactly like the dragon she'd sacrificed.

Remembering what it felt like to see the silver dragon on that ship and relate so much, she tried to imagine what it would take for her to want to continue to live in these conditions, as if she were one of the dragons, but couldn't. No one could imagine what it was like to live like that.

She forced her eyes away, but that didn't help with the smell of their feces and urine, so prevalent now that she'd seen the amount running in a trail from the cages down to the sea.

It's worse than I ever knew. No wonder Jericho hid this from students. Rebakah had never given dragons thought or consideration as more than a meaningless creature. *But the dragon aboard the ship was hurt. I saw its pain.*

When she left the ship, she might have thrown away her future with the church, but it was what felt right. She wouldn't let any creature suffer like that dragon aboard the ship, or the ones in the divot.

She could never return to the Lord, being wanted as a sacrifice and now a rogue. *Who is on my side?*

Then she spotted Isaac's friend and bunkmate, Boyd, looking back at her. He had crept out from a crevice at the other end of the cavern and waved with lanky arms, only capable of seeing so far because of his blessings.

CHAPTER 18

SECOND ERA, 113, UAIR
FIVE OF FALLING GOLD

Isaac

"What do you mean she's on her way?" Isaac asked as Boyd slipped back into their hideout amongst expired spice and withered parchment. The harbor was empty, but Isaac hadn't forgotten the dragon the Zealots lugged out from the ship, hoisted onto a platform carried on their backs. With two curved horns and stumps in place of wings likely taken by Jericho, it was undoubtedly the Chrysos, maybe even the one from his father's notebook. Its golden scales were only tinted gray—a sign of malnourishment.

Rebekah strolled into the crevice opening. Her face seemed much more serious, her piercing eyes gloomy, exchanging between them.

"I have to know how you did it," Boyd said. "Those Zealots *really* wanted you, how did you convince them to let you go."

"A pastor's trick," she said, checking her surroundings before taking up the last open space.

"We're going to need a lot more of those," said Boyd.

Isaac could see in her hesitancy, something had driven her mad. "It's a good thing you're here, but why? Weren't you just praising the Lord?"

"I know you saw it, too."

"The Chrysos," Isaac said. "From my father's notebook?"

"Does your notebook speak about that creature?" The fact seemed to trouble her. "Does it talk about the way the dragon looks when defeated? They held me captive, right beside it. When I looked over and saw the clipped wings, I realized I was no different. Lord Jericho clips our wings before they have time to grow."

She's always been intense, Isaac thought. *But whatever happened aboard that ship tipped her fervor to our side.*

"Praise the Spirit," Boyd raised his hands. "We have a chance."

"We?" Rebekah asked.

"Aren't you on our side?"

"I still follow the Spirit," she said. "Wherever it guides me. I've been too blessed to ignore the things the Spirit can do. But these sacrifices, it's not the true way. I know it. I can't stand by and watch while the Lord takes advantage of innocent souls." She looked between them both. "What those pastors were doing, that's not the will of the Spirit, the same one that encourages less suffering in the world. The dragons feel pain, too."

"What about the Lord?" Isaac asked.

"You were right. They wanted me to give my life without even telling me the reason. They want someone who will serve the Lord unerringly. That was almost me. They said I should be thankful for being chosen. I would've been, too, if you two didn't tell me of your view."

Isaac's stomach dropped at her gratitude.

"I would have suffered anything for the Lord and Spirit," she said. "But when I saw the dragon, it was different. The way it sat there, asleep, but so... I don't know, so..."

"Tortured," Boyd said.

"Depressed. I felt it, too." Her hands drifted to the necklace that pastor Nim had given her. "When I completed the test, I didn't feel much different. Jericho made me kill without reason, and I hated it. I know I'm not a true follower of the Lord, not in this church. How could anyone dedicated to serving the Spirit murder a creature that clearly felt so much?"

Boyd stepped forward. "And you didn't think about any of this when you murdered the helpless dragon?"

Isaac punched his inconsiderate friend.

"Ow. What? It was just a question."

"Something changed when you guys talked to me. I couldn't get the idea of Jericho's plan out of my head. I saw it everywhere."

"Welcome to his world," Isaac pointed a thumb at Boyd.

"So what do we do?" Boyd asked. "Jericho's most prized student and sacrifice is gone, but he still has the Chrysos. He could always sacrifice a different student. There's no shortage of Jericho-lovers around here."

"That's what scares me." Rebekah looked to the harbor. "He said even some of the Zealots would become blessed. He's planning something greater than we can see. If we only had time to let the younger dragons grow, all the other students could see how aware dragons are. You have no idea what it's like. There are millions down there covered in their own feces. Dragons of all kinds."

Isaac had taken out his notebook and turned to the final page. "Look," he said, and they looked over either shoulder. The word *gold* amongst the many arrows felt ironic. The dragon looked so powerful with its wings intact, a heroic version of its current self.

"The Chrysos are rare," Isaac read, "but the few stories about their power are the most prominent in our culture. Chrysos have been said to create whole islands from the sea, food from the soil. The Chrysos showed us how to farm, sail, and turn water for the animals to that of our own. May they continue to guide us to new heights."

"There's no question," Boyd said. "We have to stop the sacrifice before Jericho uses that power for his own purpose."

"How?" For the first time, Rebekah seemed defeated.

Isaac wanted nothing more than to find a solution. "My father wrote of a cathedral. It lies somewhere in Tempus, built by humans and dragons through divine architecture."

It took him a while to find the page in his father's notebook with a sketch of the structure. He spoke as he read, keeping his voice low so it wouldn't echo throughout the cave. "Divine architecture is when dragons provide a vision for a building, and humans construct it according to this idea. Every church has built their church this way, on every Greater Island. The cathedral of Daemonus is said to be the holiest structure ever built, conceived of and built by the dragons."

Isaac read the last few sentences on the matter. "Some say it is the holy place of the dragons and we desecrate the space everytime we enter, others claim it is a blessing for our loyalty of which we must reap." He closed the book, tucked it away. "I can't think of anywhere else Jericho would take the Chrysos."

"Do you think they would venture through Tempus?" Rebekah asked.

Isaac had forgotten she was the most promised apostle of Jericho's. "What if it isn't that dangerous? The evil spirits of Tempus could be yet another lie to keep students from knowing his truth."

"Death is in Tempus," Boyd said. "I saw Tempus for myself, and I'm not going back. I told you, didn't I? Thousands of little, life-sucking creatures, hopping around, clinging to me with gross, stupid mouths. Don't even go away when I kill them." He shivered and brushed at the stains on his cloak.

"Jericho may have lied about the dragons," Rebekah said. "But he'd never lie about the evil that threatened him. He was too cautious for that. He's not as stupid as you think." She turned to

Boyd. "If you did go into Tempus, I can only imagine what you saw. Demons live there."

"But we all saw them take the dragon that way," Isaac said. *I'll go, whether they follow or not.* "Even if evil spirits do reside there, we have no other choice."

A seagull screeched by the harbor, as if to clarify his point.

"No," Rebekah said. "We don't have another choice."

"It's the only way." He and Rebekah were on the same page.

Boyd sighed. "Then we might as well say our goodbyes here."

"Don't be so pessimistic," Isaac said. "You walked through Tempus safely the first time."

"But you weren't there when I went through the second." Boyd's demeanor had changed. He drew his odd slingshot. "But since you called me out, fine. I want to face these demons head on. At least I won't die as a part of Jericho's plan."

"We have to be fast," Rebeakah said. "I don't know how far down those Zealots will walk before they notice the end is impossible to reach. But what about the younger dragons held captive down there, in the crater. Do we free them?"

"Wow, it's like you're a completely different person," Boyd said.

"They don't deserve their suffering either."

"None of us do," Boyd said. "But that doesn't stop the bigger sacrifice from happening. You know, the one we need to stop so Jericho doesn't have world-altering power at his fingertips?"

"These lives are just as important." The rose garden came to Isaac's mind, the maggots that'd soon sprout, feast on their bodies, then mature into flies.

"I owe them," Rebekah said. "One must never leave a fellow member of the Spirit to suffer. The Spirit is in them, too. I'm sure of it."

"If we are trying to save the dragons," Isaac said. "It makes sense to save them all."

Boyd huffed. "We have to be quick. Unless you want to sneak lead-foot here past some Zealots so we can get caught."

Isaac wanted to say something back to Boyd, about his blessings and how they were from the Lord, so it doesn't make sense to flaunt them, but he was afraid his insult would hurt Rebekah too.

"I took care of the Zealots," Rebekah donned her hood. "But yes, we have to be quick." In moments she had been halfway to the crater.

Boyd twirled the slingshot, shifted it between his hands. He looked to Isaac, a glare in his eyes. "If we don't save the Chrysos in time, remember that it was because you wanted to agree with a girl."

Rage surged through Isaac. "Why do you feel like you have to make all the decisions? Ever since we got back from Tempus, you think you know everything just because you got scared. I've been saying there were evil forces in Tempus all along, and now that you know there are, you don't want to go. We're supposed to be working together, considering each other's plans, but you disagree with everything we say."

"Pfft," Boyd hissed. "Remember that next time you and Rebekah side against me."

Boyd was being immature. *We have the same views, that's it.*

But was that it? Isaac would likely do anything to save Rebekah, he was about to when he heard her screams from the harbor—just like he would do anything to save the dragons. Would he do the same for Boyd?

No...

Boyd was different. He could take care of himself.

"We don't have a choice but to go into Tempus," Isaac said. "It's not my fault you're too scared."

"I'm going, aren't I? I just don't know what's going to be there." He shouldered Isaac while storming off.

Why has he changed so much? Then again, Isaac changed too. There was no helping it, once the truth lay open.

An eerie feeling came over Isaac as he crept out of the crevice. A vivid image came to mind of a stalagmite dropping from the ceiling to pierce through his skull. Someone could coordinate the stone lance to drop if they wanted; it wouldn't even have to look like an accident. They were rogues.

Boyd's paranoia is wearing off.

By the harbor, the sea lapped up a gathered dam of chunky brown fluid. Rebekah and Boyd stood still, facing the expanded ditch. The carved storage area spanned the length of the harbor itself, with cages stacked to the height of the hole further back, and less up front. Isaac could hear tiny cries now, helpless squeals of nothing more than pain. His chest hurt at the sight, and the smell brought this morning's chowder up for another taste.

"We should split up," Rebekah said. "So we unlock as many cages as possible."

"I'm not sure if that's the best idea," Boyd replied. "What if there are evil Spirits in there?"

Rebekah turned. "Then you should fight them."

Boyd's face went red. "And when are we going to stop? If it were up to you, we'd be here forever."

"He's right," Isaac said, struggling to reinforce Boyd's confidence. "Let's make one pass through to the other side. We should open what we can, but remember what we have to do."

Boyd nodded at him and ventured into a nearby row without another word. Metallic locks crashed against the floor as the doors creaked open.

Not one dragon ran for its escape.

"See you on the other side." Rebekah disappeared before Isaac could say anything.

One row remained left to choose from, the darkest. He couldn't see what he was walking into, but he could hear. Tortured dragons warned him to turn back.

The darkness left forms to his imagination. From what he could tell, thousands of dragons were crammed into the cages. Whatever warm sludge ran along the ground soon filled his shoes and wetted his socks. Flies came in suffocating swarms, which meant maggots.

Isaac hoped not to see those wiggly spawns of the worst spirit, and luckily no more than a few inched around.

None of the dragons made an effort to escape as he unlatched and dropped the silver clasps. Few acknowledged him at all; the ones who did cried out for mercy.

How could I have been so stupid to sacrifice one of you.

Isaac resisted meeting the gaze of the infant dragons, unsure of what might occur. Instead he focused on the difference in subspecies —variances in wingspan, placements of the horns and spikes. Some had sharp daggers along their back and others not a horn or limb. Still some, an unfolding reptilian fan around their neck, sharp and equipped with multicolored fringes. A good number of the dragons had two legs and two sets of claws on the ends of their wings— Wyverns, Isaac knew. *The dragons they breed must be Wyverns.* After everything they'd seen, Isaac doubted he had any idea of how the breeding process worked.

He was unable to define specific features like gender and temperament, not in this dark place, though a trained first-era pastor could determine the personality of a dragon just by inspecting its scales. Isaac didn't remember exactly how, though he knew it had something to do with the dragons being embodiments of the strongest forces that drive us. First-era pastors trained to be in tune with these forces, allowing them to interpret and follow through with an exceeding amount of the dragon's will. Father's notebook said if one claimed they understood dragons, it was safe to say they knew nothing.

Isaac knew nothing, unable to distinguish even the difference in shades of the scales. Something still forced him to look inside the cages, though—to see the dragons as unfortunate souls subject to the will of another.

Unlocking the latches wasn't helping them escape. The clink against the floor became a sad reminder of the Lord's immunity. Meanwhile, High Silver approached, when Jericho was going to conduct the sacrifice according to Boyd. Soon the Zealots would return with more dragons and lock the cages again.

Boyd was right, this is a waste of time. What did the Lord plan to use the Chrysos for, anyway? What could the purpose of murdering such a sacred dragon be? *Many, many things...*

Isaac unlocked a cage near the row's end, and as it creaked open a skinny orange head poked out of the crowd of resting bodies; the first dragon to seem alert. Isaac caught a glimpse of lively yellow eyes, forcing himself to look away.

Will it run? He hoped it would. *Run away and never come back.*

He nudged the cage open some more, watching the orange form stir in his periphery. He allowed his gaze to drift and inspect the scales.

A dark orange, more like amber, the stone of Windhaven. Sudden memories of his home flooded back; the snow, the round amber stone his mother kept above the fireplace, mined from the very mountains that surrounded the Breath of the World.

"Here." He stuck his hand out and leaned into the cage, facing away. "I won't hurt you." He knew the creature couldn't understand him, but he had to try something to show safety, that this was a chance to be free and he wouldn't hurt the creature.

Deep clicking sounds came from the shadows and Isaac's stomach turned. *What am I doing?* He could feel his heart beating faster in his chest as the orange shade crossed the bodies toward him. Isaac tried to avoid the yellowish slime covering the iron bars as he reached further, half-inside the cage, though some of the slime had gathered at the top bars and it dripped onto his face, gooey, with the pungent scent of expired milk.

The dragon clicked again, no more than arm's reach away. The hum in its throat sounded like many-voices at once. Inside the orange of its scales were hints of an ocean's blue.

He reminded himself he couldn't look into its eyes, but he felt like a pastor of old more than ever, a mediator between humans and dragons.

Couldn't he handle it? St. Daemonus went to extreme ends to describe the insanity of draconic manipulation, telling students tales about first-era pastors who looked into the eyes of a dragon and lost their soul, going on murderous sprees, ransacking whole villages before taking the lives of everyone they loved, then themselves.

On the other hand, his father's writing spoke of the most talented pastors to ever live, how they could look into a dragon's eyes to see the future and past through a connection made possible by the Great Spirit.

Couldn't I do the same?

He wasn't trained enough.

The dragon's honey-scaled snout reached to smell Isaac's outstretched hand. A smile grew on his face, his chest warmed, but a single thought buried the pleasantness.

I murdered one of you.

The dragon's gaze was set on him, he could feel it pressuring him to look back. The snout drew closer still, youthful wings extended out a few inches. The dragon seemed to be in good shape, even healthy. *How, in a place like this?*

Isaac kept his palm held out, as his father's notebook said to do. The Wyvern's nostrils twitched, smelling him. Its head bowed to Isaac's fingers, flinched back, and reached forward to rub against him.

A jerk of energy flexed his fingers as soon as they touched the scales, his fingertips went numb, and before he could pull them back the scolding freeze of ice rushed through his body.

Weak.

He was alone in the cavern with the amber dragon, falling back, back, into a flurry of white.

The electric jolt had turned to an unforgiving cold wind. He couldn't move according to his will despite long, far-stretching arms flapping on both sides of his body to support a heavy weight.

The white flurries cleared and he tucked his arms, diving down over an open landscape of snow. His arms extended before he connected with the ground, catching the wind so it lifted him up.

Not arms, he thought.

Wings.

His body dipped around a snow-capped mountain to reveal a landscape of evenly coated powder reflecting the pale silver moonlight. He couldn't move, had no control over his body, merely a passenger seeing the world through these eyes, so sharp and clear the roaming sheep stood no chance.

Past the field of snow and white-tipped pine trees, jagged stone teeth capped in white lined the horizon. Just when he recognized them, his arms folded, sending him careening back down to glide over a frozen lake.

I'm a dragon.

He'd never experienced a feeling quite as free, climbing up until the pine trees formed a pattern below him, split by the frozen lakes. He was in Windhaven, or this dragon was. Isaac had heard of this side of Windhaven in lessons and stories. Even though he'd lived outside of town, this was true wilderness, and he never had been allowed to venture this far.

Flying over the range, long amber streaks lined the cliffside. The mountains were too dense and brutal for anyone to trek, so whatever lay inside remained unexplored and unclaimed. Father once said dangerous wind wraiths occupied most of the lower mountains, and he'd even seen one.

Maybe I'll see one now.

Amidst all the others, one mountain stood as a giant amongst dwarfs. The unseen peak increased in height and volume until swallowed by clouds. *The Breath of the World.* The wind lifted him higher. Across his nose came not the smell of the dragon's secretions or the cave, but crisp wind in long, enduring breaths.

I'm going to see the peak.

His father's notebook said that was where the elder dragons

resided, in a place too far and remote for any human to reach. But Isaac was not human, not now.

He entered clouds. When he exited them, he'd see the peak. Isaac heard a whisper from somewhere behind him, barely audible —*Helios.*

Then the cold faded away as quick as it came, and the next time Isaac blinked, it had been with his own eyes, in the darkness of the harbor's crater.

He took a short breath—humid from the sea—and felt the cavern rock tearing at his knees, his arm aching in the cage. The dragon's snout grazed across the tips of his fingers once more.

Isaac jerked his hand back out of instinct.

The dragon jumped in response.

"No," he said, not wanting to scare it away. "It's okay... Helios. Is that your name?" Isaac didn't dare touch the scale again, let alone look into the dragon's eyes. Whatever happened, it was amazing, but he didn't know if he'd return to that land for good. He didn't know what would happen at all.

The creature turned and walked away.

Does it not want to escape?

Was it a vision? Isaac almost didn't want to say so. He wasn't blessed, not in the second-era or the first. He didn't even look into its eyes.

The puny size of his body felt foreign, though the word—was it a name?—seemed familiar. *Helios.* Where had he heard it, from the notebook? If so, he didn't know where.

Footsteps approached behind him, and Isaac turned to see Rebekah's black cloak standing near. "Am I interrupting?"

Boyd emerged, on the opposite side from where they started.

Isaac was still kneeling, half-inside the cage. "No," he said, standing. "No."

"It's time to ruin the Lord," Boyd said.

"Stop the sacrifice," Isaac corrected. Before leaving, he glanced once more back to the cages, the amber dragon nowhere to be found.

He didn't tell the others what happened as they snuck quietly to the cave's side exit, where the pastors had escaped with the Chrysos.

Though it was still falling gold and the afternoon sunlight shone through the harbor's exit, Tempus appeared bathed in a thick gray fog leaking partially into the cave. Dead, barkless trees struggled to stand in their decay. An eerily cold wind filled the gaps in Isaac's cloak. The footprints of the Zealots were there before them, easy enough to follow in the damp ground.

"The Lord is up to this," Boyd said. "No way the Spirit would make me go in here again."

His friend's face was terrified, so scared he couldn't possibly doubt what Boyd had seen. Rebekah's hood still hid her expression. *At least she's on our side.*

Isaac was about to walk out, to be the first one into Tempus and show the others he was willing to give his life to save the dragons, when he saw a glistening orange shade stir out on the dock.

The Wyvern that had responded to him crept out from underneath the creaking wood, a darting flame. The others turned. They must have seen the smile on Isaac's face.

Rebekah gasped and backed up toward Tempus.

"What does it want?" Boyd asked.

"Its name is Helios," Isaac said.

The dragon paused, then trotted up slowly. It paced around Isaac's feet and made the multi-layered clicking sound.

Isaac looked at the others, embarrassed, hesitant to tell them the truth about what he'd seen and where he'd gone. He had no idea what it meant.

I still have to tell them, if we're to work together. He'd have to tell them everything. They seemed terrified of the creature in a way he'd never been. Deep down, he always knew dragons were safe.

"I should tell you about what happened when I unlocked the cages."

CHAPTER 19

SECOND ERA, 113, UAIR
TWO OF RISING SILVER

Jericho

The time has come. My kin are rising.

The thundering voice, aged a million years, echoed through Jericho's head. He rubbed his temples as they thrummed with pain. He kicked the door to his study open and stumbled through.

"Haskil!" But the servant had been off making his preparations for the day.

Ra-ko-dah! The ancient voice chanted, and its power had almost escaped the Lord like a cracking dam, holding acres and acres of accumulated water.

Jericho shot toward the chestnut cases lining red velvet walls. *My gems.*

The intricate tunnels deep underneath St. Daemonus had no windows. Although decorated with the Lord's chic style, it lacked proper lighting. Jericho had tried to compensate by filling these areas with luminescent plants familiar to the island, but it only made the underground tunnels and library more mysterious.

The Lord squinted as sweat dripped from his brow onto the cases and their glass covers. Veins on his forehead threatened to burst. He couldn't remember which case housed the gems with the power of souls already stored inside.

Jericho broke the glass to each one, feeling the emptiness of the gem's presence but never what he searched for.

The soul trapped inside of him gained more control.

You choose to ignore the rogues as they escape from the harbor. The draconic voice echoed through his head. His knees buckled. *Rebekah, your most trusted student, tricked your witless Zealots. They still wander the cathedral's depths as we speak.*

Shut your mouth. Jericho's knees buckled again and he fell, catching himself on a nearby case. A gash on his hand felt like no more than a scratch. *This was all a part of my plan. You've grown stronger, I see. I just need my power, as you use yours.*

You have ancestors inside every gem on this island. You're saying even that is not enough to hold me down? Letting the rogue students escape may have been part of your plan, but only because you cannot see a way to stop them. There is no way. For years you've tried to squash the holy spirits of the Daemonus forest, but they've managed to evade you all this time. Now they bestow gifts upon your enemies, and reap the reward for their patience.

Jericho managed to push the voice back in his mind and crawl to the next case. He peered into the glass, finally met by that numbing presence. *Yes.*

He punched the glass open with his stinging hand. The strength had drained from him, and he'd become more of a decrepit older man than he'd ever been. *If I go any longer, I'll be too weak to survive.* There was no point in hiding his panic. The dragon knew.

Blood ran down his wrinkled hand as it grasped the golden necklace. He returned to this necklace in moments of crisis. He should've known where he kept it. Bails on the golden chain held gems of different kinds. Shaking, the necklace clinking, he raised it over his chest, shoulder, his head.

He paused.

It is true, Jericho thought. *You are right. The students know of my deception, and they are headed to the cathedral. I don't know what they will find in the forest. I don't know how to fully rid the spirits residing there. But they know of the sacrifice and even now plan to risk their lives by entering those woods.*

Yes, Tiamat said. Once, when Jericho had been just a child, the elder dragon had been destined to rule the sea under the watchful eye of his father, but Jericho's own father had quickly proven that prophecy incorrect.

Holding the necklace brought back a sense of relief and strength. Jericho found the hold in his mind, the grip and feel of stability, muting the dragon's voice. He bolstered his mental fortitude upon the sheer power stored in the necklace, cultivated from the souls of his ancestors as their final wish. The strength and power condensed into the gems brought level-headedness, adding clarity to the world. Once more, Jericho's body and mind was under his control. He placed both feet solidly on the ground and stood.

He thought back to the day they infused his soul with that of the four-thousand-year-old ferocious animal, and smiled.

I still have the Chrysos, Jericho thought. *Or did you forget?*

The dragon wished to say something but Jericho's dam had been fortified, and he pushed back with willpower granted by those who came before him.

Understand, my plan is extensive, perhaps far too much for your feeble dragon mind full of ignorant ideas of peace. I have accounted for every aspect in every imaginable scenario, Tiamat. I admit my execution must be flawless, but why else would the Spirit call the chosen one to arms? If anyone can complete a task as monumental as blessing millions, it is me. The room had become brighter now, his senses adjusting. Crevices and corners came to light as he walked to the case furthest from the door and lifted the glass with healed hands. *I'm surprised you don't remember, being so bright for your breed. After all, you helped with the plan.*

The more jewelry the Lord donned, the more he could influence the natural power of Tiamat and alter this pathetic realm to which humans are condemned. Dragons lied about there being anything other than the Great Spirit, where forms were created and inevitably returned.

The soul of Tiamat was still very much alive, however, aging and gaining strength as any dragon would, but if channeled correctly, Jericho grew with equal power. He needs only carry more blessed gems.

The week prior to this equinox day, Jericho equipped himself with gem-filled teeth he'd fashioned from the last of the harbor's garnet reserve. In doing so, he stretched Tiamat's usual day's supply of power over a three-day span, which he spent reviewing the plan of the Chrysos's sacrifice.

Not only did the draconic power give him energy, but it provided a type of grasp over his knowledge that allowed him to bounce unhampered from idea to idea, accessing his own understanding of the Spirit and the workings of the higher realms to a degree even the thinkers of old never reached.

He had an idea toward the end of those three solar cycles, one that would allow him to bestow his followers in this middle realm with draconic Spirit, showing them the power that comes when worshipping him. In turn, he would have an army to conquer the higher realms. After the rogue students were murdered or changed, there would no longer be an unblessed soul in all the islands of Indus. He'd accounted for the dragon-lovers as well. They were the puzzle's central piece, and once Jericho fit them in, the picture materialized. Soon, the balance would be tipped, and no one would be able to deny him.

Jericho hung the fourth necklace over his neck, stopping because the weight had become too much to bear. He reached for rings sitting on a smooth wooden model of his hand within the rightmost portion of the case and doubled up on his left hand—a ring above and below each knuckle. His dominance towered over the dragon's will, the palpable force cowering within his mind.

Tiamat shied away as Jericho attempted to pull it forth. He tugged harder, so the creature listened, and thought: *Soon, I will distribute the essence of your Chrysos to pastors and Zealots throughout Indus, placing it in the hands of those who will bring about true peace. We will bathe in the light of the Spirit. Unlike your species, we will share our power with those who deserve it, bowing to the one true power.*

The dragon's voice came forward abashedly. Jericho allowed it to speak. *What about the power you hold? What good have you done here, in this church? All I see is evil.*

Jericho laughed aloud. *That's something your kind never understood, along with the first-era. Good and evil are subjective. Do you not think it was cruel to hide the powers you had from us for so long? How much suffering could have been lessened if you showed humans how to farm a few years earlier, how to cure our diseases? You can't tell me making us struggle in this way was good? What I bring to the world is less suffering, and that is why my followers worship me. It is what everyone wants. They only need encouragement to transcend their fear.*

Your kind is not ready for the power it took.

He could feel the dragon's anger surge. It fueled him.

We are your creators, Tiamat said. *We are forces that have been here long before you, and will be long after.*

It is a shame you brag about denying death.

This is the only reason why you can fuse my soul to yours, because you are but a part of me. Our kind guided yours with a gentle hand, but in the end, everyone must find their own way. This is what you do not understand. You think you have access to it all when you have yet to see past the first of the holy realms.

This very fuel, this anger, had given him the power to become Lord of Daemonus and drive the dragons away, putting those who used to beg at the altar in homes with food. Jericho used the natural fury of the species to his advantage, something few people would be able to handle. He could take this vague criticism.

Why not bless everyone if you want to bring about true peace, instead of just your followers? You could have a greater, larger army. Your purposes don't align with your actions.

Jericho ventured to the left side of the dresser and doubled the rings on his right hand. *Those who I allow to become blessed are those who would otherwise be under the delusion that they could build a life in this middle realm, that there would be some part of them that survives after death.*

But that is—

—a lie. Nothing escapes its return to the infernal realms, from which all has arisen. Your figment of imagination, the belief in anything outside of this, is a dream that occurs from the infernal realms and Great Spirit itself. Even you will return to the Spirit one day. Dragons are not immortal.

Wrong. It is all wrong.

Jericho converted the dragon's desperation to strength.

My kind is proof of the eternal.

I do not think so highly of your kind. Jericho sighed, tired of this petty back and forth. *It is me who saves the world from suffering.*

Chains jingled against his rings as Jericho tucked them inside of his cream-colored cloak. He sensed someone approaching and soon heard scattered footsteps—*click-clack, click-clack*—the recognizable walk of Haskil.

When humans fuse our beliefs, generation after generation, we stand a chance of matching your strength. By the end, we will all be equal in the void of peace. Death is what truly stands against time. And if you don't come willingly, I will tear down the fake world you confine us to, and allow the infernal realms to drown every inch of your holy land.

Are you not scared of death? The voice asked. Jericho sensed a lack of fear and general amazement.

It was a thoughtful question. *I have no fear of the true Spirit.* Jericho pushed the dragon spirit into the recesses of his mind. *This dull middle realm and everyone inside of it will have returned to the Spirit after High Silver. My minions will rise from the infernal realms, and together we will conquer and bring justice to our kind.*

The study door flew open and Haskil entered. The black-cloaked servant guided a string wrapped around the wool of one of Tempus' sheep.

Baa. Baa-baa, it complained.

The servant's decrepit walk yanked at the animal's neck.

"Haskil," Jericho motioned for him to drop the leash. "What is this?"

Baa. Baa.

"Claims to have information on the dragon-lovers, m'Lord. Came and told the guards after 'igh Gold, she did."

Jericho studied the sheep as the servant closed the door. The *baas* grew more jumbled, and the sheep began to cough, its tongue moving in and out of its mouth as it twitched. It stood slowly on its hind legs, growing taller, hair receding into gray skin that gained complexion by the moment. Jericho recognized the face.

Ack, the witch coughed. She fell to her knees and bowed her balding head. "My Lord." A hackneyed smile revealing a few yellow teeth angered Jericho.

A genuinely revolting sight. "Elphaba... Forgive me. I hardly recognized you."

The witch stood from her place, and Jericho couldn't help but take a step away. "And I you, my Lord. You are looking ever extravagant, as always." Her voice sounded like a bag of nails.

He forced a grin. "Your information?"

"Yes, my Lord. The rogues, you see. The dragon-lovers. You said to always watch out for them my Lord, and I never thought I would have to, you see, being on the outsides of the wall." As she talked, the remote connections in the sheepish part of her still lingered in her human form—particularly the boil and her broad nose, sticking out like a muzzle over her mouth as she talked.

"Yet I was there," she went on, a misty look in her eyes. "I grazed by the forest as I do every day, and one of them jumps right over the fence. He goes right into the forest of time." Her yellow-brown eyes were the size of the moon. "I'm sure you knew of this, but I had never seen a thing so brave my Lord."

"Brave?" Jericho asked.

"No, no my Lord, of course not brave. I meant to say reckless. I'd never seen souls so reckless and... And lost, my Lord, willing to throw everything away. But the boy, he returned. The conversation was worse, you see, they want to turn the blessed girl, the sacrifice. They intend to make her a rogue."

They already have, Jericho thought. *Precisely on time and according to plan.* He gave her a gracious nod. "Very interesting. Thank you, Elphaba. Anything else I should know?"

She stuttered, her eyes scanned for something else to say. "No, my Lord, I do not think so, no, I fear not."

"Do not fear," he said. "You provided valuable information. More than that, you did as you were told if you saw someone disobeying the Lord."

She nodded appreciatively.

"Forgive me if my worry hides the gratitude I feel for your act. *Ah,* I know just the reward for you." He shuffled over to a nearby case and clutched one of the rings. "I should reward you with blessings of your own, come equinox tonight. You've so obviously displayed your loyalty." He flicked the ring over to her. "But this should do for now."

The witch's eyes went wide as she caught the ring in midair and bit on the metal to see if it was real. She squealed. Her hideous smile flashed up at him—her God. "Oh, thank you my Lord. Thank you, thank you, thank you."

"Please," he motioned to the door, and Haskil opened it. "It seems we have much more work than expected."

"Yes, my Lord, of cou—*aaa, baaa.*" She returned to sheep form, muzzling through the door. Haskil started to follow.

"You heard her," Jericho said to the servant. "It seems I did not account for many things on this day of reckoning. I need you with me, Haskil. Let her find her way through the tunnels."

"Right away, m'lord."

The sheep stared with a low glare through the doorway as Haskil slammed the door closed.

The servant turned to Jericho, his beady all-black eyes wide, head tilted in question. "If I could ask, my lord. Will I receive any blessings today?"

Everyone is always worried about themselves. "You have a substantial amount of draconic power within you." Every time Jericho looked at Haskil, he was forced to remember the failure of his first attempt to fuse a human with draconic form. It had never been done since his father managed the feat all those years ago.

"You have more responsibility than my sheep," the Lord said. "You are my loyal servant. Focus on your task and doing it well, and you will have more Spirit than any witch could imagine." Jericho listened for the breathing or hooves of the creature outside the door. "Are all of your tasks in order?"

"Y-yes, my lord. I made to the cathedral this morning and all is correct." The servant seemed too fidgety for his liking.

"Then you shall expect a great reward." Jericho kept quiet, waited.

"Perhaps there is one issue," Haskil finally said. "But it has not to do with the cathedral or my tasks, for I did everything to your wish, m'lord. It's not an issue, really. More of a concern. I'm sure you have it managed, m'lord, as you are so capable, but it is your wish for me to tell you everything, as your servant."

"Go on." The authoritative tone crushed the puny half-breed.

"Right, m'lord. It has to do with the rogues. It is just that, you know as well as I, we do not have a hold on the forest of time. I must ask, m'lord. Are the rogues the reason why we go to the cathedral underground today, instead of with pastor Solomon?"

"You're mistaken," Jericho said, walking around the room to Haskil, avoiding the broken glass on the floor.

"I'm sorry, m'lord. I meant in no way to offend—"

"The old spirits are no more than ghosts of the past, Haskil. They cannot harm us from the sheltered place they stole. It is only a matter of time before they weaken and are forced to come forth and own up to their pathetic existence. It might be good for the rogue students to see a dying era. Did that ever occur to you? Tell me, Haskil, do you have any other doubts about my intelligence?"

"N-no," Haskil chuckled nervously. "Never doubts m'lord, never. Only a question, so I may try to understand your wise ways." He dropped to a knee.

"A measly effort, if that was the case. Stand. Let me see if you can figure it out for yourself. Think, Haskil. Why would I want the three rogue students, who are the most capable students in the church, as close as I can get them to the sacrifice?"

Haskil's face twisted in thought, trying to make sense of the intricacies and complexities.

Jericho saved him the headache, tapping the upper pocket of his cloak to be sure the little creature was still there, though the cloaks he'd designed were highly functional. "Those who are most likely to challenge their fate must be closest to the sacrifice," he said. "They are harder to convince of the true way of the Spirit."

Jericho walked past Haskil and opened the door to the tunnels, stepping into the humid dim corridors. "Pastor Solomon has guided my Zealots and cargo through the forest without issue. The Dyra are too weak to stop the Spirit, as they always have been. Our conquest over their realm begins in the equinox moonlight, and from then on, we will bathe the heavens in the sweet cloak of the void. Meanwhile, I have a reward for your good service."

The servant snorted and dribbled as Jericho locked the door to his quarters by removing a single ruby gem from the top lock.

"A reward, m'lord?"

He can't hold it in. Jericho ignored him, reaching into his cloak to fetch the tiny scaled creature. He removed the one-sided dagger from his hip and brought it across the creature's throat, careful to hold it out before him so as not to stain his cloak.

A string of glowing beams rose from the dragon's body and swirled down through the tunnel, the swamp green color of the creature's scales. It would guide them through the tunnels to the cathedral.

Haskil had been slurping up the blood of the dragon. Jericho whistled and threw the servant the body. It crunched between jagged rows of teeth. Moments later, the servant looked up, licking its lips. "And the sheep, my Lord? Surely she couldn't find her way through here. Why did you send her on her way to be lost?"

So he does pay attention, at least to the things he finds worthy.

Jericho waved the servant on to track the sheep. "Be sure to save the ring."

CHAPTER 20

SECOND ERA, 113, UAIR THREE OF RISING SILVER

Boyd

Boyd had no way of knowing how the dragon would act. Neither did Isaac or Rebekah, no matter how young it was. Just because it listened and stuck close to Isaac's leg didn't mean they could trust it. The way it slithered and sniffed the ground alongside them seemed deceptive to say the least. Boyd noticed the exaggerated playfulness. A young creature so blessed would have a power they knew nothing about, not to mention its unpredictable, untrained Spirit. Regardless, Isaac had invited the creature along without asking the group, as if it were proven harmless simply because it followed him out of the harbor below. Isaac seemed to have convinced himself, bragging about a fake vision to Rebekah.

Aside from it all, Boyd couldn't say anything. There was no time to worry about whether the dragons could befriend humans—not here in Tempus. As Isaac and Rebekah conversed on the path ahead, following the dry footprints of the Zealots through crushed twigs and broken trees, Boyd lingered back to keep watch on the forest depths and the orange dragon.

The trail and footprints of the pastors had been easy enough to see—another reason why Boyd suspected someone tricked them into the forest. They had found what they looked for too early. The danger that surrounded them, however, would reveal itself only when it became too late.

For now, the shadows of the forest proved empty. Boyd's gaze hopped frantically from shadow to shadow.

The two looked back every few moments, probably to see if he followed. He was staying quiet on purpose, listening to them talk. They seemed to prefer it that way.

They probably wish I'd leave them alone.

He would have preferred that too. He could focus on the actual dangers of the forest, the tasks at hand.

The oppressive scenery wasn't helping him get over the bitter feeling in his stomach. Tempus proved just as lonely, dead, and terrifying as the last time he entered. The dwarf creatures, whatever they were, likely discovered their arrival by now, hopping their way through the swamp and shrubs to consume them. *It won't be long until we are fighting their way through the waist-high demon horde.*

And how would the dragon react when the demons came? Would it be able to do anything more than turn the monsters to mist? Boyd chuckled at the realization they'd have.

Isaac glanced back.

"Are we almost to the cathedral?" Boyd asked.

"I believe so." Isaac returned to his conversation.

What does he know about directions here, Boyd thought, watching with contempt as the dragon trotted near him. A creature so powerful, yet an outlier among its peers at the harbor. A unique one among the crowd of dying animals that just so happened to take a liking to Isaac.

It was all so easy for him, so catered to his plan. *It's too good to be true.* Isaac was falling right into the trap, likely planted by Jericho himself. *The dragon has no reason to stay and fight for the humans that tortured its kind. It doesn't care about us.*

Part of it had to be Rebekah. Even she might not be worthy of trust. She'd been the Lord's protegé, changing her mind from everything she'd ever known in just a few hours. Yet there Isaac was, tapping her arm as he talked, taking in her smile. He tried so hard. A shot at taking the equinox test, thinking he's strong enough to take on the Tempus creatures, and now Isaac was mentioning visions? *Next, he'll think he can breathe fire.*

Dark flashes in the woods made Boyd jump. It had been the darkness playing with his mind once more. He still hadn't gotten entirely used to his increased perception.

He focused again on Isaac and Rebekah walking side-by-side, the dragon at their feet. *They're far too comfortable. It's a good thing I'm so alert.*

"In the old days, they encouraged pastors to look into a dragon's eyes?" Rebekah asked.

"There was talk about other realms in the first-era, places only trained pastors could visit by meeting the gaze of a dragon."

Boyd remembered the stories he'd read a million times in that dusty old notebook.

"We never got the chance to try it at St. Daemonus," Isaac said.

"Why would someone want to do that?" Rebekah asked. "I mean... It'd be too unnatural for me."

"It took time and effort to learn, but it was worth it. Apostles would see advancements that we could try and recreate here in this realm, and often did. Boats, farming, herding, it was how they found out about the island of Daemonus and every other discovery the dragons gave us since Vulcan, the first Chrysos."

"So to have a vision, you have to look into a dragon's gaze?" Boyd had to know because of the vision Isaac claimed. If his friend had been crazy enough to look into one of the dragon's eyes while he was unlocking the cage, untrained in the ways of the first-era except for reading that outdated notebook, he'd be suicidal for taking such a risk. *Does Isaac want to prove he's right so bad that he'd risk his sanity?*

"That's what the notebook says. But that's not what happened when I received the vision from Helios. It was hard not to look into its eyes. I wanted to. It took everything I could, but I promise that I didn't."

"So what happened?" Boyd asked.

"When I reached into the cage, it leaned forward and touched my hand with its nose. Then I became very cold, and I couldn't stop falling back. I didn't know what was happening, but the next thing I knew I was back in Windhaven."

"Why would it bring you there, of all places?"

"I'm not sure. The vision didn't seem to mean anything. It happened so quickly. I felt weird when I returned, like the world was unstable."

Boyd wanted to laugh at the absurdity. *Who does he think he is, to be gifted a vision by a dragon?* It sounded like he tried to compensate for the dragon he murdered, forcing the world of his father's notebook to come true. It was all Isaac ever wanted for the dragons to be friendly. It seemed like quite the coincidence for him to be chosen for a vision immediately after he'd been rejected by the Lord and humiliated by Rebekah, after trying every other possible path.

Boyd studied the amber dragon, considering the different ways Jericho could be tricking them, convincing them of another false world—one that appealed to each of them. Jericho could have even placed the forest here to deceive them. *Let's not forget the sacrifice they both made earlier today. They both could be under the influence of Jericho.*

Rebekah stopped, bent to inspect a worn footprint on the ground, and moved forward. "Something similar happened to me," she said. "When I touched the scale of the Chrysos, I—"

"You were next to the *Chrysos*?"

Boyd hushed Isaac. Thankfully, no child-like laughter returned.

"How big were its scales? Did you see the wings?"

He sounds like an excited child, Boyd thought, studying the same footprint as Rebekah, weakly pressed—rushed.

"The scales were pale, maybe dying," Rebekah said. "White and gray. Lifeless. It was dark below the ship, I couldn't see much. But it felt like I was in a furnace, and when they pressed my hand to the scale, that same feeling paralyzed me, except it was a terrible heat. I couldn't move for the longest time."

Isaac agreed too hastily. "When my vision started, my body may as well have been frozen."

They shared a lingering gaze.

"I could only imagine what it was like to visit another island, if only for a moment."

A fire erupted in Boyd's stomach. "If I touch the dragon now, I'd have myself a vision?" He leaned down near Helios, sticking out a hand.

"I wouldn't," Rebekah said.

"I don't know what would happen," said Isaac.

He agrees with every syllable that leaves her mouth. Boyd would find a way to prove that Isaac lied about the visions. You couldn't travel to a completely different place by touching a dragon's scales, and Isaac wasn't unique or hadn't done enough training to receive a vision.

Boyd bent to touch the dragon's scales, and it jumped away faster than he could ever hope to move, helped by a flutter of under-grown wings.

Come here, you little freak. Boyd stepped forward, lunged again.

Not even close.

The dragon bounced back.

Boyd ran forward, missing another snatch. Leaning down, he noticed something missing from the dry Tempus trail.

"Hold on," he said. "Where did the tracks go?"

Rebekah walked up next to him, inspecting where the Zealots's tracks ended. "This isn't good."

"They were just right here," Isaac said. Helios sniffed around, sitting idly by Isaac's leg.

Boyd backed away from the dragon. "We're lost. I told you." The fog of Tempus, low and blue, started to thicken. "We never should've come here."

"Wait," said Rebekah. "Do you hear that?"

The laughter. It's the gnomes. As he went to draw his slingshot, Boyd paused and lowered it back into the holster. The sound of bright, ringing bells played in a random pattern—sonic gold from somewhere deep within the fog's curls. "What *is* that?"

"It's amazing...." Isaac said, his voice falling away as Boyd couldn't help but run toward the tone, searching. The distinct sound spoke of truth, a pure perfection one would feel silly hoping to attain, but here it was. The footsteps of Rebekah, Isaac, and Helios followed somewhere behind.

"Should we be going this way?" Isaac asked.

They had deviated from the path, but nobody answered him.

Boyd knew it was some absolute form of the Spirit. Perhaps it would help them defeat Jericho.

Legs scraping through the dead shrubbery, the fog took on a fainter texture, the collective chimes growing louder. *I'm close.* Some of the dead shrubs looked as if they were coming to life—greener, fuller. Boyd caught sight of a single blooming petal, like those in the library. It glowed as they neared.

"Look," he told the others, though he felt disconnected, unsure if he could reach them with his voice. It felt like he'd spent a few seconds admiring the soft petals, far brighter and more intricately grown than those of the Daemonus garden, but when his head raised again, Isaac and Rebekah were far up ahead through the growth of many flowers and budding leaves.

They laughed. For a moment, Boyd worried about what the chimes did to him and why, but then he followed their gaze out to the forest, looking around. Tree trunks had widened, and the arms grew by the hundreds, extended to intertwine and hug nearby relatives. Magnificent flowers of every color, shape, and texture blossomed everywhere in a contrasting glow to create a calming interplay of glowing auras. Red speckled dots marked the leaves on the trees filled with new life, and every now and then, the whisper of wind would knock down powdery red dust, like snow, and it fell atop fungi with domed and spotted caps.

Shoulder-height arched doors began to appear on the left and right, carved into the tree-sides. *The gnomes.* Though, the doors had been too nicely decorated for such a despicable creature. When he worked up the nerve to try and open one, the long and thin gold bar holding the door wouldn't move. A peek inside the tiny circular window showed nothing but darkness.

Boyd looked up the massive trunks that had tripled in size, giants of their past form. The moon poked through their branches. He had the momentary thought that concern might be necessary, then the sound of rushing water called to him, riding the wind—a melody beneath the colorful chimes.

Helios jumped onto a series of jutting mushroom caps like platforms. Isaac ran around the tree, after the dragon, laughing. It was too fast for him.

As Boyd moved closer, he found sharp marks carved in the bark; six dashes, three on top of three. He couldn't believe it, digging into his pocket to retrieve the rock he used for his slingshot, making the seventh mark under the others. *It's different since the last time I came. Better.*

The tree before the bog was giant this time around. Boyd hadn't seen any sign of the jumping gnomes. The fog cleared. He reached out, touched the rough bark, and rubbed the marks. Faint colors moved within the timber, blotches of violet and yellow.

Hold on.

Comparing the two, the wood of his slingshot matched the bark exactly, pulsating with the same inner glow, even seeming to link in timing when Boyd brought them close together.

As he ventured around the tree, he saw Rebekah and Isaac exploring through a grassy clearing, a crystal spring lake where the bog used to be.

"I think this slingshot is from here," he said across a stream that led to a smaller pond at the clearing's far end. "Wherever here is." He tripped over a tree limb.

"This isn't Tempus," Rebekah said, pacing near the lake. "We went off the path. Where did the chimes go?"

Boyd hadn't noticed they were gone. The immediate silence brought a sharp sense of worry.

Isaac seemed almost groggy, slouching near the water. "The notebook never talked about a place like this."

"This is what we should be following," Boyd said. "Not what Jericho says or promises of a vision. But how did we get here, and how do we get out?" The question hung in the air. It seemed silly to suggest. Who would want to leave a place like this?

Perhaps, there is something here that could save us. Boyd looked out over the fresh spring, so different from the bog. The water provided a wavering blue view of the sand on the bottom—thousands of buried gems reflected with a wavy sheen.

Isaac appeared next to him.

"Be careful," he said. "Just because this place feels good doesn't mean we can't get lost."

"Yes," Boyd said. *That's what I was trying to say.* "We have to find the cathedral before it's too late." But as he spoke, what was said got lost in Helios' commotion.

The dragon ran out into the brush. Rebekah and Isaac followed, but Boyd thought it best to have some space from Isaac and Rebekah for a few moments. Then they would hunt for the cathedral and the footprints of the pastors again. Helios wouldn't go far.

He became encapsulated with the lake's depth once more, trying to hone in on the feeling of the Spirit, the thousands of untapped gems, an effort to locate and cultivate the feeling for good. The effort brought tears to his eyes, and he found himself overcome by an intense hatred for Jericho, the one who lacked enough heart to disturb a cluster of gems as sacred as this for his own selfish purposes.

Boyd would dedicate his life to making sure this form of the Spirit went untouched by humans and dragons. *That is what Rebekah meant when she said she still followed the Spirit, even though she didn't trust Jericho. But is it what Isaac meant when he agreed?*

He's confused, willing to kill a dragon just to fit in. He expects us to believe the dragons chose him to receive a vision. The thought of Isaac's arrogance dulled the beauty of the gems.

As Boyd stood from his knees, neither of the two were within sight. He searched the line of luminescent brushes, growing anxious. *They couldn't have gone far.*

He ventured into the forest, where they had followed Helios. "Isaac?" he called. "Rebekah?" Faint chirps and groans from unknown animals returned.

They couldn't have gone far.

The descent into panic seemed terribly familiar. Boyd strained his ears to listen for the slightest laughter or sign of fog as he crept over tree limbs and under giant leaves, heavy to lift. The more he walked, the more a flaky, red substance on the plants and trees covered him. He began to use the caps of the growing mushrooms on the trees as stepping stones, climbing high to the thick branches. Despite the beautiful view, there was no sign of his companions.

Balancing and jumping between trees proved easy due to Boyd's blessings. He felt in tune with the environment. The foreboding silence was traded for crashing waves.

Even the ocean looked different, the waves perfectly aligned.

Boyd turned at the sound of a snapping twig, hoping to see a friendly face. Every muscles in his body went into shock at the sight of snarling fangs, dual daggers sticking out of a yawning jaw. Mouth closed, dripping with saliva, the face of a jungle cat stared at him with bright green eyes, a mane of white swirls amidst night-black fur.

A sniff and the creature jumped to the same tree branch Boyd stood on, its bend doubling. Boyd stepped back, balancing in the little space he had left. "Good cat," he said, looking around for an escape to the long distance below.

The cat lashed out, Boyd jumped, missing the branch he intended to grab.

This is it, he thought, falling for what seemed like forever to finally bounce atop a mushroom cap. A strawberry-colored burst of red dust flew up, and Boyd used the cover to slide away.

When he looked up, green eyes peered over the branch from above. The cat's head disappeared, then its body blocked the starry sky as it fell toward him.

Terrified, Boyd thought to run once the cat landed and its claws dug into the plush cap.

He fumbled for his slingshot and fired at the creature as he ran, but the rock no more than bounced off the creature, and he caught it again mid-stride.

The creature's paws thudded against the forest floor as it weaved through low branches in the autumn trees. Unsure of how to get back to the spring, without time, Boyd tried one of the doors on the trees, and to his surprise, the bar lifted.

He stumbled into darkness. In the center of the tree, there was a staircase, and he ran up.

A few moments later, the door burst open behind him.

The scent of lavender became prominent, and a blue light leaked in from the cracks of a door at the top steps. But when Boyd emerged, it wasn't the tree branches and high overview of Tempus he saw, but he was on the ground level of trees; only the plants had grown more numerous.

He didn't know how much longer he could survive. The door behind him burst open, and again the cat followed. *I was hoping you'd relax a bit.*

A sharp right under bunches of leaves, Boyd ducked, tripped, and fell into an open clearing.

Out of breath, he lugged himself to his feet and took a few steps forward, only to drop to his knees again at the sight of ghostly figures floating ahead.

It can't get any stranger, he thought, staring at ghosts as clear as day—outlines of forms, faded and faint. *This has to be another realm, another world.*

The beings floated toward him, no more than a collection of wisps from the shade of gray to blue. Boyd could barely see their faces but for their bright green eyes. The most prevalent sign of their presence was the pulsing shade of color inside the gut of each one. For all he knew, these beings were impervious to his slingshot as well. And what good would it do? There were hundreds.

A heavy thud sounded behind him.

The floating creatures gasped all at once and retreated into the carved doors of the trees.

Boyd turned to see the enormous cat prowling out from under the leaves, its fur rough and mangy, ribs visible. It hadn't seen a meal in days. The hungry eyes cut through him.

Boyd threw the useless slingshot on the ground out before him, hoping the creature would accept his plea for mercy. When the beast stalked directly past it, he found a sense of acceptance as he raised his hands to his face and prepared to die.

A ferocious snarl.

Boyd heard pounding feet leave the grass...

Then nothing.

Was it that quick?

He lowered his arms to see the forest and bushes, the translucent floating beings approaching once more. He thought more had emerged this time around. *Their bodies are clear as glass, airy as the wind.*

"There is no need to be scared," said one, separating from the group to fly out toward him.

"Where is the wildcat?"

No answer.

These flying creatures seemed to pose no threat, given their lack of physical structure. The one who approached had a band of white feathers around a golden crown on its head and wore nothing else, overdressed compared to the others. Boyd couldn't keep his eyes from drifting, but the creatures had no sexual organs to leave exposed.

"I know you're confused," it said, no more than a few feet away. The voice felt like a warm hug amidst the chaos. The whitish glow emanating at the creature's center morphed and moved like an orb within its body. The others fluttered near the grand trees and maintained their distance, whispering.

"Where am I?" Boyd asked. An expression of curiosity fluttered across the nearby being's face. "Y-you won't hurt me?"

"We'd only be hurting ourselves," the creature said.

"You're not wrong," Boyd said, trying to be intimidating, but someone near the trees might have giggled. "I mean, why is that?"

At the same time, the floating beings drooped to the ground, making a relieved sound. *"Ahhhhh."* The aura at their center flashed the pale purple of lilac for the shortest moment, then settled back to white.

"What are you?" Boyd rose to his feet. "What happened to the thing that was chasing me? Where are my friends?" It felt weird that he called them that, but he didn't know what else to say.

The creatures giggled, rising into the air. The closest resisted laughter, though a smile was on its face. It floated down to meet Boyd's eye level, no taller than half his height.

"You're the first to see this realm for as long as we can remember." With a smile, the creature bowed, its headwear jingling from various bells and chimes strung together. "We apologize for your journey here. It seemed to be rough. Yet, it had to be for you. You are that which is brave. The warrior."

"Have I died?"

The older creature laughed again, the others following—something they seemed to do often. "I apologize," the being said. "I forget how different our world is from yours, and this is only the first realm. Can you imagine the others? I doubt we would recognize them.

"I suppose it is important to tell you, we are empaths. We feel the feelings of others and cannot help it as much as you humans breathe. And my, we haven't felt such intense emotion in years." The creature soared up into the air, a stream of continuous wisps around one intact ball of light. "We the Dyra would like to thank you for allowing us to empathize with your struggles and relief. In times like these, we must savor positive feelings, as infrequent as they come."

Another creature approached him, looking so similar to the other except for its black and white bandana of fur. "It wasn't hard to scare this one. I almost had to change into something less frightening. He was about to pee his pants. I felt it."

Suddenly Boyd recognized the texture and pattern of the fur on the Dyra's head. "You were the wildcat?" The creatures that called themselves Dyra erupted into laughter. "What is so funny about that? I thought I was going to die."

"Nothing at all," said the Dyra with the bandana, floating down to him. This Dyra was younger, more brawny, but it had the same knowing presence. "You confront things a normal human would be too scared to face. My kin are experiencing the vast range of human emotions for the first time in years, and struggle to handle themselves. Don't blame them for having a little joy." The Dyra flew back toward the other, and a shock of spring green light passed between the glowing orbs in their bodies.

Boyd had so many questions. How could they shift into other animals here? Where was here? But he needed to know how much they knew about him first, less whoever was playing this trick gained the upper hand. "What is that?" he asked, pointing to the lights in both their guts.

The creature with the headdress looked down as if never noticing the light before. "We are empaths, and cannot help but feel the emotions of the beings around us. So why would our bodies hide them as well?"

The creature floated down toward Boyd. He watched as the light inside pulsated midnight blue. "We cannot hide our own feelings, no matter how much we try. Whether we feel them ourselves or absorb them, the emotions take the form of color in our bodies. It doesn't take long to learn what color means which, about the same as it takes to learn the name of all the feelings." The creature floated away, raising its arms at the surrounding forest of light. "This is the realm of promises, where nothing can be hidden." The creature looked back his way. "Does my knowledge of your feelings offend you? We can teach you the corresponding colors and emotions, if you like."

Boyd wanted to say no, but it was very odd. He couldn't bring himself to lie to the creature. It would know. He couldn't bring himself to offend the being, either, so he said nothing.

Then the two Dyra looked at the other and began their laughter. *Childish and giddy.*

"You've done us a great favor in this time of sadness," the Dyra with the black and white bandana said.

"I'm not sure how. But I suppose I'm happy for you."

"*Ahhhh,*" the Dyra near the trees sighed again.

This time, he needed only to give the leader a questioning look.

"Saying the way you feel goes a long way."

Wherever this was, he'd seen enough. "I need to find my friends."

"No need to be scared," the floating Dyra with the tall crown said. "I promise you, you are safe. We want to see the Lord fall."

How could he be sure they weren't some conjuration by Jericho meant to appeal to his wishes? It wasn't like the Spirit he felt earlier, the one he knew to be true. "Why?"

The one with the crown answered. "The Lord seeks to destroy every being that does not bow to him and vow to serve. We can sense his pain and sorrow, and do not want any part in it."

Boyd perked. "You know of the Lord's sacrifice?" *Yes,* he thought. *Jericho's conjuring trick would know of the sacrifice too.*

"We know much more that we hope may aid in your battle

against the Lord. You judged us because of our differences, but I'm afraid no fate is as simple as a cat chasing a mouse."

"Show him his things, Legola. You must always keep this one occupied, he learns quickly. Already, he grows impatient."

Boyd wanted to object. He couldn't deny the sense of unease, but it was because of everything unfamiliar. He had deviated so much from his task. "I was with others. We were on our way to stop the Lord. We have to make it to the cathedral before midnight."

The Dyra they called Legola looked at Boyd, a smirk upon its face. "Your friends are okay. They are reaching this realm through their means." The Dyra pulsed a familiar dark blue. "Our Elder is correct. You are restless. Such is the way of the warrior. You also need to be calm in your critique of the world. Look to the sky, young Boyd, and tell me what you see."

Boyd looked, saw the moon and the stars. "I see that it's close to High Silver."

"And it has been in our realm for the past hundred years, but never has it reached that time." Legola paused. "You are confused. We will tell you everything when your companions arrive. In short, we've been hiding from the Lord here, right in front of his eyes. It won't be that way for long. Our hold on this time is fading, and the Lord grows stronger." Legola sighed and pulsed with a cloudy gray hue. "Now, let me return you your things."

Boyd followed Legola as it flew through the camp toward what they said were his things. Midway through the camp of flowers and logs, they stopped and lifted the bar to one of the towering trees and the door opened with a creak. The main floor of the space was wide open, a fire pit at the center despite the house being wood, and a kitchen on the far side. Moonlight leaked through cracks.

Other levels of the tree were accessible by a stairwell placed right in the middle. Boyd crouched to inspect the knick-knacks lining the shelves, doll-like recreations of creatures of many different forms, including the ghosts. Legola walked along the floor in here with a confident jaunt. Boyd followed to a jumbled brown blanket at the corner of the room.

The Dyra lifted the blanket to show his daggers gathered in a pile.

Boyd scoffed. *It was them all along.*

Legola pulsed a bright shade of yellow. "Not so fast." The Dyra flew past him, no more than a rush of wind, and picked up one of his silver-hilted daggers. "Allow me to show you the proper way to use these. Do you still have that slingshot from the first-era?"

CHAPTER 21

FIRST ERA, 1,999, UAIR FIVE OF RISING SILVER

Rebekah

T hey'd searched everywhere around the clear spring lake except for inside, and Rebekah refused to venture in there. Enough had taken place to show her they weren't in control anymore. The dragon that so quickly became a sign of momentum against the Lord had disappeared into the moonlit forest, seemingly for good.

We can't let ourselves be distracted again, Rebekah thought as she wandered back into the clearing, admitting to having lost Boyd as well. Whatever this version of Tempus was, wherever they were, everything had too much meaning to ignore. The beautiful sights and sounds—the chimes, wind, and glowing leaves raking together, no animals present—it tore them away from each other.

The clear water of the spring drew her attention. She fell in love with beautiful crystals at the bottom, like tiny promises of the Spirit that Jericho always seemed to hide for himself.

"Do you think the Lord found out about Helios?" At the edge of the clearing, Isaac stepped over and through the line of glowing fauna. "Just when you think you have something, Jericho goes and takes it away."

Rebekah wasn't so sure the Lord had power over all of Tempus, especially a part as unique as this. He had always preached against entering the forest of time because of the evil spirits that would fill one's mind with insane ramblings of the first era. The texts of the St. Daemonus library mentioned nothing more than the inevitable death that lay inside.

Rebekah never considered that this part of the forest could exist, the world filled with random plants, gems, and trees that gave her more peace than what she felt worshipping Jericho. She couldn't ignore the beauty of this forest, especially with the blessings, allowing her to feel so much.

"Helios," Isaac called again, inspecting crevices of gem-filled rocks near the water.

Did he even notice Boyd was gone? He had mentioned some sort of fallout they had before meeting with her, but never elaborated on what happened.

"Helios," he called.

Rebekah had seen the last moment Isaac touched the amber dragon at the harbor. She emerged around the corner, about to say she finished unlocking the cages in her row, when she caught Isaac halfway inside the cage, and stepped back to watch in silence.

His eyes were closed, making her doubt he ever met the creature's gaze, but to touch a dragon without reason was reckless enough. She tried to forget the burning emptiness that had come over her when pastor Solomon held her hand to the sleeping Chrysos, looking down at the wrinkled marks reddening her palm.

Boyd's recklessness, his urge to end everything Jericho stands for, none of it is warranted. We still have to be able to trust someone, she thought, looking at Isaac as he called the dragon again.

"Boyd likely went into the forest to look for us," she said. "We should do the same. He couldn't have gotten far."

After he searched a while more, Isaac agreed.

It was getting dark. They would have to leave Tempus soon if they had any hope of saving the Chrysos. The moon had neared High Silver faster than Rebekah knew possible. Perhaps the time had moved more quickly in this place.

"I don't know how we ended up here," she said, trying not to seem overwhelmed by the silence replacing the chimes.

"I hope it wasn't a mistake," Isaac said. "We left the trail just to follow a pleasant sound."

They trekked through the bushes, branches almost moving with their stride, providing dim light in the growing darkness that would soon end their search. Isaac jumped onto a few squishy mushroom caps growing up a tall tree, climbing as high as he could to search outward. "Where could he be? He was our only chance at saving the Chrysos."

"It seems like you're more worried about Helios than Boyd."

Isaac gave her a puzzled look. "Who is going to help us most when it comes to stopping the Lord? It's not like Boyd would go along with a plan we came up with."

Her perception of his emotions felt more significant here. Suddenly, the plants couldn't distract her, and she focused solely on him, finding millions of small actions to notice—the direction he looked, the posture he took, and the way his eyes lingered on her own. "I just thought you guys were close friends," she said.

I hope he can tell I only speak from curiosity.

"Boyd was the one friend I had in the church. He lost his mind when the equinox neared. He became a different person. Always arguing and trying to prove he was right. Everything became a challenge. We didn't always fight like this."

Isaac walked down a path lined with the luminescent shrubbery, balancing on an enormous root running the narrow length. A faint chime jingled with every one of his steps. "We used to dream about my father's book and the adventures we were going to have as heroes. For five years we ignored what was going on in the church, not caring about what murderers would say. I mean, the Lord's other followers. Not you."

"I thought you were different," she said. "But not in a bad way. Not until the idea of being Jericho's best student got to me."

"We never cared. We went through whatever class we had, waiting to explore the world of the notebook after. It's like we knew what was true all this time. When our fifth-year came around, we were forced to consider our other options besides killing a dragon or ending up as Jericho's slave. I ignored the topic for as long as I could, that's probably bad, but the day finally came, and it ends up we thought differently."

"What exactly happened?" Rebekah asked, thinking back to her roommate Priska. *I should've spent more time comforting her. She didn't deserve such pain.*

"We were trying to come up with a plan to leave and Boyd planned to escape without telling me."

"He was just going to leave you behind?" *Like I did to Priska.*

"After I told him it was stupid to leave, yes." Isaac was beginning to get involved with the story.

"It is impossible to leave the island as a blessed one," she assured. "Hasn't Boyd read about the Lord's sigils, his eyes throughout the island?"

"Boyd has read very few things in his life. I told him that escaping was impossible and he didn't believe me. You can't tell him anything."

The story made sense of their insistence to contradict each other. Rebekah felt wrong about criticizing Boyd without him here to defend himself, as wrong as it was to speak negatively about the Lord, and wanted to know more about Isaac's view. It had been his authentic dedication that convinced her.

"How did you want to change things?" she asked.

"After looking for a natural way to stop the Lord in my father's notebook and finding nothing, I wanted to convince everyone that the dragons were friendly. I knew it had to be over a long period of time. Nobody would believe in the miracles of dragons unless they saw it themselves. To me, it was obvious. I had to join the church and change it from the inside out. That's why I went to training and took the test, even though I didn't have blessings."

Rebekah couldn't find anything dishonest about the statement. "I'm sorry about training, by the way. I don't know what came over me."

"It's alright. Not like I was going to become blessed anyway."

"You weren't a terrible fighter."

He half-laughed and grinned.

The path narrowed, closing the distance between them.

"This seems like the forest, renovated to fit the first-era," Rebekah said, batting at one of the giant palm leaves. A cloud of shimmering red dust leaped off.

The path forked, and Isaac hesitated to choose the leftmost direction. "What did you think about me before today, when you didn't understand?"

She supposed it was her turn to elaborate. "The others called you a dragon-lover, teasing you and everything, but I never joined them. You interested me. I admired how you always stuck to your ways, but thought you were confused. I see the irony in that now. The Lord and church were all I ever really knew. There was no other path but to become a great apostle, and you were so far from it. I never considered you much, if I'm being honest."

"That's funny."

She glanced at him. "Is it?"

"We were both encouraged to be great apostles, me from my father's notebook and you from the Lord, but we were trying to be two completely different things."

She thought for a moment. "Less funny, more a strength that we have to play into. Maybe the only thing we have to fight with."

He didn't respond to that, and she cursed herself for ruining the good tone. She turned, about to thank him for lightening her mood when he twisted toward a sudden rustling in the surreal brush.

An orange figure darted into one of the tall trees, through a crack in the misshapen door.

"Helios!" Isaac ran in after him.

So much for not losing each other. Rebekah hurried, climbing up short brown mushroom caps on thick stalks to the hollow tree's entrance.

Segmented levels filled the tree's inner height, a spiraling staircase to access them all. The place seemed like something had lived there many years ago, and nothing had visited since. Rebekah squinted to see supplies lining the far wall; kitchen utensils, much too small for use, yet intricate and seemingly complex. Isaac ran up a staircase in the center. She followed, and to her surprise, emerged to the same forest floor of Tempus, as if not having climbed through the tree.

Isaac ran through a garden of neon purple-blue, pink, and yellow petaled flowers so abundant there was no option but to step on them, releasing more of the flickering red dust into the air.

"I saw him running through here," Isaac said, referring to the dragon.

He. Rebekah chewed on the reference to the dragon's gender, something Jericho never allowed. "I saw him too," she said.

A fountain lay across the clearing. The gargling whisper of falling water called Rebekah closer.

The fountain water appeared as blue as the spring. She sat on a short stone wall circling the water, feeling the smooth lines of many different gems cutting and weaving through the rough gray texture. Her fingertip reached the source of the trails—a singular gem buried far within the stone bench, even larger and more magnificent than the others.

By far, the most beautiful gem she had ever seen.

The broad surface cooled her palms. A lone, roaming blue light inside of the rock called to her. At first, she thought the gem was blue, but when she drew closer, it seemed to contain a piece of every rock she ever knew. A swirling collage. Her earlier dismissal of Uri's gem fascination felt hasteful.

"Helios!" Isaac's voice was somewhere far away.

Rebekah forced her eyes back up to the fountain.

I need to be more careful. But it was so hard. She could forget about everything that had happened to her, that she had killed a dragon, trading its life for the Spirit and the feeling it gave her here. *What is so wrong with that?* This Spirit was accessible at the slightest glance, an endless wealth within the littlest things.

"Helios!" Isaac called the young dragon again. "It's useless. This place is too big."

"What if we wait here and see if they'll come to us? We weren't looking for him before, when we saw him in the bushes."

"I guess it wouldn't hurt to rest." Isaac walked over. "If Boyd is as scared as he said, no doubt he's searching for us." He sat next to her on the circular stone.

"I'm not sure if he is," she said. "Things changed when we entered here. We can get distracted so easily if we aren't careful."

"Is that a bad thing? Did you ever feel this happy when you were at the church?"

She hadn't. The sacrifice felt more like a win for the pastors and Jericho than it did for herself.

"There's a reason why Jericho didn't want students to come out here," he said. "Whatever this is, it's not evil."

Isaac reached into his cloak and removed his father's notebook. He brushed off the cover, so old she thought it might crumble in his hands, and flipped through. "I just wish there was another entry here that would show us how to defeat the Lord, or how to get out of this place. We probably won't be able to find the cathedral, let alone Boyd and Helios." He searched the text furiously.

All this time, he'd been truthful, even when he wasn't sure of himself. Rebekah had never met anyone so set in their way, and wished she had been the same. Maybe it would have stopped her before the sacrifice. Everyone else wanted to be the next Lord, including her, but Isaac could look past the glory. He had no problem believing in something everyone thought was a joke.

She plucked a fluorescent flower, grateful for the decision she'd made to go against Jericho. *It was almost too late. I would've been his pawn.*

She wanted to thank Isaac for saving her but struggled to express such a strong feeling. The soft wind lulled her attention this way and that. The living strings of gems weaving throughout the stone bench fascinated her, and she could feel herself slipping into the face of the rock embedded between where they sat.

The colors danced and called to her from within. She might've heard the chimes. If she reached out, her hand would slip right into the silky violet. She leaned over the stone face, unable to resist its pull, and felt Isaac's shadow draw closer as he leaned in from the opposite side.

As she stared into the gem, its colors slowly began to swirl, the middle growing with that tiny blue spectral light. Faster and faster, the swirls increased, and when she realized she could not pull her eyes away, she ceased to care.

The scene morphed into something familiar. For a moment, Rebekah mistook it for where they were now, though it *was* them. Her and Isaac. They seemed taller, and older, her hair the curly brown color from before her blessings, and she dressed in clothing far too extravagant for the padded grass on which they stood. She wore a white gown, shades of pink cast upon it, the same light shade as her floral crown.

As the swirls settled on the sides of the gem and Rebekah became immersed in the picture, she noticed the light pink shades on her dress were a result of hundreds of petaled trees, limbs reaching out like delicate protectors over a small audience. Members of the audience sat on stone chairs, and there were types of creatures she'd never seen, some with skin the color of the sky and others with faces like elephants and hair covering their bodies as thick as a wolf's pelt.

They faced toward where she and Isaac stood.

A centaur stood between them, bushy eyebrows furrowed toward the crowd. Behind him, a cliff dropped away, and a painted sky extended on to infinity.

The being recited something, but Rebekah couldn't hear.

The audience stood from their seats.

Rebekah and Isaac reached out and held hands.

At the exact moment their fingertips touched, the sky filled with the wings of a dragon, and the force of the flapping wings caused a whirlwind of pink petals that pushed her back, back out of the scene, past the sky and into swirls of colors and spectral flowing light.

The scene collapsed to become a solid gem once more.

It felt like a chore to lift her head, but she saw Isaac staring back when she did.

He seemed almost saddened.

A rustling came from the trees.

They both turned, but there was nothing.

The chimes had returned, ringing lightly over the clearing, and a harmonic voice spoke. "Some need only a slight nudge in order to see their holy path." It seemed to come from everywhere and nowhere at once.

The feelings of hope suddenly turned to blame for letting herself lose focus. Fear gripped her heart.

"Do you see anything?" Isaac asked, on his feet with a dagger drawn.

She donned her hood, felt the inside pocket of her cloak for her own.

"Then again," the playful voice continued. "A course correction can always lead to an *over*correction. It's easy to get carried away, in all honesty. But that's why I'm here." The voice was high-pitched, more of a whisper, carrying across the flowers, lightly through the chimes and the wind.

"Where are you?" Isaac repeated. "What are you?"

A childish laugh danced through the air, growing louder with the breeze.

That's what Boyd warned us about.

The wind picked up in the luminescent brush. Gusts gathered in clusters, mid-air before them. A figure slowly defined itself within the flow of air, a whitish-gray body. Its form showed in glimpses only when the creature turned. The face was innocent and youthful. At the center of its ephemeral being shone a white light, and Rebekah watched in awe as it flew closer.

"What do you want with us?" Isaac asked. "Where is our friend?"

What was it I had seen in the gem? Can it help me now? The gem had called to something inside of her and showed her a vision.

Isaac.

It was nothing. I got carried away.

That was what the creature had said. It stared at her and Isaac with bright green eyes, never hovering in one spot for longer than half of a moment.

"Wait, I think..." Isaac brought a hand to his chin. "Yes, I know what you are. I should've known all along. My father wrote about you in his notebook. You're a Dyra. Pastors spotted hundreds of your kind when they used to explore Tempus."

"Precisely, but my *name* is Oswaldo, and I prefer you'd address me however I prefer." The Dyra twisted in the air. The orb of white light at its center pulsated a burnt orange. "I suppose you really are as knowledgeable about the other realms as the Elder claims."

"Other realms?" Rebekah asked. "As in, that's where you're from? Another realm?"

"That's where you are." Oswaldo giggled. "In the times of the first-era, the time when Isaac rightly claims there were sightings, we used to visit your realm now and then. Mainly because every Dyra must feel as much as we can, and humans are all over the place with their emotions." The creature laughed again. "One moment you're happy, the next you're craving. There were a lot more of us before

Jericho invaded the forest. We haven't quite recovered. But we'll talk about this later."

The Dyra fluttered from place to place, looking around suspiciously with those shining emerald eyes. "Now that I have done my work and guided you here, and you've had your visions and seen your path, I can take you back to the Elder. But first...." The Dyra buzzed down right in front of their faces. A sweet scent filled the air. It whispered quickly. "I must say, it was beyond wonderful to feel the love between you two. Tell me, did I time it correctly? Were those the first amorous feelings you two have had for one another?"

She felt Isaac looking at her, but she didn't look back.

"What are you talking about?" he said. "We don't have armorous feelings."

"It's amorous." For some reason, his words disappointed her. She wanted to change the subject. "How do you know our names?"

"So many questions. I suppose I would be the same. My kind has been watching over you for ages, but I never knew you were so *timid*." The Dyra swirled back, up in the air. "Oh, how I missed youthful passions and humiliations. I remember them like it was yesterday. A romantic I've been and always will be, I'm afraid. How could I resist the greatest feeling there is, to love and be loved?"

"We are not *amorous*." She sounded contrived, but it was true, and the Dyra was beginning to annoy her. "Can you tell us where we are, or if you've seen our friend?"

The Dyra gasped. "You really aren't going to admit it?" The amber color of sap pulsed within the being's aura. "Oh, *no-no-no-no-no-no-no*. We have to tell *everyone* when such wonderful feelings overcome us. My dear Rebekah, don't you want to fulfill the sight of your desired future? To live the vision you had in that gem?"

What she wanted was to make this creature disappear. "I don't know what you're talking about."

The Dyra looked next to her. "And you, young Isaac. Do you know the meaning of what has happened since you entered the forest?"

"I just know Tempus was never fully explored. The Dyra were said to be the first glimpses of holy beings other than the dragons."

The Dyra giggled again. "Elder always says that it is the inability to agree on an issue that keeps humans from seeing their path. If you ask me, it's the lack of transparency. Humans can share emotions too, you know. They need only make it a point." The being zipped down to their level once again. "Let me fill you in before we make it to the Elder."

"But our friend—"

"Boyd, yes? Helios, too."

"But—"

"Will you please listen to me, for a second? For a *sliver* of eternity?" Just for context...." The Dyra took a sudden massive gasp of air, its stomach growing almost twice in size. "The problem is that your middle realm doesn't let you know of any emotion that you don't feel yourself, so all you humans are stumbling around, hoping everybody means what you mean with their promises, but only a few humans get lucky enough to find someone who doesn't betray them, and even less often do people ever really mean the same thing when they talk about something because words aren't the greatest communication tool." Its aura pulsed many shades as the Dyra caught its breath. "It's even rarer for a human not to betray themselves. That is something the ascended have come to understand."

"How would one do that?" Isaac asked. "Betray themselves?"

"The same way they would betray anybody else. They would make themselves a promise that they do not mean to keep, or simply not look at their feelings. Every human does it, in fact, and you two are right now. But, that's what it all comes down to in the end. In this realm, no one can hide their emotions. Not around us. That's why everyone comes here to make or renew their promises.

"What I'm trying to say is that it took a little effort to get you to see your path." The aura pulsed the sweet red. "And I don't want to take credit, but I did do a pretty good job guiding you two to see your lovely little path. Once I set the scene with the fountain and the flower light, you felt comfortable enough to stop to talk to each other. And once you looked into the gems..." the aura pulsed a deeper red. "We all know what happens when humans do that."

Please, stop.

"I don't, actually," Isaac said. "But I'm okay."

The floating creature looked between them. "No? Well, I'm not explaining the intricacies of gem visions to you. Not now. I just think that I should be rewarded, that's all." The Dyra glanced between them. "What, nothing? Not even a brief little description about how it felt to see your love? You don't understand. I don't get any romance here. All you have to do is give some thought to what happened, it's not much. I can feel it if you relive it as a memory. That's enough. It's all the same to me."

They were silent, and the Dyra fluttered in one spot longer than ever. "Fine." The aura pulsed light blue. "Anyway, you saw what you saw—and wasn't it unlike anything else? Nothing is more mean-ingful than love, I'll say it a hundred thousand billion times, and once more for good measure. I'd been waiting since you arrived at Daemonus."

"You've been watching us for that long?" Isaac asked.

"Longer. In truth, you being the first humans to ascend to our realm was as much our work as yours. Thank you very much. We searched a long time for you two. Boyd, too." A windy sigh. "I guess my efforts will have to go unrewarded."

"What about the Lord and his sacrifice?" Rebekah asked. "He's strong, and if he sacrifices the Chrysos, he's going to be unstoppable. We just need to get through Tempus, then we'll be on our way. We mean no harm, but we have to stop him before it's too late. Just give us back our friend." She couldn't take any more of this uncomfort-able place. Her hood hid her blushing face.

"That's not what you were concerned about a moment ago. But let me calm you, and as a result, calm me. Look up at the moon. Have you seen it move at all?"

Rebekah did as she was told, peering through thick branches. Uair Four of Rising Silver. *It should be closer to High Silver by now.*

"We are not in your time, young Rebekah. When you return, you will find that time has moved but a second for every hour you spend here. This is where we've hidden from Jericho all these years. In the past, a time he cannot reach. My has it been long since I've felt such confusion. Now follow. The Elder is at the hovels waiting for your love."

The Dyra flew up and across the clearing, looking back when it reached the edge. They hadn't moved. "You better get over that fear soon if you two ever want to walk a holy path. But, the promise will take care of that."

For the first time in a while, Rebekah turned to Isaac, surprised to see his face blooming with bright red color. *Had he seen anything in the gem?*

"My," Oswaldo said. "There is quite a lot of fear between you two."

"Then why bring us here?" Rebekah asked. "Why separate us, hide all these years just to reveal yourselves now? If you've been in Tempus all this time, why didn't you ever try to defeat the Lord yourself?"

"You wouldn't expect to stop the infernal Lord by yourself, either. Would you? I hope not. Besides, a Dyra doesn't fight. Even if we tried to rebel against the Lord, the moment we killed someone, we would be crippled by their pain, not to mention the fear that comes with dying. We plan to help you stop the sacrifice, I feel that much is obvious. But it will come with a price."

"A price?" asked Isaac.

"It is none too different than any other choice, the basic cost of choosing one thing over another. Also, the Elder may want to keep your sacred dragon." Oswaldo turned, floated a few feet away before falling into a laughing fit. The aura pulsed a jungle's green. "No, I'm only kidding, don't be so frightened. Dragons are far too prideful to keep as pets."

CHAPTER 22

FIRST ERA, 1,999, UAIR FIVE OF RISING SILVER

Isaac

The Dyra, who called itself Oswaldo, led Isaac and Rebekah up and around fungal structures and into broad towering trees like the one Isaac had chased Helios through before they entered the garden.

Isaac still looked for the dragon behind the creeping, glowing fauna and inside the tall tree houses even though the Dyra said it was with the Elder, where they headed. Because Oswaldo knew their names and could make such alterations to the world, Isaac felt like he had no choice but to follow the creature. It had come straight out of his father's notebook.

As they walked, Isaac recalled more stories about the Dyra playing tricks on unfortunate souls, aiding those in need if they were proper servants of the Spirit.

Given what Isaac had seen in that gem and the way things have transpired, Isaac thought it best to cast aside his doubt of the Dyra for the time being. Not to mention the moon above them hadn't moved, and the surreal texture everything had here. *This must be what it is like to be blessed. What would father say of me now, venturing through realms unknown with a Dyra by my side?*

He crept through another of the carved doorways, arches studded with gems, and entered an empty room with a staircase in the center.

"You guys live in these things?" Isaac asked. Neither of them had said anything since leaving the fountain.

Oswaldo fluttered to the stairs and climbed. "Not these gross things. These are old hovels, occupied long, long ago." It was funny to watch the creature's tiny feet speed up the stairs.

"I see. And why are there steps here, when you can fly?"

The Dyra huffed a light jingle. "It would be nice if you could open your mind even a little bit. Why do you have chairs or beds? Flying here, there, and everywhere makes me just as tired as running does for you."

The Dyra pulsed a deep red. "I was only joking, no need to be hurt. Anyway, a long time ago, there were the most extravagant decorations in every Dyra home. Homes, yes, is what *you* would call it. Think sculptures, art. The very best, none of that mass produce your Lord has placed in all his churches. There was enough emotion in those pieces to last one Dyra an entire life. And the food, oh *the food*. We would never be in the sad state we are today if we had the same Rikouwa as before."

"You have Rikouwa here?" Isaac asked. "Wait, is that all the red dust?" He looked to Rebekah, but she wouldn't lower her hood.

"That's what the red dust seems like, but it's not real. A recreation, perpetuated in this particular moment of its existence, just like the trees and everything else here. The Rikouwa used to be this bountiful, before Jericho stole the spice and sold it as a luxury to fund his uprising. Beings from across the realm used to say our

Rikouwa Bun was the best dessert in all the land, and they wouldn't be wrong." The orb inside the Dyra went black. "Oh, how I miss those delectable things. When you ate them, you felt as if you had all you ever needed in this wicked old realm."

"How long have you been here exactly, in Tempus?" Rebekah asked the question from behind Isaac.

"Let me think... We were here far before you humans found the island. We Dyra have inhabited the realm in the Daemonus forest since the island came to be. I know Dyra that lived longer though, in places outside of Tempus. We Dyra began living all over the human realm after venturing out from our home. I used to have friends everywhere in Indus."

They followed the form past the empty third and fourth-floor rooms. "Over the years, we've had to expend a lot of energy to stay hidden from Jericho. After a while, we Dyra had to begin giving our life forces, one-by-one." Oswaldo's stomach pulsed gray. "These were the bravest Dyra we ever knew, but our resources were diminishing. We had to survive somehow. At one point, every hovel in Tempus used to be bustling with Dyra. But, we will all give up our ghost before the Elder ever departs. That's the way it has to be."

They walked up the swirling staircase, and Isaac looked into the upper-floor rooms, vines invading the walls and floor. Each room had a particular theme. Cookware he wasn't sure how to use consistently appeared on the bottom floor. The upper floors consisted of sculptures of the creatures or paintings of luscious landscapes that seemed entirely nonsensical. They reached the top floor, opened the door outside, and Isaac was amazed yet again to see flat ground.

"This is ridiculous," Rebekah said. "I feel so incapable here." She'd never sounded so disturbed.

"It's only the process of ascension," Oswaldo said, standing in the spectral version of Tempus. "It's not supposed to feel normal, you know. It's tough as a human, sure, but there's nothing to fear. There never is. Oh, unless you're going to the infernal realms. But nevermind that. I mean, forget it. We're almost there."

They strode into another nearby tree.

"Our Dynasty only fills a few hovels next to each other." Oswaldo sighed. "You can only be entertained by the same people for a certain amount of time. No romantic is meant to be in the same place for so long. That is why the Elder sent me to watch you. I cannot bear to be alone, subject to the same dull interactions with the same tired bores repeatedly and repeatedly.

"Elder says I should be grateful, but you know what I think? I think that it is only a matter of time until I don't have to deal with anyone anymore." Oswaldo stopped at the top of the stairs. "Enough of me, though. We are here and arrived."

The door opened, and Oswaldo floated out to dark towering trees and a bounty of glowing plants of every kind, much like the garden from before, but without a fountain. Bouts of wind floated above it all, playing together as interweaving pockets of light. The sound of their laughter was the same as what led them off the path— wonderful golden chimes like the silk of all tones—the Dyra's laughter.

"Look who I've brought!" Oswaldo sang, and the chimes ceased. More Dyra emerged from the trees, doors on different levels and heights. They gathered at the center, around Oswaldo, who looked back and gestured for Isaac and Rebekah to join.

"Do you think it's fine?' Rebekah turned to him.

"Probably," he said, happy to be talking to her again. "I don't think they could hurt anyone if they tried."

The Dyra's laughter returned. Many of them pulsed a sweet red color.

Isaac stayed back as she walked out into the garden of glowing fauna, greeted by yips of delight. The Dyra flew in a whirl around her, flinging the hood from her head to throw about her silver hair, mumbling to themselves in a quick language of whispers.

With a curious caution, Isaac walked out onto the soft grass and looked up to the moon. It hadn't moved. *This really is another realm, and that's no moon I've ever seen. That's the moon of the past.*

Something hissed past his head, missing by a few inches. He turned and watched as what looked like a dagger zoomed through the trees, disappearing into the night.

Out of instinct, he reached for the dagger in his pocket, searching the forest. From behind one of the closer trees, the thin stature of Boyd emerged— a blessed white-haired rogue in a tattered white cloak.

Isaac dropped his arms and smiled at the sight of his friend. "Did you throw that at me?"

Boyd strolled up with a grin. A Dyra floated next to him, green just leaving its aura.

Isaac ducked, hearing whatever object as it zoomed back through the air, grazing his head. When he looked up, Boyd gripped a familiar metallic gray dagger in his hand.

"Is that from your collection?" Isaac asked.

Boyd twirled the dagger like he used to and tucked it into a sheath on his side. "Got that right," he said, walking up to slap Isaac on the arm. "Legola taught me some things while we were waiting for you. Turns out the creatures of this forest aren't that bad after all. You can learn about them over a span of, I don't know, however long you kept me waiting here." He laughed that short chuckle. "Where have you guys been?"

How had Boyd become so accepting of this place? Gift him a dagger, and he is convinced.

"Wasn't that long," Isaac said.

"It's been a total of two minutes in the middle realm, four uairs here." The Dyra spoke sternly, and for once, Isaac saw Boyd listening in respect. "Time moves differently in this realm."

"You really like to talk, Legola, you know that? Are you sure your path isn't the talker? From what I've seen, you can talk better than you can fight."

So Boyd knows about the paths, too. The romantic path Oswaldo claimed Isaac and Rebekah were on made him hesitant, especially if he had to fulfill the vision he had when looking into the gem. He wasn't worried that he'd seen himself being rewarded in front of millions with medals of what seemed like honor, Rebekah too. It was the fact that Boyd had not been there that led him to study his friend and try to disregard the topic of paths altogether.

Isaac laughed at the absurdity. "You have to stop getting lost. Where did you go this time? When we got back to the lake, you were gone."

"More like where did you go," he said. "You guys ran off after Helios. Speaking of which, where is Rebekah and the dragon?"

"Boyd!" Rebekah ran up to them. She gave Boyd a hug and Legola pulsed red. "It's so good to know you're okay."

They separated, and Boyd looked elated. "Don't you believe me now? There are Spirits out here. It turns out they were good. The things I saw earlier that I told you about, the jumping gnomes, it was Legola. She was training me so I was able to find my path when the time comes. This whole time the Dyra guided us. Tell them, Legola."

"It was necessary for your progression," the Dyra said, its voice deeper than Oswaldo's. A black and white patterned bandana wrapped around its forehead.

Boyd shrugged. "Aren't these things weird? They can shift forms, too. Legola turned into some sort of cat and made me think I was going to die. They said it was the only way I could reach my path."

"The warrior path is one of bravery," Legola informed. "Bravery is most commonly provoked by fear."

Isaac glanced at Rebekah, her face still.

"Yeah," Boyd said. "My path is the warrior—kind of figures when you think about it. You were right," he turned to Isaac. "The beings out here are helping us. I'm pretty sure they put that new entry in your notebook too, but I don't know why. Did you ever find out?"

Isaac shook his head. "They may have wanted me to follow the Chrysos."

"The reason why they gave me the slingshot was so I could learn how to catch something that comes back to me after I release it. Did you see how I could make my dagger return like that? We're going to be unstoppable against Jericho." Boyd seemed to glow like the plants. "You guys are so quiet. What about you? What was your path?"

Boyd so obviously showed off for Rebekah. He had feelings. Isaac knew it the moment they talked about confronting her inside the church walls. He acted so desperate around her. Boyd wouldn't take kindly to Isaac having a matching path of romance. It'd mean the end of their journey working together to defeat the Lord. And what if Isaac told Boyd he saw their future, and Boyd wasn't anywhere to be found?

"I'm not sure," Isaac said.

"You mean you did nothing to ascend to this realm?"

"We explored," Rebekah said. "That is it."

Isaac couldn't help but be pained by the comment. It didn't feel good lying to Boyd, but apparently, they had both agreed it was better not to speak of it. *Forget it ever happened. I guess I can do that.*

"Interesting," Boyd said. "Your paths must be exploratory. Legola says there are a lot of different paths, so many the Dyra don't even know. And what about the colors in their stomach? Legola tried to teach me how to read them, but we figured out we can't see many of the colors that the Dyra—"

A whistle interrupted Boyd, accompanied by a high-pitched giggle, and they all turned to see Oswaldo zipping toward them from across the clearing. "There are my lovers!"

Isaac's heart dropped when he saw the look of contempt fill his friend's face.

"Lovers?" Boyd asked.

Oswaldo reached them before Isaac could think of a reply. "I see you've found your snow-haired friend. Perfect. It is time the Elder sees you now, and promises are made to follow your respective paths. There is no time to waste. We must get you back on your way to stop the Lord."

"I thought we agreed on being conspicuous about the humans's paths, as they are up to interpretation," Legola said, trying to escort Oswaldo away.

"There is no need to hide such great feelings as love and affection, you sorry brute." Oswaldo shrugged the other Dyra off, and Rebekah followed them into the garden without so much as a glance back, her hood drawn.

Boyd shook his head. "Lovers..." The short laugh. "That's a nice path." His face twisted downward, everything except his dark red eyes. "Don't know why you lied to me."

"I didn't lie," Isaac said. "We stared into a gem, that's it. There was a vision, but nothing between us. I didn't even know what it meant. Then the Dyra showed up and started calling us lovers. It's not something I chose. Or Rebekah." His words seemed to strike an impenetrable barrier. "Besides, you saw her. She hated it as much as me."

"Here we go, gifted with another vision. How convenient that it was a vision of you and Rebekah, huh? What's next, your dragon will speak to you? I saw the way you were looking at her. Yeah, I'm sure that path is awful for you."

"Don't be that way. I'm not lying when I say I'm not interested in that path." Isaac knew he was interested, though. As sure as the sun shines, he would walk down any path with Rebekah.

Boyd raised his gloomy gaze. "That's why you two left me by the spring, so you could run off and be together. I knew it, too. I left you to your privacy. I suppose it was only a matter of time until you chose her over me, over the truth and saving the dragons." He turned without a word and followed after Rebekah into the garden, entering the open archway of a far tree much taller and wider than the others.

Isaac stood there alone, watching all of the Dyra fly into the centermost tree. Some glanced in his direction and pulsed a subtle orange, but they weren't laughing. There were gasps and surprised shouts from the vaguely blue forms as Boyd stormed through the arch.

We have to leave as soon as we can. We only get along when we are focused on stopping the Lord. All these distractions and emotions are getting in the way.

They couldn't leave yet, not without hearing what the Elder Dyra had to say. It was their only hope of stopping the Lord.

CHAPTER 23

FIRST ERA, 1,999, UAIR
FIVE OF RISING SILVER

Boyd

T he door of the tallest tree matched the same gemmed archway of every other hovel, opening up to a room of benches bordering the walls inhabited by spectral beings as they laughed and flitted about.

Just before the spiraling staircase stood a massive stone goblet infused with a ritualistic green flame. Many Dyra darted in and out of the wavering fire the same color as their eyes, giggling like clinging bells when a creature would come close. As Boyd walked nearer to the goblet, following the guide of Legola, he felt no heat radiating from the flame. It didn't illuminate the room all that well, either, though the mood-shifting auras within the guts of the Dyra were much more perceptible in the low glow. They whispered, inner moods pulsing beside one another, racing to seats along the walls and upper floors as Boyd followed Legola's instructions to sit on a red pillow—one of three laid before the goblet. He chose the cushion furthest from Rebekah, who hadn't acknowledged his entrance, making her hatred for him all the more evident. *Not like she ever liked me in the first place.*

Dyra treated the moment like a celebration. Some had decorated their wings with shimmering gems to make them look like the scales of dragon-wings, making colorful shapes in the air as they hovered. Others wore intricate headdresses donned with leaves and stems of the glowing fauna Boyd confronted on his way here. You would never think millions of dragons suffered horrible torture nearby. Boyd remembered. It was much easier to maintain a clear mind when he wasn't suffering from the delusion that he was chosen to save the Chrysos and defeat the Lord, like Isaac.

I'm not any more special than anyone in Indus, Boyd thought. *But Isaac would never admit that to himself. Nobody is ever the chosen one.* It might have been better if they hadn't read the tales Isaac's father wrote about, so the ideas never entered their head and this trick wouldn't be possible. *The Lord would still figure out some way to manipulate us. That is what he's best at. I won't follow anything but the purest Spirit. Only what I can control myself.*

Boyd began to wonder why they were still here. What were the Dyra going to offer that would help them now? They have a dragon and his daggers. Regardless of what the Dyra said about time running slower in this realm, sitting around while Jericho prepared the sacrifice wouldn't help. *Isaac and Rebekah should feel the same.*

The door to the hovel creaked open, moonlight spilled through, and Isaac was the last to slip inside save for a few Dyra zipping through as the door closed, soaring past Boyd and the goblet to the upper floors.

"Saved you a seat." Boyd tapped on the red pillow between him and Rebekah.

Isaac sat without a word.

The ogreish flame of the goblet danced upward. Legola and Oswaldo took a seat on the nearby steps.

Boyd looked up the spiraling stairs to see hundreds of the sparkling emerald eyes staring over the edge, down at them.

Then a hush fell throughout the room as the door to the top of the hovel opened, way above the stairs. Silver and blue light poured down the staircase like flowing water. The Elder who first greeted Boyd entered, fluttering down the many steps, its golden headdress a commanding presence over the dense green flame rising through the wooden home without heat.

"Do I sense jealousy," the Elder said. "Fear?" The voice was like a thousand chimes.

None of them responded.

"The human life is too short, and quite frankly, mortally grue-some, for such emotions to turn to habit." The green flame of the goblet gained in volume as the Elder neared, stretching high up the stairs to brush the second floor. Dyra flew out and danced just above. "Sometimes, I forget how much humans don't know. You are preciously ignorant for all that your soul is worth. I suppose it should be that way."

I forgot she could sense my feelings. Boyd balled his hands into fists. *Good.*

There was a silence, then this time the Elder laughed, something that triggered a laugh in the other creatures, and the room tinted red as did the inner aura of all the Dyra.

"You need not feel threatened," said the Elder. "We Dyra brought you here to show the truth as we know it. We promised a way to stop the Lord and his sacrifice. But to have the best chance of conquering something, you must understand its inner workings. So I ask, or rather, the question you should be asking yourselves is... What is the power we must stop, and how did it come to be? Only when you know these answers will you defeat your enemies."

"That's easy," Boyd said. *She wants us to reveal all we know about the Lord.* "Jericho steals his Spirit from the dragons. Then, he teaches his students how to do it. Everyone wants power, that's why they follow him. And how did it come to be this way? I think you know that better than us."

The Elder pulsed a darkened blue. "I believe we do."

"I think it's pretty easy to put together." Boyd scoffed at the silence. "Killing dragons, equals bad. Either way, this doesn't feel much like stopping the Lord of St. Daemonus. More like sitting around on a fluffy mattress, talking. Isn't that what you've done for the past hundred years?"

The Elder laughed—high-pitched, beautiful, and genuine. "Apologies, young Boyd, but you do not know what stopping the Lord feels like, for you have never done so. Is this true?"

"I've never had the chance."

"No? What about the past five years?" The Elder pulsed a violet-black under her golden headdress, a sole emerald gem displayed at the front. "You have more worries in your head than there are Dyra in this room, and each one draws you further away from your path. Change occurs by choosing one issue out of many, for there is an infinite amount, and solving that issue entirely. Then you move on to the next. Now tell me, which of your worries do you most desperately want to solve?" Chimes sounded from the upper levels.

They're laughing at me, Boyd thought. *They think I'm a fool.* "How I choose to live is up for me to decide."

"Agreed. Now please allow me to continue solving the issue of Jericho while you contemplate your fate."

The Elder hovered down near the goblet and cupped a hand, dipping it into the flame to retrieve a separate ball of the light. The Elder blew gently, soft chimes in the wind, and three bouts of the crystal green orbs rose in separate directions through the air.

Rebekah and Isaac gasped.

All Boyd could think of was how much he wanted to leave. *The Lord believes he can distract me with all these sensations, fake stories, and amazing shows,* Boyd thought. *I know better.*

The flames morphed and floated through the air like cloudy bubbles, each one approaching their respective seats on the floor.

Boyd watched as it drew closer, hand on his dagger. The texture altered shape grossly, growing legs, arms, wings, forming into a dragon.

"Already you know," the Elder began, "we Dyra hid from the power of Jericho over a hundred years ago, here in the Tempus forest. We knew something was wrong when we felt the emotional shift in the church as Jericho's rebellion began. A shift from hope to despair. He murdered the last great Lord of Daemonus, and as much as I would like to be rid of it, that pain still haunts me.

"Our kind sensed an immense sadness that reverberated throughout Indus, though we knew not what occurred. So we did as any Dyra would and retreated, unable to fight, and in doing so, trapped ourselves here, away from our kind."

The wispy green dragon flame in front of Boyd fought the two forms next to Isaac and Rebekah, pastors celebrating as they drove the creature up and away, back into the fire.

Slowly, the flame leaked and flooded about the room like a cold green fog.

"From our place of hiding, we've watched the Lord's rebellion grow into the dominant belief of Indus, only a few islands withholding the first-era means of worship and respect for dragonkind. Jericho now has thousands of followers at his disposal, all of them believing the dragons to be bloodthirsty mongers who hid from humans an ancient power that rightfully belongs to your race."

The orbs next to Isaac and Rebekah also returned to the green formlessness. The fog cascaded around them like ocean waves. More of the other-worldly substance leaked from the goblet, rising to the upper floors. If it weren't for the minuscule pupils and white aura of the Dyra, the creatures would've been imperceptible.

Stay aware. Boyd couldn't help being inspired by the beautiful sights and sounds. *They... they're trying to trick me again.*

"For decades, none of our Dyra had been brave enough to venture out of this moment in time to discover what happened that day. That is, until Legola and Oswaldo refused to hide any longer. For the past twenty or so years, only a third as much in our time, they searched the backward land of Indus for those who still believed in the old ways of the first-era."

The Elder's aura pulsed orange, tinted by green. "I know you are wondering why us Dyra did not venture out earlier and try to help. Surely there are other ways of winning a war other than outright combat, you might say.

"The fact is that Oswaldo and Legola risked their lives by isolating themselves from the dynasty. Many of our other Dyra have surrendered their ghosts trying to stop the Lord. In vain, I'm afraid.

"As our numbers dwindle, our collective strength is weakening, and our grip on the past is slipping. If you were observant, you might have noticed the forest lacks any sign of life other than the plants and ourselves. We are too weak to keep up this retreat, and eventually, we will be forced to return to the present-day Tempus forest, where we will confront the Lord."

Boyd could hear the sadness in the Elder's voice. Its aura remained blue for a long time. A desire to remove the blue color arose for a short moment. Boyd quickly dismissed the feeling. *I won't fall for sympathetic tricks.*

"It would be wrong to blame ourselves for what happened that day. We were full of panic, sadness, and the paralyzing thoughts of death. Never had any Dyra seen a dragon fall, and the day the Lord conquered the church, he slew many. The Dyra would have felt each momentous fall... our souls would have been scarred forever if we did not hide here. Not even I have the means to overcome such tragedy. Not in the span of one life."

Boyd glanced at Isaac. He sat on the edge of his pillowed seat, hanging on every word. *They'll tell him whatever he wants to hear about his father's notebook and more.*

Two orbs reappeared from the fog, taking on the shape of two pyramids. One prism matched its base with the other to form a diamond; between, an empty rectangular space kept the figures divided. The segmented diamond twisted in the air at the spin of the

204

Elder's ghostly fingers, one end facing up, the other facing down, like a fat spinning top.

The Elder Dyra hovered in-between their place on the pillows and the spinning figment of smoke. A rich vanilla scent followed. "Powerful forces work around you, many of which the average human cannot perceive. These forces influence your decisions, from what you eat to who you love."

The Elder pointed a translucent finger toward the middle space, a rectangle dividing the two pyramids. "You and the rest of humanity have been confined to this space, the middle realm. Above you are the seven holy realms, and below, the infernal."

This is crazy, Boyd thought. He vaguely remembered the mention of other realms in the notebook of Isaac's father, but crazed rantings preceded that section, and that was the point of the notebook when he thought Isaac's father had lost his mind. *The savior boy is eating this up.* He couldn't believe how up-front the Dyra were with their manipulation. He thought they might be more competent.

"In truth, there is not merely one Great Spirit as the Lord preaches. Two forces exist in unity, the holy and infernal, to make one Spirit whole. That result, the fusion of these forces, is the Great Spirit the first-era worshipped."

"I knew it!" Isaac said.

Of course you did.

The Elder's aura pulsed red. "Holy forces are derived from the seven realms above, and the infernal forces from below. When these fuse in perfect balance, they create the true Spirit. The true Spirit is life, the light that allows you to see and the void from which you arose. Everything that has ever known or will be known, and nothing at all. There must be constant conflict between these forces. Balance.

"The human soul is a result of perfect balance between holy and infernal forces. This balance is creation, a direct spawn of the Spirit, and the only way a new soul may come into existence. The human form is the one thing most similar to the Spirit, the soul untouched, the form unshaped, and as a result, it is the target of manipulation from both realms. The higher realms for creation and growth, the lower realms for submission and destruction."

It couldn't be so simple as good and evil, Boyd thought. *That's not how anything works.*

"As the human soul moves throughout the world, it chooses between two great forces every moment of its life, and thus, becomes more familiar with a given side. As you invite more holy energies into your soul, you will naturally attract this force. It is a simple law that mimics itself nearly everywhere throughout the realms. Those who have more money will attain more, same as those with power.

"At the end of one's life, the human soul appears like a record of past influences, a balance corrupted by either force. Come the day when a human must give up their ghost, the soul ascends if it is filled with more holy forces... or descends, if it is occupied by forces infernal."

Boyd caught himself contemplating the decisions he'd made in his life, whether they were influenced by holy forces or infernal. "How could we possibly know which force is behind which action?"

"That is something your kind has worked hard to develop until the Lord altered your progress with his claims. In truth, it is impossible to be absolutely sure of one's tilted balance until the soul has passed and taken a new ghost in a new realm.

"For example, we Dyra ascended to the first holy realm. Our soul was infused with a ghost fit for this particular space, where we will be exposed to the lesson that Yewha believes we must learn, should we ever be capable of doing so. There are many different forms throughout the realms, and likely many lessons, but there is one thing that distinguishes the holy realms from the infernal. Creation and destruction."

Boyd never read about this in Abraham's notebook, but he didn't doubt the text mentioned it. Everything inside the notebook made sense in this context, which was precisely what Isaac needed to be influenced, claims that the dragons were some holy force reincarnated. *Another convenience too good to be true. The world could never be so simple.*

"How do you know all of this?" Boyd asked—a reasonable question, he thought.

The Dyra turned as slow as the pyramid in rotation. "As the soul ascends or descends, it gains the necessary knowledge needed to care for itself. We oversee your realm, and can enter it as we please. Our kind has some knowledge about the structure of the realms, but we do not claim to know more than what we share. When the soul reaches its fullest progression, evolving through all seven holy realms, it may serve its final purpose."

"And what is that?" Boyd asked. "When does a person get to do what they want, instead of serving some force?"

"Serving, an interesting word. Both realms require serving, I would say, but only the holy realms allow you to serve willingly."

"Willingly? Why would I serve something willingly when I can serve myself?"

"The final purpose of a fully realized soul is something a human cannot imagine," the Elder said. "Even if I told you, you would not comprehend."

Of course not. Boyd crossed his arms and chuckled.

"When you complete your path through the seven realms, your soul has been tested and tried, proven stronger than any force within. A soul works its way through the universal structure the same as a caterpillar changes form, though the stages are many, and nearly indivisible based on the path one takes.

"The dragon is the final form of the ascended soul. You three are aware of the magnificence of the creatures, yet still have no grasp of their true power. The only knowledge humans gained was gathered on the slight occasions the beings would descend to your realm.

"However, when they descended, the dragons were only passing through. Being the most powerful creatures in the holy realms, the dragons must fight the constant war of keeping the infernal realms at bay, maintaining the balance."

"Why would the Spirit make dragons do that? Why wouldn't it get rid of the infernal realms once and for all?"

"You ask questions to which we do not know the answer. Since our existence, infernal forces have been trying to invade and tip the balance in their favor. Dragons defend this, but I do not know why we have been placed in this position, nor do I doubt the Spirit's motives."

Just like the Lord, making us think we are too dull to understand the motives of something so great.

"We are all ultimately subject to the Spirit's control, but that is not to say we understood all of its actions."

The creature contradicts itself even as it speaks.

"We are not sure what form the soul takes in the last of the infernal realms. As far as we can tell, infernal forces do not seem to be individual souls progressing through the realm based on their wisdom and aptitude, but rather a mass of souls, united under the power of the void. That from which everything arose. The infernal realm is a fundamental rejection of life.

"Jericho has invited infernal forces into your middle realm with ease since the fall of the first-era. He has used the power of these infernal forces to spark a rebellion across Indus, claiming he will bless his followers with ancient power the dragons once showed. In truth, he has mastered the method of converting the holy spirit to infernal.

"These days, the Lord can gain a follower by charismatic manners of expression, flashing his white hair and red eyes. He was not always like this. Long ago Jericho was once an unaltered soul, balanced in the Spirit, the same as every human soul begins. Some would say circumstance doomed him to everything infernal, but I prefer to believe he had a choice. The bravest of our dynasty left Tempus to feel the emotions of the past, and discover how Jericho's era came to be."

"Wait, into the past?" Boyd was sure the explanation would fall apart at the slightest prick. "If you could go back in time, why wouldn't you change things and never allow Jericho to become Lord?'

"When you reach the higher realms, you find that time is something to be navigated quite easily, depending on your perspective. Time is something the Dyra play with like a cat does yarn, throwing it up and viewing it from different directions, but our abilities are limited. We see the past of the middle realm through a layer of glass, unable to touch or alter what is on the other side. The Great Spirit only allows us to feel what happened in those days. We do not influence events of the past and have little to no say over the future, though it is fairly predictable when humans are involved."

The Dyra went gray. "I know this hardly seems logical, but I'll be the first to say we are far beyond the logic of your middle realm. It is best to believe us, and act accordingly."

"That's what you'd like." Boyd said. "Wouldn't you?"

"You will discover these things for yourself after you stop the sacrifice. For now, I will let that brave member of our dynasty who felt the past with their own light come forth, so they may speak for themselves." The lead creature fluttered back to the stairs.

BOYD'S DOUBT rose and subsided along with the mist's curls. The green twisted and solidified to display the inside of a building with tall towering bookcases. Gigantic slabs of stone took a greenish, foggy form, cracked and broken. Around the two flattened rocks stood a group of hooded pastors, all made entirely of the cold glow.

Legola appeared next to the scene, white and black bandana standing out amidst the green.

"You don't believe this either, do you?"

The Dyra cast him a judgmental gaze.

I didn't take you for a simpleton.

Legola pulsed red. "As churches arose in honor of draconic worship, there were those, typically on lesser islands, who never trusted dragons to begin with. They thought the dragons were devious and serpent-like, repulsed by their appearance and general control over the world. In all reality, they feared the dragon's power. Over the years, this movement grew, this fear, and out of their beliefs a cult arose dedicated to lessening draconic value in the church. As our Elder explained, this type of worship invited the most infernal of forces."

Boyd tried to raise his voice but found his will pressed back by something unknown.

"Lord Jericho is the descendent of a long line of cult leaders. His bloodline has dedicated itself to studying and harnessing draconic power. The cult discovered specific actions catering to the infernal realms and repeated these until infernal forces became strong within their line. It was soon known to the cultists that the sacrifice of a soul was an immediate way to harness vast amounts of the Spirit— the more rare the sacrifice, the greater the return.

"The possibilities became endless for the cult leaders, and they filled with an envious pride. The only thing that mattered in a sacrifice was the murderer's intent, as this would direct the essence of the soul and determine its infernal role. In most cases, I have felt this intent to be desire." The Dyra looked at Boyd, pulsed green.

"The Lord and his pastors preach this," Rebekah said. "He says nothing is impossible if you can imagine it, and know the proper technique." She lowered her head. "All I wanted was to become a respected apostle."

"And when you attained that, what would you want after? Indeed, it never ends... This desire and hunger for power was demonstrated best upon the birth of Jericho. The Lord was the first-born son of the greatest leader the cult had ever known, Dromethius. It was brought to the attention of Jericho's father that, with the right sacrifice, he could have the greatest son in the land, only needing to bless him with the sacrifice of a dragon. A certain pride filled the leader then, one I have not felt otherwise."

Legola fluttered down to the floor, next to the scene of fog, and spun her finger in a circle. The mist turned into a tornado, and the familiar form of an infant dragon appeared. Legola placed it atop one of the scene's shattered stone slabs. "The Lord was a perfect child. Always respectful. A good listener. His greatest happiness was to please his father." Again Legola spun a finger, and a new form was introduced onto the second slab beside the dragon. A young boy, no older than Boyd.

One of the hooded pastors separated themselves from the group. They raised a dagger and brought it down upon the dragon.

The pastors staggered back as a bright flash of green light emanated from the sacrifice, flowing into the seizing body of the young boy. The bright light overwhelmed everything, and soon the fog drowned the scene once again, breaking and splitting into the mist.

Lies. There is no way.

"So, what happened?" Isaac asked, breaking a long silence.

"The Lord's soul was fused with that of a dragon. He was the first of what you call the blessed."

"And where were the dragons then?" Boyd asked. "They didn't do anything to stop this?"

"The dragons attempted to retrieve their youngling as soon as they discovered it was captured, but the infernal realms had been long at work, and the power of the underground cult was mightier than they had foreseen. They had no choice but to retreat and try to develop some plan of attack. In truth, it was their turn to fear.

"A few days after the boy Jericho became blessed, dragons chose to reveal a vision of the island of Daemonus to their most trusted apostle, in hopes that the humans would progress faster and prove themselves worthy of the power they stole.

"From the higher realms descended the white dragon of Akraan, and he granted a vision to the apostle Alyosha, foretelling an island out east, where they will find the holy spirit in a form they'd never known.

"When the boats arrived at Daemonus, a few things impressed

the pastors, but by no means was there a spirit that equaled that of the cult. The outcast boy and fourth-generation apostle, Jericho, was one of these members who went along on the underwhelming voyage.

"The fact that the dragons weren't present looked even better for the cult. By this time, Jericho had accumulated a wide following, hidden under the eyes of the church, though mainly consisting of its worshippers. At this point, the church was already more infernal in its praise than holy. Jericho had an underground empire. Followers called him the divine son. Not even I feel such emotion toward my Elder, not in an unquestioning manner. In return for their servitude, Jericho promised the same abilities he wielded. Pastors filled with a desire to change the world followed along, first wishing the old ways to crumble and burn. It was a spiteful hate that fueled them, a hatred of the dragons. The Lord was an example that humans could be as powerful as the creatures of the higher realms, if not more.

"On the night of the equinox, Jericho held meetings with church leaders, slaughtering the few who refused to bow at his will. This pain, the reverberation of the death of holy beliefs, was enough to bring every Dyra dynasty throughout Indus into seclusion, most to the second holy realm we call home.

"The next day, the Lord used a form of first-era praise to summon the dragons from above. Some of the creatures were wise not to come, others simply refused to respond to the call of humans, but that day, many did answer. The result was the power of hundreds of draconic souls handed into the Lord's possession. With each slain dragon, he grew stronger, absorbing their divine forces and converting them to infernal. He shared with his followers but always remembered to remain the strongest, storing incalculable amounts of draconic spirit in the ancient structure of gems. Jericho was able to do something his forefathers never could. He overtook the church, and began a new era."

Inside the cloud of green, there were pastors moving thousands of chained, caged dragons over land, hundreds of ships spanning across waves in the green sea. "Jericho has refined his practice of cultivating draconic souls and transferring them to his followers. The blessings you possess, young Boyd and Rebekah, are a product of a holy spirit turned infernal. They are not blessings, but curses. The draconic spirit does not sit right with you, eating away at your form and corroding your human ghost, taking the color away from your hair and eyes. Your inner balance is tipped."

The problem was that Boyd did not feel the soul of a dragon in his body, or any infernal forces at work. *I am the same as I've always been.* Besides, he never killed a dragon or even partly believed in Jericho's ways. How could infernal forces have influenced him?

"This is the purpose of the equinox test," the Elder drew closer in the fog as Legola spoke, as did the Dyra they called Oswaldo. "Each student must absorb the Spirit of an infant dragon they have killed, vowing your soul to the infernal realms."

"What about me," Isaac asked. "I acted according to the infernal forces just as much as the others, and I'm not blessed... or cursed, whatever."

"I sense your guilt," the Elder Dyra responded. "You must let go of the act you committed. It is in the reconjured realm of the past, which is never a true recreation. The only thing you can do is vow to act in light of holy forces."

"I will," Isaac said, and Boyd almost laughed at his eagerness. "I'll save the dragons."

The Elder pulsed red. "That is the type of will holy forces require from followers. As far as we Dyra know, it is when one performs acts for others that they invite the higher forces to influence them. You ask why you are not blessed, Isaac." The fog swirled and took the form of a book Boyd recognized; he'd read it twice, through-and-through.

This was the Dyra's final touch, the presentation that would sway Isaac for good.

"Ever since the Lord's reign had taken over, we Dyra were looking to do our part. Legola and Oswaldo ventured throughout the islands of Indus to try and find humans capable of reverting to second-era beliefs, raising a rebellion, and defeating the Lord. We began to doubt ourselves, feeling hopeless as we neared our hundredth year of hiding without a single hint of hope, and our dynasty dwindled to what you see today.

"Then we had word from Oswaldo, who we sent north. He spoke of humans on a lesser island, influenced by holy forces, untouched and removed from society. They found you, Isaac, on the island of Windhaven, near the sacred mountain."

"My father used to tell me about it," Isaac said. "'At the peak is the home of the dragons,' he would say. You could see the mountain from my house, in the distance. The peak always hid in the clouds."

"It was so. Oswaldo witnessed your father trekking down from the mountain, dragging you behind him in a sled, though you had entered your calling age already."

Boyd sat up straight. "Down, as in he had already climbed the mountain?" This was impossible.

"None of the Dyra saw him climb," Oswaldo chimed lightly. "But that's what it seemed like to me."

Boyd remembered how Isaac and the notebook had described the highest-reaching mountain in Indus. A behemoth, towering steeply into the sky—impossible to climb. He looked to Isaac, about to ask if he really believed this nonsense, stopping himself when he saw his friend's wide, hopeful eyes. *They have him.*

"We are not sure what happened on that mountain," the Elder said. "But Oswaldo followed your father, seeing a way that you could influence others, as Jericho did so long ago.

"We watched you grow, saw the difference in you as a boy. You had a proclivity toward holier forces, despite your rather uncomfortable means. All your feelings were pure, even the angered ones, and we believed you would be the rare human to find the path early on in existence. We were wrong... But not far off.

"The notebook your father gave you is something he worked on his entire life to complete, of this, we Dyra know quite well. The only reason we can think of for your immunity to the infernal forces is the amount of care your father imbued into that notebook. Even when you carry it now, its affection radiates like a glow to me, and I feel the years of struggling devotion. I do not believe any infernal force could penetrate that text, as its intent was as holy as the dragons themselves. The effect seemed to have worn off on you as well, lasting throughout your years at St. Daemonus.

"The Lord could never get through to you. Even when your actions showed that you wanted to follow the infernal ways, he couldn't unwind the protective forces your ancestry created."

Boyd was confused. Wouldn't he have at least accumulated something over the years to block him from the infernal forces? He'd read enough of the notebook for the holy protection to wear off. "What about me?"

The Elder fluttered closer and pulsed a darker green than the fog. "What about you?"

He ignored how the creature spoke like it was better than him. "Why do I have the Lord's blessings when I also read the notebook? We both wanted to save the dragons. Wasn't there anything in my life that would defend me against the infernal forces?"

For a moment, he thought the Dyra would say no, and all the suppressed anger rose at once.

"The Lord intended to use you," said the Elder. "All of you. The way that the Lord recruits students for his school is by searching the land for whatever capable souls remain, and corrupting them at first chance. Jericho invited you to St. Daemonus because you showed a propensity toward all things good. The power of this Chrysos is the last thing Jericho needs to bring infernal forces into the middle realm and tip the balance in its favor. Then, he will be too powerful for any holy force to stop, and your souls will be his."

"That doesn't explain why I became blessed," Boyd said. "Over the years, I was exposed to that notebook."

"It has much to do with your earlier life. Rebekah was blessed with the infernal forces as well. Though, let us take a moment to recognize these blessings for what they are—curses. Isaac was raised by his father and others who held much of the holy beliefs inside of them. He was different from the beginning. Nevertheless, you can change what's been done, by focusing on what you can do."

"Now that I think about it, I remember feeling the infernal forces act through me," Rebekah said. The flashing lights and fantastic shapes the Dyra conjured must have been enough to convince her. "It took over when I dueled with Isaac. Something made me push him off the tier. I didn't want to, but there was a force I couldn't resist." She was reading into things. The infernal Spirit she thought she felt was probably a natural desire to win. Nothing more.

"The influence of your curses today likely felt stronger than ever," the Elder said, "but we are here to rid you of them entirely. This is what we will do to help you stop the Lord. We have managed to bring you three to ascension and tell you all that we know. There is one last reason why you stand here in the past."

The Elder's crown shimmered with deep green color as it lifted its head and began to hum a light, melodic tune. Whispers of wind picked up with the rhythm, and soon every one of the Dyra joined in. The fog moved with the wind, picked up in speed, and flowed throughout every level in a whirlwind.

Gusts filled the tree, and the Dyra continued to sing their lullaby, their ghostly forms lost in the foggy tornado. Their voices carried here, there. Eventually, the hums settled as the fog descended from the topmost steps.

The green cloud shone brighter, gathering near the bottom where they sat. As it finished its bout, the vapors condensed next to the Elder into a mirror of glowing white, the exact shape of the oval mirrors in every room at St. Daemonus, except the inside shone so brightly it hurt to look.

The Elder floated nearby. The chorus of hums came to a sharp end, and a curl developed at the corners of the Dyra's transparent smile. Wise green eyes wrinkled, fixing on them. "This is the realm of promises, where one cannot hide their emotions." The Elder spoke over the high-pitched ring of the oval white mirror. "We Dyra have had many years to feel the wide range of emotions and learn how to share them, but now, with the holy forces we have left, we believe it would be most wise to rid you of the Lord's curses. Those you can see, and those you cannot."

Boyd stood. He knew what they were up to. "So you're just going to cure us of whatever work the Lord has done, that easy?" *Nobody will tamper with my soul like the Lord. I don't care if what they tell me is true.* This was coming to be the same ruse, redefined to fit Isaac's world. *The only person left in Indus to trick.*

"You need only vow to walk the path of the holy realms," the Dyra stated. "As the church discovered years ago, a simple promise to follow forces draconic and holy with the right intent invites a wealth of holiness into one's life."

"I will make the promise," Isaac said, standing.

"Of course you will," Boyd said.

Rebekah stood in the shadows, looked between Isaac and the Elder. "What about defeating the Lord? Without the abilities the curses give us, we don't stand a chance."

"Right," Boyd said. "I'm a much better fighter with the curses." He looked at Isaac. "I bet you couldn't take me anymore, not with my new daggers."

"You're fighting Jericho, not me."

The Elder pulsed a darker, wine red. "The Lord can appeal to the infernal forces inside of you as long as they linger. It is best to vow to a holy path."

"No," Boyd said. "I refuse to be messed with and weakened. I'm not going to let some *thing* alter me because they told me what I wanted to hear."

"We made many decisions that could be the same." Rebekah looked at him from across Isaac. "You won't do this in the name of stopping the sacrifice? Not after the risks that I took?"

"If we were stopping the sacrifice, we'd be on our way to the cathedral by now."

"This is our chance," Rebekah said. "They brought us here to help defeat the Lord. You heard what they said about his power. We'll never be pure enough to defeat the Lord until we vow to walk our holy path."

"What if I don't want my path? This is the same message the Lord says: believe in this, and we will give you what you want. Live like this, and you will be fine. This vow, promise, whatever you want to call it, it's just another form of sacrifice and giving your soul away. I'm not doing it. I'm capable of defeating the Lord with these daggers. That should be enough trust for them."

"We strongly advise against harboring your curses," the Elder said. "Even the ones who take the vow do not lose the capacity to succumb to the infernal realms. It is the consistent upkeep of the vow that defends them. If you do not have this as your shield against the infernal forces, your soul will be manipulated."

"I see it differently," Boyd said. "Is it so wrong that I want to do things my way? Can't I reject your precious path?"

Isaac turned to him with a look Boyd remembered from the previous night, before he escaped over the church walls. "Maybe it's best if he doesn't take the vow. We'll have someone different from us, just in case."

Boyd froze. *Does he think he's gaining the upper hand?*

"I suppose it's not my path to walk," Rebekah said.

There was an eerie silence in the room as the winds shifted, and the white glow rang so beautiful and distracting. "We cannot make decisions for you," the Elder said. "We cannot force you to act a certain way, or force our emotions upon you. In bringing you here, we had no choice but to fit you to a path of ascension. We chose the best path we could, but by no means is this path permanent. Your path may change at any moment, however Yehwa sees fit. To choose no path opens one to the influence of all that is infernal."

"I don't wish to follow any path but my own."

The Elder pulsed red and flew behind the glowing image. All was dark except for the spectral arch. "Very well," the Elder's voice resounded. "Step forward, those who wish to be cleansed, and through your will, vow to walk the holy path wherever it may lead."

Rebekah was the first to step forward. Timidly, hood up, she walked directly into the glowing white and disappeared.

There was a sharp ring, the light weakened, and the voice of the Elder spoke. "Now you, Isaac. Quickly."

Rebekah returned to her seat with a graceful walk. Boyd couldn't glimpse her hair or eyes.

Part of him wanted to get up too, to walk through the light of the Dyra, but he knew even if he did, it wouldn't work. He still had doubts.

I won't be swayed by another false story. Nobody would alter him unless it were of his own accord. That was how he'd never be overcome by evil forces.

Once Isaac had walked through the glowing light, it was but a cloud, which soon returned into subtle flame atop the goblet.

It seemed that none of the Dyra that had been cramped upstairs or on the lower floor had returned. In front of the dimly lit goblet fluttered the Elder, Legola, and Oswaldo, their aura fading from black into white.

"I feel... different," Rebekah said.

Boyd looked around at the empty portions of the tree, much less cozy than before. *Hollow,* he thought. "Where are the other Dyra?"

"It takes a great amount of effort to undo the Lord's work," the Elder said. "The act we performed has rendered us less in number, but better in essence." The Elder nodded to Legola, who flew past the stairs into higher levels of the tree.

"Do you mean they gave their lives to rid us of the Lord's curses, without a second thought?" Rebekah sounded like she was about to cry.

The Elder giggled. "It certainly wasn't without thought. We have been alone in this forest for over a hundred years. Besides, they did not give you their lives, but their ghosts. It was the right thing to do when it comes to stopping the Lord and I am sure the Spirit has rewarded them."

Was that directed at me? Boyd donned his hood, feeling unwelcome. *Never mind this illusion. They didn't do anything but make some light go away.*

Legola came walking back down the staircase leading an orange dragon hardly grown enough to fly.

"Helios!" Isaac said. "He looks so clean."

"It is customary to treat a dragon with the utmost respect when it visits your realm. We rid the scales of the grime from the harbor below. Our dynasty has truly been graced by its presence."

The dragon reached the bottom of the steps and sauntered to Isaac, sitting next to him.

"We Dyra did not plan for you to escape the harbor with a dragon. Never have we seen the creatures act so confidently toward your kind."

Boyd wanted to drive in his point, convince the others of their mistake. "So, how do you expect us to stop the Lord without any blessings?" Boyd asked.

"There are powers greater than those you can conceive," the Elder said. "Such as this creature. It is by having faith in these that you will defeat the Lord. This is the only way."

Boyd was struck with a sense of comedic tragedy. Faith wouldn't stop an army of Zealots and pastors. Faith wouldn't stop the Lord. "Let's go," he said to the others.

"That is a warrior," said Legola.

"He's right. We've done all we could," the Elder said.

"I feel like we owe you," Isaac said. "Thank you."

"Believe the dragons will rise again." The Elder rested on the wooden staircase. "Remember your vow. Seek the aspects of the higher realm that appeal to you, that which you saw in your vision. This is how you can repay us. This is the antidote to everything infernal."

On his way to the staircase, Legola pulled Boyd aside. The

swollen Dyra handed over the backpack taken when he'd first stepped foot outside the wall. Bright eyes studied him. "I know you don't believe us, but a warrior must take proper caution."

Boyd shook his head. "I won't need them." But the Dyra shoved the bag into his arms, and it felt comforting slung across his back.

The Elder fluttered in front of the bottom stairs. "Anything else you wish to ask us?"

No one spoke.

Oswaldo started sobbing, pulsing a dull black. Legola tried to provide comfort but didn't seem very skilled at the task. The Elder appeared hopeful somehow, smiling in the faint outline of its frail face.

"We will place you near the cathedral when you leave this realm. Sneak in and stop the Lord. Your dragon will help you."

When they reached the top of the stairs, they exited through a gem-filled arch and emerged to the Tempus he'd always remembered—cold and desolate. Boyd stepped into the moonlight, looked up, and saw the moon hadn't risen but a sliver through the sky. *It's still not far from High Silver.* They'd have a little over a few shades to stop the Lord.

He sighed and glanced back toward the archway, seeing nothing but dead bark.

CHAPTER 24

SECOND ERA, 113, UAIR THREE OF RISING SILVER

Rebekah

U pon their return, the dead Tempus forest appeared painfully barren compared to the adorned world of the Dyra, sadder still because of Rebekah's lack of blessings. She could hardly distinguish the location of Isaac and Boyd as they sauntered close next to her, the little dragon's steps no more than patters.

This morning, Rebekah would've traded the world to become blessed by the Lord. She had practically given her soul away. What would Priska say if she found out Rebekah gave up the very blessings they dreamed of having for years? Rebekah had wanted to help her bleeding friend on the floor, but she looked so pathetic next to the broken mirror, she couldn't bring herself to console her. Weakness wasn't worthy of her time. Rebekah had bigger things to think about, her own blessings to earn. *I thought I was more worthy than anyone else. Considering the Lord's plan to cultivate evil spirits... Perhaps I was.* If she could do it all again, Rebekah tried considering how she would have acted differently, but she didn't think she could—not then.

If she saw Priska now, she'd have the courage to console her. Once the blessings left her body, a change happened. For the first time in years, Rebekah was nervous about what others thought about her, specifically Isaac. It was like some closed off part of her had finally come to light and changed every instant of the world. Ultimately, luck brought Isaac to her, or the Dyra, but it was too late for Priska. *If only he'd come a day earlier.* No hope remained for Priska anymore. The unblessed would not be treated kindly considering the Lord's supremacy.

They aren't blessings, she reminded herself. *They're curses. The Lord manipulates us. He takes our decisions away.*

Boyd claimed the Dyra did the same, but she knew better, having been a true follower of the Lord. Faint differences showed in the recent promises she made.

In her promise to follow the Lord, she murdered an innocent dragon from a place of pride and determination to succeed. The other promise, the one that took her curses away, she made out of a need to repent. To undo all the harm she'd done.

That was the difference.

She made sure to stay behind the group as they trekked down the well-worn path the Dyra placed them on, wider than the last though no less frighteningly muggy. Rebekah checked to see if her hood could fit over her head any tighter.

She loathed the return of her tangled brown curls and unimpressionable eyes. Never again would the other students gaze at her as she looked back and saw appreciation and love.

Curses, she reminded herself. *Stolen souls aren't blessings.* None of that mattered anymore.

They walked in silence. She studied the footprints, and the insignia printed in the center like a stamp. The same one on the bottom of her own sandal. *I would have been such a good apostle.* Her white cloak felt heavy and just as lifeless as this version of Tempus.

"This isn't the same path we were on," Boyd said. He spoke with disdain; less detectable without her blessings, but still obvious. Ever since Oswaldo proclaimed her and Isaac to be lovers, Boyd refused to make eye contact with her.

She couldn't explain the pit that appeared in her stomach when the flower-filled vision of her and Isaac came to mind. *The audience looked at me with appreciation then. With love.*

Boyd was wrong, though. She would never give up something as useful as the blessings proved to be for another person—deep down, she hoped Isaac wouldn't either. The Dyra said their path was bound to change, anyway. At least three or four times. To believe such a dream with Isaac would be ridiculous.

I gave up my blessings to save the dragons. Nevertheless, her body felt slow. A remarkable weight filled her limbs and she felt less aware. She tried to move with more grace but her body wouldn't obey.

It worried her that Boyd had been so defensive in the first place. She tried her best to watch closely without him knowing, aware of his remaining curse and the abilities they granted.

I don't remember any other students being as blessed as he is. For a moment, Rebekah couldn't help but wonder if the tables had been turned, whether Boyd would have escaped from the harbor and tried to save the Chrysos, or if he would've served the Lord.

Boyd claimed to be against the Lord, but his actions didn't match. It doesn't matter who killed a dragon. As long as he was cursed, Boyd would be manipulated. That was what the Elder said. *As long as we agree on stopping the Lord, we'll be okay,* she hoped.

Golden caps on the cathedral towers emerged over the treeline after a long, curved turn.

"Look," Isaac said. He turned back with excitement, but that quickly vanished when he saw her and Boyd. "This must be the path to the cathedral from the church, built in the first-era." The cleansed orange dragon stalked by Isaac's side. Proof of the creature's ability to cooperate still amazed her.

"High Silver will be soon," Boyd said. "We wasted too much time speaking to those... whatever. We wasted too much time."

"The moon didn't change a shade while we were there." Rebekah knew the Dyra likely didn't judge time by sun and moon dials, they had compared it to a ball of yarn if she remembered correctly. She couldn't let Boyd go on spewing nonsense.

"Time is a factor," said Isaac. "But, she's right. We shouldn't rush. The Dyra said to find a way to sneak in. Let's take some time to look around, maybe we can find a way around the main entrance."

A pressing, awkward silence.

"There's a drawing of the cathedral in my father's notebook, it might help us out. I mean, the Dyra were real after all... I can't help but wonder what else in my father's notebook was true."

"And right on time," Boyd said.

"What do you mean?"

"I mean, that's exactly what the Lord wants." Boyd's steps grew faster, harsher as he rushed past Rebekah. Despite her loss of blessings, she could sense his anger.

"I just don't know how you expect us to defeat the Lord with *hope*." The last words carried out to the forest. "At least Legola had the right idea, arming me with daggers. That was the only one of those creatures who had any sense. Guess that's because it was meant to appeal to me." Boyd wound up, and threw one of the silver daggers out in front of them.

Isaac ducked after it whizzed past his head. "What was that for?"

Boyd stepped up next to Isaac, they stared eye to eye. He stuck his hand up and Rebekah lunged forward, thinking she might have to break up a fight, then he caught the dagger. "Call me crazy, but I'm still confused about what use a dagger like this and a tiny little dragon will be against the all-powerful Lord. The same one who can't be defeated by even the strongest draconic power."

Isaac turned, continued to walk down the path. "You heard what they said about my blessings. We just have to trust in them."

"In who, some random creatures we met in the Tempus forest? You expect me to trust a vision that showed you kissing a girl?"

For a moment, Rebekah thought he may be right. The hope the Dyra preached required a blatant ignorance. But at the time of her vow, the very fact of their existence was enough to convince her.

"We have to believe we'll stop him," Isaac said. "That's what's kept me... us, protected all these years. The belief that we can."

"Don't you think the dragons tried to *believe*? You don't actually think you're more capable than them, do you? Then again, you've always been gullible. I suppose you might if some special beings from your father's notebook told you you were chosen."

Isaac ignored him, stepping over monotonous branches.

Rebekah tried to do the same, but Boyd caught her glance as she passed by.

"Fair enough," Boyd said. "What about when you looked into the dragon's eyes, at the harbor?"

"I told you," Isaac said. "I didn't look into Helios's eyes. The vision started when I touched the scales. I saw my home island, Windhaven. It was like I had an overview of the entire place, shore to shore, flying in the form of a dragon. I know it sounds ridiculous, but that's what I saw."

Rebekah believed him. It was the way he spoke about it. Given the feelings they shared in the forest, she could tell when he was truthful. Besides, she'd seen him jolted by the dragon's touch as he knelt in the filth by the harbor's cages. She saw how the dragon approached him itself, nothing if not seeking an escape of its own.

"It ended with me flying up the Great Mountain," Isaac said. "I almost saw the peak."

"And that's what you're wagering the fate of your soul on. Think about it. Seeing a mountain you've already seen, in some dream. You know, the Lord could make you see that easily."

"No, this vision is true. I know it. Just like I know the Dyra are real," Isaac said. "I'd say that's enough not to give up my curses from Jericho."

"You think that you know," Boyd said, "but you can never be sure. We're just as ignorant as the rest of the students. It's not like you were there a hundred years ago."

"We all want to stop the sacrifice." Rebekah said. "Isn't that enough?"

"It won't be," Boyd said. "We can't stop the Lord just by wanting to, that's what you two don't understand. As of now, we're going there to die. You're so scared of strength that you don't want any for yourself. We should've left the Dyra and spent this time gathering swords, bombs of fire, anything to help our fight. But what, you think we're going to defeat him with some advanced combat train- ing? The Lord knew that you would fall for some first-era vision, and he exploited your weakness. He knew you wouldn't be a true follower, so he tricked you both. Now we're on our way to certain death, and there's nothing we can do."

He glanced at Rebekah, and laughed. "I don't blame you for giving away your blessings. You're probably confused after discov- ering your Lord wanted to sacrifice you. That doesn't mean it wasn't a terrible idea. Be honest with me, you don't really think we're going to defeat the Lord, right? Go ahead, it's okay to admit it. It's healthy."

Rebekah kept her head down, following the curving path. Boyd mumbled behind her, but she couldn't hear what he said. The Dyra had said a being can fall prey to infernal forces, even if they vow to serve higher realms. She wouldn't be one.

Isaac stopped. "I think we made it."

The moon's shadows presented a collapsed, deteriorating half- structure. Their path led directly into the main entrance, which wouldn't provide much cover as its ceiling had given way to the natural decay of time. *An infernal force of its own.* Next to the lobby of rubble were several hallways with missing walls. Wooden crates lay everywhere as if the cathedral had been in use over the past years. The only standing portion that still seemed in-tact was the domelike, stained-glass ceiling, which overshadowed the rest of the structure in an oppressive mood of unobtainable beauty.

Isaac removed the notebook from his cloak, flipped through the pages. "The cathedral is a combination of human and dragon architecture. Imagined by draconic minds, built with human hands. My father drew this picture before it was finished. It's what he thought it might look like."

Rebekah glanced at the notebook. "He wasn't far off," she said, looking back toward the sunken structure. It must have taken years to build. How long before it was destroyed? The past version of Tempus the Dyra lived in would've fit well with the picture in the notebook. "It's quite the drawing."

Isaac pointed at a path along the side. "I was thinking we could enter through here. The river runs underneath the cathedral, and we can find our way up to where Jericho is keeping the sacrifice. Then, we free it."

"All with the sharpened sword of hope. Only one thing, the river is dried out." Boyd pointed to the dusty remnants of the water channel running beneath the cathedral's side. Shattered stone and wood lay in a dry patch of dirt just in front of a grated tunnel, welcoming them to what looked like peril.

"Even better." Isaac closed the notebook and looked at Rebekah before she could avert her gaze.

For both their sake, she looked away.

She'd always hated the way she looked without blessings. It was part of why she wanted them in the first place, to look like her favorite apostles. *He likes this version of me less.*

CHAPTER 25
SECOND ERA, II3, UAIR THREE OF RISING SILVER

Isaac

I saac forced himself to look away from Rebekah, returning the notebook to his cloak pocket. *I have to be brave,* he thought. *For her.*

Her old appearance startled him, causing faint feelings of a lingering connection—the version of her he'd always known, the version that everyone at St. Daemonus loved her for, the version that showed so much promise so early.

Isaac would be brave for both of them. If he gave into hopelessness and despair, they would be captured by the Lord and influenced by infernal forces. The Dyra said even those who took the vow could still fall prey to the Lord's ways. *If only the Lord wasn't so subtle.*

After a cursory glance, he made his way out from their hiding place in the forest, following footprints of the pastors, then leaving them behind for the side of the cathedral and patch of dry dirt that marked the tunnel's underground entrance. Helios stayed by his side. Rebekah followed long after, then Boyd.

Where the dead river met the cathedral, a metallic gate had been destroyed, a tear in the center as if punched in by a hand much stronger than his own. Bits of crushed gems speckled the dirt. Filthy mud water lingered at the entrance, marking the start of a narrow underground tunnel.

As Isaac peered inside, a sudden heat covered his face. Rotten leftovers from the river made him gag—bones and organs of what had once been great fish, nibbled on by mice and eye-sockets filled with... maggots.

The amber dragon entered without a second thought, weaving between the mess. Isaac lost it in the dark.

"This thing is going to collapse on us," Boyd said.

"It won't," Rebekah said quickly. "The Lord wouldn't bring the Chrysos here unless he was certain he could sacrifice it."

"You heard the Dyra," Isaac said. "Follow the dragon."

The darkness of the tunnel enveloped him.

As always, there was a certain truth to what Boyd said. The instructions seemed so meaningless and vague. But what else could they do, really?

The burnt orange sheen of Helios led deeper, far ahead. Isaac guided himself with his hand along one of the rocky walls. Soon, the stone turned to soft dirt. Puddles gave into a cramped heat. Dry bones crunched beneath his feet. Isaac's cloak clung to his skin, beads of sweat dripping into his eyes.

"We have to be close," Boyd said.

The tunnel had grown so dark, Isaac was forced to listen for Helios's guttural clicks. Regardless, the tunnel only seemed to lead one way. Orange scales came to fruition within a dull purple and reddish glow, so faint Isaac doubted its presence.

"There's light," he said, confused by the formless, touchless substance seeming to hang in the air. It made Isaac think of the tent and the sacrifice.

"We're close," Rebekah said.

The tunnel grew ever more hot and damp. *Nerves*, Isaac thought. His breaths slowly filled less and less with dirt, and more with the dense air.

He kept pushing on. Something called to him, a voice he'd heard his entire life, tempting him to give in. *It's so hot,* it said.

Helios stopped before them. It took a few moments for Isaac to notice they'd reached the tunnel's end. The air hadn't gotten any cooler despite the surrounding walls opening to an expansive cavern.

"The notebook never said anything about a cave," Isaac said, looking out over Helios. Sweat dripped from his face.

"No," Boyd said. "I don't think very many people have been here at all."

"What is this light?" Rebekah asked. "It stings, like the Lord's worship. And the sacrifice."

"Yep," Boyd said.

Isaac stepped to the tunnel's edge and looked out over Helios. A single narrow bridge continued out from the tunnel where they stood, leading to a sole, circular platform. The platform rested in the center of the void, floating if it weren't for a long connective pillar, leading down into the forever of the purple and red hue. *That is where the heat is coming from.* Isaac knew it as his face burned, gazing into the tempting call to believe they had no chance. The heat clawed at his legs, begging him to kneel, fall.

He forced his eyes up and scanned the rest of the vast expanse.

In the center of the dirt ceiling high above, silver moonlight shone through a small hole in a series of shreds, casting reflections upon a ladder that connected down to the single platform.

Boyd tried to force his way past Isaac.

"Hold on." Isaac stopped him with his arm. He considered his next words carefully under Boyd's analytical gaze. "Don't look down."

A metallic creak echoed off the rock. Moonlight overcame the darkness as the grate above the ladder lifted.

They retreated into the tunnel as a stubby, snickering form hidden by shadows descended the ladder. Isaac would have recognized the form anywhere, though it took him a moment. The Lord's servant only vaguely appeared as himself. The lump on Haskil's back had become a set of luscious black wings, guiding him down as he dropped from the opening to the platform with a few easy flaps.

Isaac wasn't surprised. The Lord promised draconic power.

Haskil spent a fair amount of time grumbling near the bottom of the ladder. He removed something egg-shaped from his cloak, threw it into the void, and ascended with another series of flaps to the grate. It almost didn't make sense how the small wings carried his pudgy body, but he maneuvered with a quickness they had to be sure to avoid.

A metal clang sounded as the grate slammed shut.

"We're too late," Boyd whispered. Rebekah hushed him, but he waved her off. "I can hear them above us. The Chrysos is in position. That was the servant's final check. The Lord beat us here."

"But it's not High Silver," Rebekah said.

Boyd looked between them, fumbling for his daggers. "They must have known we were coming. It doesn't matter whether the sacrifice is during High Silver or not, it's a *Chrysos*."

This time Isaac wasn't able to keep his friend from darting onto the bridge.

Helios ran out next.

They neared the ladder as a group. Isaac could hear soft murmurs coming through the grate.

Boyd finally drew his daggers. He neared the ladder, glancing up.

Isaac placed his hand on one of the metal rungs. "I'll go first." He felt scratching on his leg, looked down to see Helios clawing at his side. The dragon dug into his skin, flapping its wings, as if asking to climb onto his shoulders.

Boyd's hand fell from the ladder. "Be careful we're not made into sacrifices, as well." He moved aside.

The damp air made the climb difficult by the tenth rung. Helios's scales tore into his shoulder. At times the dragon would flap its wings to take off the weight, but even so, the claws buried deeper. Isaac looked down, curious to see how the others were doing.

He was met by the disorienting immensity of the void beneath him. It expanded deeper the longer he stared. He found himself inspired to loosen his grip and fall.

Helios flapped, the pinch of claws bringing him back to the moment. Isaac shook his head, tightening his hold on the metal.

The cool air of night provided fresh relief as he neared the top of the ladder. Isaac heard conversations between the pastor and Zealots. Their speech was solemn and short. He was still too far to understand.

Helios shifted on his shoulders with another flap. *He knows what's ahead.* Isaac convinced himself to grip the final rung and lift himself up, peering through the grate's metallic segments.

Nothing but dark cathedral walls.

"Hurry," Boyd whispered. He feared Boyd might take the liberty to run out and face the Lord himself. It wasn't eve Boyd he dealt with anymore, but a braver version of his old friend. *Too brave.*

Isaac almost fell as he released the latch and lowered the grate by its hinges with a single hand, silencing the metal as best he could. Helios jumped from his shoulder to the cathedral floor and hid behind a wooden crate. It took Isaac's last reserves of strength to crawl through the opening.

Dozens of the wooden crates lay around, few intact. In one direction of the hallway, moonlight seeped through to the sunken lobby entrance, and on the other, the cathedral's deconstructed room of worship.

Isaac searched the fallen segments of stone and intact crates for cover. A wooden box large enough to hide them all stood on the left, though it might have been too close to the cathedral's nave.

Boyd followed, then Rebekah, each taking place at his side, behind the crate. "They're about to begin," Boyd said.

Isaac's breath hastened, short and choppy as he peered over the wood.

The nave of the cathedral seemed larger on the inside. *Another thing like the sacrificial tent.* He wondered if Rebekah noticed. The domed ceiling lifted higher than the ladder below them would have reached, built with a glass of magnificent colors Isaac had only seen in the realm of the Dyra. The patterns created pictures, imperceptible from where they hid. Isaac wanted nothing more than to decipher the story they told. *Father only dreamed of seeing this place.*

But not like this. Moonlight spilled in from broken walls. Zealots and black cloaks moved in and out of the shadows. Pastor Solomon inspected his sleeping gray captive with a sober demeanor the Zealots lacked. The sea-faring henchmen hardly kept their weight on the chains subduing the massive creature.

The dragon's head took up the entire space, pews shoved as close as possible to the shattered walls. Isaac considered the Chrysos might have grown on the trip.

Pastor Solomon walked in a crescent shape around the head's perimeter, stakes holding the chains around the thick neck firm. Sharp, curved horns extended from the dragon's head, three times the size of the pastor maneuvering next to them. The rest of the dragon stretched out into one of the hallways. They only needed it down to the neck.

To see the magnificent Chrysos so close but weak and malnourished, it was no wonder Rebekah changed her mind after the harbor below. Isaac's stomach turned at the scarred gashes on the creature's back, where there once grew wings. The Lord took away any hope the dragon had of escape.

A ghostly cry called up through the grate behind them, from the void. A wild heat surged past Isaac, sandals burning the bottom of his foot. The floor of the cathedral rumbled and quaked, forcing their grips onto the nearby wood. Helios jumped onto the crate.

The heat ended abruptly, as if priming the entry of a transient voice. "The touch of the Chrysos. You've suffered worse to get here."

"I have, my Lord," said Pastor Solomon.

"Soon, your suffering shall end. The eye of the Silver Goddess looks upon us. Equinox moon has risen."

Jericho lumbered out from a hall much like the one in which they hid, fit in a blood-red robe that matched the two glowing beams of light inside the hood. Around his neck, wrists, and fingers were necklaces, bracelets, and rings, each adorned with many gems. He lowered his hood in stride to reveal a thin, youthful face, no older than its thirtieth equinox, white locks of hair falling beside eyes of a blessed red.

"The sacrifice is in position," the pastor said.

What can we do? Isaac looked around desperately, but the others just watched. Even Helios did nothing from atop the crate, the dragon's spiked tail flitting about. *It is just as nervous as me.*

"We await your order."

Zealots doubled over the chains.

Rebekah gripped Isaac's arm.

The black-cloaked pastor reached into his cloak to draw out a dragon, smaller than Helios. In his other hand, he held a dagger.

There's no way to stop them. The heat made it apparent, seeping through Isaac's skin, slowing the blood in his veins.

The Lord remained in the nave's center, fixated on the Chrysos.

"Now?"

Jericho nodded. "The natural way."

The pastor shut his red eyes, a long pause.

When he opened them, he muttered an imperceptible word, likely a spell of awakening.

Isaac flinched at the slice; he always did.

Silvery-blue wisps swam through the air like Dyra and entered the scales of the Chrysos. Its scales flashed an array of colors as its eyelids blinked once, twice.

Another wave of heat surged from beneath the cathedral. The

walls filled with red like a furnace, invisible fire rippling through the air. A few Zealots collapsed from the harsh atmosphere, and the resulting earthquake threw the rest off their footing. They recovered, doubled over the chains. Some wouldn't dare venture close to the groaning dragon, despite their barking pastor.

The Chrysos had been subdued from the neck down. This didn't stop its head from lifting, slinging henchmen across the room. Those smart enough to drop their chains ran into a nearby hallway.

Now, Isaac thought. *We can overtake them now.*

But his body didn't move. He could only look to the Lord, who held his ground, then to Boyd. Isaac could see the horror reflected in the red of his friend's eyes.

The dragon's enormous head stretched as far as the chains allowed, grunting once it reached resistance. Smoke-filled bouts tortured the room with heat. Meanwhile, the scales settled to solid gold.

The Chrysos shifted, searching for comfort. The creature's structure would have been perfect if its wings weren't clipped. Wide was its mouth, capable of consuming a human in one snatch. Instead, the dragon gazed at the glass ceiling.

Isaac expected a blast of fire, surprised when a piercing screech filled the room. The volume rose to rattle his brain.

Glass shattered.

He watched, hands cupped to his ears as colorful shards rained down upon the Zealots, pastors, and the Lord. Fragments shattered and ricocheted against the Chrysos's golden scales. Red blood pooled on the nave's tiled floor.

The few unlucky ones who could not find cover were impaled where they stood. Rebekah shielded her eyes. Boyd watched along with Isaac in unmoving silence.

It ended, and cloudy debris of blood and glass filled the air.

In the center, the Lord stood unphased. Around him, a perfect circle marked where no glass had landed.

For some reason, Isaac expected the Chrysos to be free after the display of force.

Zealots stumbled back into the room, taking up their places on the chains as if it mattered, slipping and falling in the blood of their companions.

The worst part was how the Chrysos went along with it.

Has it lost hope? Perhaps even the draconic species had given into the temptation of the infernal realms.

Haskil stumbled out of the Lord's same darkened hallway, wings flapping subtly. The servant held a wide leather sheath. He giggled, bowing and presenting it to the Lord. "M-m-maaaster."

Jericho gripped the handle and removed the sword, which rang as if met with equal steel.

"The sword of Daemonus," Boyd whispered in disbelief.

The crafted masterpiece, as silver as the moonlight, shot gleaming rays at them as Jericho admired the blade in the air.

He knows we're here. It is time to act.

Isaac looked for the amber dragon and found nothing. Helios had moved from the crate, a few paces away. He wanted to reach out and grab his tail, yank him back, but he couldn't risk having another vision.

But he realized the heat wouldn't berate him when he focused on the small creature. There also seemed to be a change in thought whenever he looked at the so-called monster, as if it were the sliver of hope that remained. He did his best to foster that feeling as Helios crept forward and Lord Jericho approached the throat of the Chrysos, silver blade held at his side.

CHAPTER 26

SECOND ERA, 113, UAIR FOUR OF RISING SILVER

Boyd

W*e're too late.* Boyd couldn't take his eyes off the Lord, watching him saunter in front of the yellowish skin of the Chrysos's neck, chains jingling in the moonlight.

I have to stop him.

But when he told his body to move, it wouldn't obey.

It's no matter.

They stood no chance.

The Lord looked directly at us. He knows. All that effort, and we're forced to sit here and become sacrifices. He did something to the cathedral, made it impossible to move.

They would never have stayed in the realm of the Dyra if Boyd had any say, but of course, he didn't, and that's why they arrived late, confirmed by the thick air of the Lord's power threatening to boil his skin. The slightest movement through the darkness with a subtle purple tint took every fiber and muscle he could muster. To intervene undoubtedly meant death.

We're dead if we try and we're dead if we don't.

But he couldn't find it inside himself to run out into the scene and give his life away. This wasn't like escaping the church, when he'd been sure there was more to discover. There would be nowhere to go if he left from behind the crate. There would be nothing at all. Only more of this mind-bending dark. Even though he was the last one capable of fighting in the group, the Lord's draconic power would make quick work of his throwing dagger trick. He'd die with no apostles around to witness or write psalms about his valor. The sacrifice would wipe out opposing forces, holy or otherwise, completely erasing the ways of the first era and any other means of existence.

Jericho stood still, paces away from the dragon's neck.

We are all his sacrifices, Boyd thought.

The determined expression on the Lord's face lacked emotion—professional. Leftover pleas from those dying by glass wounds called out over the Chrysos' heavy breathing, but the pastors and Zealots who remained had fallen silent since the appearance of the Daemonus sword.

The only textbooks Boyd thought worthy of reading spoke highly of the sword forged at the beginning of Jericho's reign from a rare stone called Spinel, forged within the infernal realms.

Per the operational structure of the second-era, the Sword of Daemonus captured souls. Texts and pastors boasted of it often, but much like the stone from which it had been forged, none knew of the sword's precise location. Boyd had written the blade off as a myth, another tale told by the Lord to ensure his followers stayed in line, lest their souls end up trapped. The fact that the sword shone in front of them now proved the Lord's speech more accurate than any —more true than the Dyra or the notebook of Isaac's father.

The Law of Utility: What is most true will remain.

Is that how the world should be? Whoever has the most power always wins? Then again, it didn't seem to matter what Boyd thought about anything. It never did.

Act. Boyd told himself, feet and legs blending with the heat. Melting. *Do something.*

What, die? He found himself at least able to grip the twin night-fall daggers. *I might take out a few pastors on the way, but it would be worth nothing.* The leather hilts burned his hands, and he pulled away.

Jericho mumbled mantras Boyd couldn't hear—quicker whispers than any human ever spoke. The Lord lifted his gaze, surveyed the pastors and Zealots who adored him with the same timidness they seemed to have with the dragon. "Today is the day rogue souls become blessed. We will turn day into night, fire to ice. Humanity will be gods after my sacrifice, due to the efforts I've endured."

The Zealots chorused. "Yes, my Lord.'

Jericho looked to the ground, then to the sword held out high before him. "Great Spirit, purveyor of souls. May you grant my followers with blessings from this sacrifice, the Chrysos we return to you."

Boyd just realized Isaac had left from behind the crate, crouching near the hallway's opening, the orange dragon stalking next to him. Boyd wanted to call him back, but Isaac lacked blessings, and wouldn't be able to hear unless the Zealots did too.

It's not like the Lord doesn't know we're here. Besides, if Isaac wanted to die so quickly, so be it. *As long as we are letting each other make our own choices.*

Rebekah seemed able to do no more than stare in angst. The tips of her curled brown hair clung to her damp skin. The darker shade of her eyes seemed much better at expressing emotion than before, easier to read.

Weaker, Boyd knew.

The Lord raised the silver-stone blade ever higher. With a grunt, the blade whistled through the air.

The Chrysos bleated like a sheep as the slice ventured halfway through its neck. Halted by dragon bone, the sword stopped as blood darker and thicker than curdled milk leaked from the gash, soaking the Lord and the floor in a pool.

Rebekah buried her face into Boyd's cloak, but all he could think about was how he didn't have so much as an adverse reaction to the scene.

Isaac sat near the hallway's exit, watching—as did Helios.

It is too late.

Jericho tugged the sword out from the dragon's neck. A dripping trail of arteries and tendons followed. Inanimate eyes of the dragon, so filled with grief and life before, stared blankly out over an open mouth and limp tongue. The dragon died, gradually.

Jericho screamed in triumph as he brought the sword down once more, connecting despite his foot having slipped in the blood. The severed head of the Chrysos plopped limp onto the floor without grace. The Lord breathed heavily as he backed away, eyes wide in fervor.

Not a soul moved in the cathedral's main room.

A silver shred of moonlight seeped through a crack in the ceiling in a sad, intervening sliver of gray.

High Silver.

Boyd stood frozen. They had lost, and the thought made him weak and unable to run, let alone fight.

Gasps arose from the Zealots as golden wisps lifted from the Chrysos' scales and gathered in an orb near the severed head. Slowly, a spectral ball of gold formed, shimmering with high frequency as white bands circled around it. The scales of the dragon were left gray and defeated, and the orb grew in size with a subtle *wub, wub, wub.*

A devious smile sprouted upon the Lord's face, bathed in the acquired shine. Jericho began a crazed laugh as icy, tundra-like wind picked up inside the broken structure, disorienting, swirling up into the night. Boyd wanted to escape, but he couldn't look away, oddly fascinated by the spectacle of his demise.

Even Isaac sat staring, exposed near the hallway's end.

A stream of gold and silver leaped from the orb, pounding into Jericho's chest.

Zealots cried out, retreating with murmurs into the halls.

The Lord had finally completed his task. Now, he reaped the rewards.

The orb grew brighter than the moonlight, approaching the size of the Chrysos' head. With a growing vibration, the cathedral quaked longer, more furious than ever. Boyd kept a steady balance holding a nearby crate but couldn't help from shielding himself as a shock-wave created by the orb flooded the room in silvery golden light.

Boyd felt helpless as the shine reached them and slammed into an invisible barrier just before where they stood, as if some wall had been placed in front of Isaac and Helios at the hallway's end. The spectral glow continued to crash and flood into the transparent barrier, never entering but spreading in a flat pan outward to every direction until the room looked brighter than day.

Boyd leaned forward, wanting to witness the light. The rays seemed staved off by infrequent, pulsating blue streaks like lightning strikes throughout a clear shield as tall and wide as the hallway's edge. Isaac and Helios became silhouettes. Isaac dropped onto his knees and elbows before the encompassing light, crawling forward, almost inside.

Boyd reached for a feeling of sadness but could provoke none, not in this space where followers worshipped eternal death, welcoming the Lord's vision of a lightless, burning nothing.

Still think hope will save you?

Isaac fell to his stomach and went limp.

He chose this path himself, always claiming he'd been chosen for some vision, wanting to be the savior.

Even his promise couldn't save him.

Boyd needed water, his throat clenching in the terrible air. His body felt swollen. Yet, he somehow knew this was only the beginning. He wouldn't be able to quench this thirst for a long, long time. If ever.

Through the clear shield, a reddish outline developed around Jericho's twitching body. Within the gold and silver swirling vortex, millions of serpent-like shadows flew in a chaotic tornado. Bodies of Zealots flew by, unable to control themselves in the force of it all. The scales, skin, and muscles of the Chrysos evaporated on the floor, its skeleton collapsing onto the ground, then picked up by the growing fury. The Lord had managed to make quick work of the most sacred creature in all of Indus.

Then the light fell, and the main room came to fruition within a few moments's time. It was apparent the shield the little dragon created hadn't protected Isaac. He lay unmoving. *Dead,* Boyd thought without a doubt.

Rebekah ran out from behind the crate and laid silently next to him.

Somehow, the dragon Helios lived. It turned to Isaac's lifeless body on the floor.

It had been with the Lord all along.

The Lord did not stir—his arms outstretched, basking in the aftermath. He looked to the night sky, cloak ripped and torn.

Boyd followed his gaze to see that a starless purple void had replaced rays of moonlight. The temperature opposed that of the cave underneath, a cool space where he could see the vapors of his own breath. *Jericho has unleashed his true power.* Boyd tried working up the courage to retreat down the ladder, his body only beginning to move, when Helios nudged the limp body of Isaac with its snout, and the eyes of his unblessed friend blinked open at the touch.

Rebekah shook him. "Wake up," she said. "Isaac, you have to get up."

She wouldn't be doing any of this if it were Boyd there on the floor. *They would be gone already.*

Just go.

But he couldn't stop from watching as Helios entered the nave. Boyd tried to understand its purpose as the dragon creeped into the midst of the destruction. Even as it did so, the amber creature seemed larger than before. Not the size of the Chrysos, less childish and clumsy. The dragon had disappeared around the corner before he could determine anything else.

Rebekah gave Boyd a skeptical look as she helped Isaac stumble behind the crate, over to the ladder. *She thinks I follow the Lord, that I had something to do with the Chrysos's death.*

A groan sounded from deep within the tired structure of the cathedral, and they stopped to look around at the collapsed hall.

No sooner had there been a maniacal, stuttering laugh from the nave. The servant Haskil rose from behind the empty skull and extended horns of the dragon. Haskil laughed a sinister giggle, his shapely body more round than ever.

Wings spread in both directions out from behind the roundish form, the servant rose. Blood dripped from his feet back down to the floor. Haskil's head tilted, lips twitching into an ever-widening grin, and the servant dipped through the air, starting toward them.

Surely this would be enough to shock him into flight, but Boyd's limbs still wouldn't move, and he could only watch the servant's face grow bigger than the moon.

Haskil bared his teeth, jaw expanding into a sharpened trap, when an orange form plowed into the servant's side, taking him out of view.

Boyd stood breathless. *Helios?*

Moans and grunts from the Lord's followers sounded from the wreckage. Burned, beaten bodies screamed in agony as they rose, shouting into the night from decrepit, deformed postures like newborn insects. One by one, they howled, and their backs split open as undergrown wings sprouted.

Something gripped Boyd's arm; he jumped.

Isaac's hold felt terribly weak. "We have to go."

Finally, Boyd found himself able to move. Holding the nightfall daggers sideways over the metal bars, he descended the ladder into the underground cavern. By the time they reached the bottom platform, where the bridge extended across the chasm to their escape, rumbles had rendered Boyd's hands numb. Whatever Jericho's followers became, Boyd realized he'd do anything to escape that fate. He'd even take the vow of the Dyra. Then again, perhaps the Great Spirit, whatever it was, meant things to be that way, and they were meant to die here.

The Law of Utility.

He dropped from the ladder and followed Isaac and Rebekah after they made a break for the tunnel. They seemed to still believe in escape. *There is no use,* Boyd thought more with every stride. *Our time has come.*

The freezing temperature rendered no feeling in his legs, each step heavier than the last. Midway across the bridge, he found himself on his knees, gazing into the forever darkness below and contemplating the solace he might find. He pulled back once the cold became too much for his face to bear.

As he stood, again the cathedral shook, throwing his balance. There was nothing to grip this time, but by some luck, none of them tumbled over into the abyss.

The ladder snapped first.

Boyd turned in time to see the floor of the cathedral split into hundreds of pieces above, raining debris of stone, dragon bone, glass, and dead Zealots onto them. Amongst it all, there was the shout of a dragon, a roar that Boyd felt in his groin.

Remnants of the cathedral floor fell all around, but Boyd hardly believed it when he raised his head and realized none had touched them. Just as he became grateful, a large rock connected with the bridge ahead of Isaac and Rebekah, breaking their only path into two ends with a gap far too wide in-between.

A second shriek followed—a clicking, predatory sound from much closer. Boyd turned as it closed in on him out of the dark, too fast to think. He looked down, locating the sound in the dark with just enough time to throw a dagger at a pair of glowing red eyes rushing toward him. His blade struck the creature, its clicking shriek cut off with a gargle, and a ripped yellow cloak glimpsed light before it dropped away, back into the void.

A Zealot... At least, it used to be. Boyd caught the dagger as it returned up to him from the void, hardly feeling it against his palm.

A series of long, clicking sounds rose out from the void in response, at least ten at once. *How many Zealots had there been?*

Two of the creatures flew up ahead, slashing with claws at Rebekah and Isaac, heavy wings beating the air as they began to tear cloak and flesh. *They can't see them coming without the blessings.*

Boyd threw his daggers, and both creatures cried out, falling back, over the narrow path and into the void. "Jump," he said, pointing across the gap in the stone bridge. "I'll give you cover."

They had no time to reply before another one of the creatures arose from the dark.

He planted his dagger between its eyes. "Run!"

Isaac watched the whimpering creature fall again, and nodded. Boyd could see the trust in his friend, and at that moment, he thought he might have been able to take the vow with a pure belief. It felt contagious after seeing the determination, different from the Lord's. Isaac showed he was worried; then, that he was brave.

The creatures stopped attacking, and the clicking quieted to a dull buzz.

Boyd walked up to where the bridge split and peered into the nothingness, making sure it was only for a moment—the void blinded as well as the sun. *They know they can't defeat me if they attack. They're waiting. They have forever.*

"Hurry," Boyd said, twirling the dual blades and stepping back.

Rebekah had taken some space to run, bounding down the suspended platform.

Boyd focused on the void. It spoke to him. *Hope... or peace?*

As the clap of her feet drew close, flecks of red appeared.

She ran past him, jumped.

Shrieks sounded, and a few moments after he launched his daggers through the screaming mouths of two Zealots. Boyd caught the weapons as they returned and looked up to see Rebekah hanging off the other side of the bridge.

She lifted herself and made it a few paces from the gap before a second Zealot attacked. She dodged at the last moment, claws snatching nothing but freezing air.

The sound of Isaac's feet pounded down the bridge's length. At his leap, Boyd put his dagger through another one of the creatures— just one. Isaac made it across, and more swarmed the other side of the bridge.

They learn fast. Boyd backed away from the gap, struggling for his next breath, his lungs pleading for rest. One of his daggers almost slipped from his loosening grip. He wasn't himself here, deranged and incapable.

There's no point. Boyd couldn't stop himself from thinking it even as he stared across the gap. He didn't know how long he truly felt this way, but he kept returning to look into the darkness, seeing not hungry red eyes, but a part of himself that he had lost—the part that would have made him go out and challenge the Lord instead of cowering behind a crate.

The distance between the two bridges seemed much further now that it was his turn to jump. Nobody would defend him from the screeching souls. The muscles in his body began to tense, lock.

Boyd twirled his daggers in hand, running before his body wouldn't let him move at all. As his foot left the stone, he looked down to see countless pairs of red eyes, slender hands with long talon-like claws groping out to snatch him.

He threw his daggers to the other side of the bridge and watched them bury into two Zealots overcoming Isaac and Rebekah.

Boyd's trajectory changed at that instant, and he was yanked down by sharpened clamps on his ankles. His hand scraped the opposite bridge, and in seconds he was overcome by an unbearable cold.

The Lord's followers pulled him down even faster than he would fall, skin slowly hardening, crystallizing with flakes of ice the further he fell.

All the while, Boyd felt awake but distant. For some reason he couldn't quite put words to, it was good to finally be done.

CHAPTER 27

SECOND ERA, 113, UAIR FIVE OF RISING SILVER

Rebekah

Rebekah ran breathlessly through the dark tunnel tugging the weight of Isaac's fatigued, bleeding body. He helped out every few steps. Screeching calls behind them were the only thing that jolted her forward. *How much blood can someone lose and still remain alive?* It had to be less than what poured from the gashes on Isaac's leg.

She'd seen the yellow-cloaked menace slash him, unaware of how hard the blow connected or the sharpness of the claws. He'd been defending her against the creatures, with Boyd.

She'd hardly spent long with Isaac's best friend, and liked him even less, but the sight of him falling into the darkness made it harder to go on. She tried to bury that memory under the necessity of the moment. Wheezing, Rebekah struggled enough in the thick, dry air. She remembered something pastor Mary had taught her.

In the fog of war, there is little time for emotions.

Keep pushing.

A faint purple glow occupied the underground corridors, carrying the screeches and spine-tingling clicks out from the void of anti-light; again, Boyd's red eyes flashed in her mind. But the purple glow seemed to stretch past the tunnel into the night. They'd reached the puddle at the broken grate where once a river flowed, and Isaac collapsed. When she turned, she found him crouched like a child against the wall—like Priska—head buried into his arms, body heaving in sobs.

"We failed," he said, speech muffled by his cloak. "The Chrysos is dead. *Boyd* is dead."

She knew he thought it was only a matter of time for them as well. Without blessings, she heard no more from the foreboding tunnel than the clicks turning to screeches, unsure if the creatures had grown any closer. But they couldn't stay here—the longer they stayed, the shorter their lives.

Do I have to leave him behind, too? She would do everything she could not to, but a strong sense told her to get away from this cursed cathedral as quickly as possible.

She kneeled next to him, keeping an eye on the void. It wouldn't make it any better if she panicked. "It may seem bleak, but as long as we're still alive, there is hope. You saw Helios, he escaped. Maybe he can stop the Lord." Screeches sounded from the tunnel, and she jumped. "We can't stay here."

"Helios didn't try to save us. The dragon just watched while its own kind was murdered. We all did. Why would he save us now?" When Isaac looked up his eyes seemed darker. She thought she'd glimpsed red.

"What happened up there, when Helios woke you?"

"I was asleep. I felt the last of my energy leave me…. I-I thought I was dead. I don't know why he woke me up, just to watch everything die again." Isaac licked dry blood from his lips. "It watched the Chrysos get murdered. There's no way Helios is on our side."

"No," she said. "Helios saved us. You were still waking, but he stopped the servant Haskil from attacking us in the hall. The servant is part dragon, too. One of the Lord's creations, like the other followers. Helios probably still battles him. Come on, we have to leave, before those... *things* get here."

"*Pfft...*"

The screams sounded louder. "Isaac, we have to go. Come on. Please." She tried to grab his arm, but he tore it away.

I have to leave him behind.

"Helios saved us, but what about Boyd? The dragon liked us better for some reason. That's how it always was, even with the Dyra. We were too blind to see it, but that's what he was trying to tell us. Boyd never got a chance. The Dyra didn't care that he didn't take the vow. They wanted him to die. He was the only one brave enough to try and escape the church. If I would've listened, we would be long gone by now, probably on a ship to another island. He would still be alive."

She knew what he meant—if they hadn't tried to save her, they'd be long gone. If Isaac got the chance, he'd probably trade her back for Boyd. She looked into the dark tunnel, sure that Isaac would rot there. Still, a part of her had to give him one more chance. "Get up. This isn't you. What about all those things you said about hope? About saving the Dyra?"

Isaac had been the one to open her eyes to the Lord's malevolence. Unable to help him, she'd never felt such pain, magnified and distorted into something like anger.

But it had first been pain.

All at once, at the shriek of a Zealot, her anger flipped and took hold. The truth was, she had no choice other than to stand and back away. She wouldn't let her battle end here, because Isaac gave into his sorrow. Curled up and vulnerable, he looked rather different than that person she knew who'd changed her mind in the church halls.

"Don't blame yourself," she said, fighting back as her tears welled. *He almost made it.* "Boyd didn't want to forfeit his curses. It was his own choice. The Dyra only allowed him the freedom to make his decision."

"You didn't know him like I did. Boyd never wanted to follow the Lord. If the Spirit my father described was fair, he never should've been cursed in the first place. His intention was always to save the dragons, not fall dead because of the Lord's power."

A lesson came to mind, one she'd been taught by the Lord himself. "The Spirit isn't fair."

She had backed out of the closed tunnel, finding herself oppressed by a blackened sky. The anti-matter of the void seemed to have stretched and swallowed the stars. "That wasn't your friend, not the one you knew. The infernal forces were too strong inside of him. He had nothing to keep them at bay."

She was beginning to see the very same forces gaining strength inside of Isaac now.

"Do you remember when he saved us?" she asked. "The higher forces are stronger. The forces of your father."

Isaac looked at her as he fell onto his side, reaching, and she caught a glimmer of hope.

Or was it the distance?

"Isaac," she called back to him with all the sincerity she felt. "We have to go."

He planted a hand on the ground, and stood in a slow process.

She couldn't help but let the tears flow, giving into her emotion despite the words of pastor Mary.

His cloak hung by threads where the gash on his calf stood pronounced. "You're right." He shook his head, glancing back at the cave. "We have to go."

A weight lifted off her shoulders, and hope seemed easier to find. *Holy forces are stronger.* She hadn't been sure when she said it, only wanting to get him moving again, to push on. But now the truth was evident, yet a part of her still struggled to believe they had a chance at defeating the Lord. How could they lessen the power of a Chrysos?

A cloud of doubt hung around that she couldn't shake. She blamed it on her surroundings.

Isaac had managed to stumble toward her. "Dyra said the intention upon one's death affects where the Spirit guides your soul. Boyd sacrificed his life for us. If what the Dyra said was true, his soul would have ascended, right? To one of the higher realms? What's more noble than giving your life for others?

"We have to go to the Elder," he said as they entered on the dead forest's main path. "Oswaldo and Legola. There's a chance the Lord hasn't reached them yet. Maybe they can help us."

Rebekah recalled her vow never to lose hope, having difficulty cultivating the corresponding feeling. "The Dyra don't fight, remember?"

"But they know more about the realms," Isaac said. "We might earn some ability to fight, like Boyd. Who knows what they can do."

Rebekah didn't think that was how it worked given everything they said about life paths and trajectories, but there seemed to be no other option. The Dyra appeared weak on their last visit, and if she remembered right, only the three that Isaac mentioned had survived the removal of the Lord's curses.

The air of the forest swarmed with depressing cosmic light that had replaced the very stars in the sky. *Where all is one, and one is nothing.* Rebekah used to sing the Lord's verse amongst others before she went to sleep, reminding her of the infinite peace she would feel upon giving her soul completely to the Lord and Spirit.

She stepped over a fallen trunk where termites feasted in hordes. *I suppose there is still some life here.* But it was so unlike the beautiful, holy realm of the Dyra's past.

First, she heard the high-pitched chimes, soft and infrequent—a musician preparing to play. The high tone didn't have the same brightness as she remembered, sounding broken, irregular, and defeated. Pursuing the sound around blackened trees, they walked into a familiar open clearing.

A once great tree lay dead across the length, divided by a break in the center. Wide, hollow segments of the tree lay exposed. Twice the size of the others, the tree lost life and strength in front of Rebakah's eyes.

The Elder Dyra lay on its back next to the break. One of its wings twitched, the ethereal blue form struggling to free itself of the bark's light weight. The Dyra's hums became stuttering pleas, and the aura in its gut held the colors black and gray. Isaac ran up to the wispy body, lifted the tree, and Rebekah carefully pulled the creature out from underneath. She almost expected her hands would go right through the body, but it's ankle felt soft, wrinkled and cold.

"Elder," Isaac said. "What's happened to you? Has the Lord come this way?"

The creature rolled to its side, off its broken wing. The frail Dyra managed a smile. Its golden headdress lay a few feet away. It reached in the direction weakly. Rebekah helped by handing the crown over, and for a moment, the glow in its stomach seemed a little less dark.

"I appreciate your worry and aid, but this is nothing less than inevitable." Its voice was a echoing chime of the beautiful harmony that once elicited shivers and praise. "I don't feel prepared. Another Dyra may have done more in my position. There have been those better than me, I know it. There are many of your human emotions I've never felt, moments I never saw." The Elder sighed with a sad laugh. Once again, its aura mimicked the night. "I suppose every soul feels this way when it comes time to give up its ghost. I may have said the same thing the last time my soul passed, for all I know. We have no more say about our time of death than a drop of water over a current."

"What about hope?" Rebekah asked, her voice quivering. "Isn't there anything we can do to save you?"

"My time of ascension is here, young Rebekah. You can be sure there is no saving. Rather, it seems you must focus on yourselves." The Dyra coughed, a clanging series of bells. "Your dynasty is one short."

Rebekah wanted to talk about Boyd, but she didn't know where to start. That feeling of pure anger arose.

The Elder pulsed red. "Please Rebekah, spare me your sorrow. I have enough of my own as it is. The Lord has succeeded in his sacrifice. By no means are we Dyra fortune tellers, but we have seen the life paths of many, and know the emotions that lead to certain actions. It was not hard to see your friend's inability to resist the infernal forces."

"But he saved us," Isaac said. "Just before he died. Boyd gave his life so we could escape. Doesn't that have an effect on whether he will ascend, isn't it about a person's choice and intentions?"

"Intentions matter, this is true. As does a promise. Though these things cannot alter the great current of the Spirit. You must give in, before it is too late. This is why the Lord will never win, he will never be more powerful than that which even the dragons serve." The Dyra coughed, a series of clanging bells. "That's what every visit with the Great Spirit is, I think. A humble reminder that we will never compare. No matter what your friend's intentions were, he will stay on the Spirit's intended path, and this is how it always will be."

The Elder's black aura deepened. "Even I have dedicated my life to ensure my path is holy, only to realize that I am helpless before the Spirit's fate. It is only right that I have not lived enough. It is the ultimate truth of the Spirit. There will never be enough time for living. We must embrace all we have now, all that we feel, before we flow downstream."

It hurt to see the wise creature so vulnerable. Rebekah had trusted the Dyra, gave up her blessings for the creature, assumed its invincibility as much as she had the Lord's. Who was supposed to guide them now?

She choked up at the sight of someone she respected so terrified of what lay ahead—the great current. *Would the Lord feel this fear before death?*

No matter. She wanted to force it upon him, even if it was her last action.

Blue light within the creature's body dulled, blending with the darkened trees and grass.

You can't go. Not yet. "What if we aren't sure what the Spirit wants, Elder? What if we get lost along the way?"

"The path," the Elder entered a coughing fit, lighter clanging bells. "I'm afraid no one can be sure of their path. Though I found certain feelings guide a soul to more holy outcomes than others. Hope, love. Those are two." The Elder took another clangy breath Rebekah feared might be the last. "Those feelings that have gone stale at the rise of the second-era. But it is amazing... amazing how the Spirit always finds a way. This morning, I was doubtful... meanwhile, everything fell into place."

"But the Chrysos is sacrificed," Isaac said. "The Lord is all-powerful."

A light chime, a laugh. "Not against the current. The Spirit will balance all, eventually."

The lower stubbish feet of the Dyra had evaporated, surrendering to the void's nothingness, so it seemed.

"I fear..."

A long breath....

"I fear my time has arrived." The Dyra laid its head back and exhaled. The darker blue outline of the winged body began to fade, withering with a slow play of bells, then the lighter inside portion of its torso and legs. Its inner black aura turned to wisps, and faded into the night. The Elder was gone. Left on the ground was the headdress, embossed with a golden necklace and gem. Rebekah hid her tears within her hood, bending to grab the necklace as something to remember the Elder by, so cold to the touch.

Alone once more, the domed, endless void encapsulated them.

Isaac wouldn't look at her. "I've had enough of the infernal forces."

She turned the necklace in her hand, put it on. A bright white line, a beam of wisps, flowed slowly out from her stomach to Isaac's. She gasped, about to take the necklace off for fear something would happen, but Isaac hadn't seemed to notice the beam suspended in mid-air.

He looked at her, curious. "Is everything alright?"

"Just... sad," she said. When he turned away, speaking more about the Dyra, she reached out to touch the flowing line.

It felt band-like.

Over a short moment, white wisps of the beam took on the color orange, and as it occured, a flow of the desire for things to be different steadily enveloped her, more than she could handle. It lingered moments after pulling her hand away.

She removed the necklace, tucked it into her cloak, and the subtle beam disappeared.

"...that's why I say we go back to the church and try to steal a ship." He turned to her. "What do you think?"

She couldn't help but stare, wanting nothing more than to rid him of the crippling pain the band exposed her to, thinking: *Is that how he always feels?*

"We don't know how to sail," she said. "Where would we go? The nearest island is Windhaven, weeks away."

Isaac nodded, walking around the fallen tree. On the ground lay pieces of the Dyra's stone statues and odd kitchenware. "The Lord will find us if we stay here. We must be the only rogues left in Indus. It would be just as hard to survive on Daemonus than out at sea."

"We could hide in one of the caves."

"He'll find us there," Isaac said. "On other islands we won't be safe, either. We have to figure out how to reach the holy realms."

Neither of them would be able to survive a fight against the Lord or his pastors.

"I'll figure out how to work the sails," he said. "I'll do whatever it takes for us to escape in the meantime."

A strong clap of thunder sounded, and the two twisted to see streaks of lightning course through the dark purple sky.

Helios, a sleek amber arrow, grown and deadly, twisted through the air. A gash of silvery-blue light opened like a tear in the sky, and the dragon entered into it. Not long after, the servant Haskil followed him with half of the same stealth and precision, and their cries echoed as the tear in the sky patched up like stitching.

"He still fights," Isaac said.

"But where?" Rebekah stared in disbelief.

"I don't think we're in the same realm as we used to be. There is no moon here."

"So... We're in the infernal realm?"

"Or the infernal realm is here," he said. "With us. The gap in reality Helios entered might be a way to escape."

"We'll find a way to enter, when he returns."

They agreed that had been their sign to move on. The central path through the forest led back toward the church. In the middle realm Rebekah had always known, Tempus occupied a small portion of Daemonus, which wasn't very large in itself. In the realm of the Dyra, they trekked for what seemed like hours through beautiful springs. Here in the Lord's realm, they had already arrived at the entrance to St. Daemonus, tall and sheltered with dragon scales. The drawbridge hugged tight to the desolate guard towers. As they snuck through the bushes onto the white-sand, tinted a darker hue, she felt their hope lessen. "No ships."

"Where is everyone?"

A risk came to mind. "Well, there is a second harbor."

Isaac glanced toward the church's main entrance. "The last place I want to be is inside that church. We have to think about where the Lord might be."

"We don't have time to think," she said. Nevertheless, she agreed —running blatantly into the church would just get them caught. *If only the Elder had told us where to go.* The waves crashed melodically onto what used to be a gem-filled shore.

"What about around back?" she asked. "We'll jump over the wall on the south wing, where nobody goes. We can sneak through the secret halls I showed you before."

"We have to be silent."

"As silent as the cursed ones." It would be near impossible with their lack of blessings. *Curses. They are curses.*

They snuck back to where Tempus met the watchtowers. Voices carried over the humid wind, singing in rapture. She recognized the hymn as they neared the back wall, verse twenty-four of a chapter written by the second-era apostle, Lewis of Vitria—composed the day the Lord overcame the first-era, written from aboard the deck of a ship as the apostle watched dragons falling from the sky, colorful wisps evaporating, bleating cries of those who were supposedly oppressing them by keeping their natural power for themselves.

They turned the corner and saw groups of white-cloaks, arms raised to the void above them. Pastors and students sang in unison. Amongst them also sang a group of older individuals robed in cloaks of wooly black sheepskin. They sang in unison, harmonic layers no match for the Dyra, and far too joyous for the moment.

Father of the night,
We hail to you.
We see your light.
What is great,
May never fall.
One secret kept,
But never saw.
To be in light,
One will always fall.

She used to sing the hymn with Priska when they couldn't fall asleep. To see it from the outside and know the truth of what happened that day, it was none of the pastor's faults for believing the Lord's lies. They worshipped all they ever knew.

"They look crazed," Isaac said. The worshippers cried and laughed at once, hugging each other, shouting praise to the sky. "We might be able to sneak by without them noticing."

Rebekah squinted at a burly black cloak pacing near the edge of the wall, separated from the others. "Wait, is that pastor Nim?"

Isaac took a few steps forward. "I think so. Why?"

"Everyone says the library pastor inherited the position. That means he hasn't sacrificed a dragon. He's not like the others who took a vow to follow the Lord. We might be able to convince him to help us escape."

"Jericho already committed the sacrifice. The infernal forces are stronger than before."

"No, I know him. Pastor Nim was a good person, driven by holy forces." The makeshift necklace he made her held a certain power against infernal forces as well. It freed her from the Zealot's watch down at the harbor below. "He's part of the reason why you were able to convince me. Perhaps he can show us a quicker route to the harbor."

Isaac stayed quiet for much too long. "I'll defend you in case Jericho comes. If he agrees, try to get Nim away from the others. They can't be good influences." Isaac unsheathed his dagger and turned to the forest. It wouldn't do much.

The Lord's followers started a new song as Rebekah neared the wall. She recognized this one as they rounded verse thirty-eight. Further down the wall, pastor Nim paced about, mumbling to himself.

"The worthy do what they must, they do what they must..."

"Pastor," Rebekah whispered. Too quiet at first, she wanted to be cautious of the other pastors's curses. "Pastor Nim."

He turned on a pivot, rabid eyes spotting her over the wall. He squinted. "Rebekah? Is that you?" He hobbled up, following her down the length of the wall as she distanced herself from the main field. "No," he said. "It can't be. You're a rogue. Lord Jericho is looking for you. A-and what's happened to your blessings?"

Where do I start? He remained convinced of the Lord, but she had been too until Isaac gave her the notebook of his father. *My necklace isn't strong enough. The notebook is the key.* She had to get pastor Nim to hold it. *Holy forces are stronger.*

"Pastor, please believe me when I tell you things aren't the way they seem. Lord Jericho cannot be trusted."

"Wh..." He stepped back with a strange look, glanced toward the pastors. "What are you saying? You don't sound like the Rebekah I used to know."

"I'm not the same," she said. "You shouldn't be, either. It isn't blessings the Lord bestows to his followers, but curses. He wants to tip the balance of the Great Spirit, to stop the progression of humanity and keep all power for himself."

Nim chewed his nails. The lightning throughout the sky connected in endless tendrils every now and again, and every time the thunder bellowed, he flinched. "I d-did see the dragons," he said. "*Full-grown.* They were fighting in the air. Other pastors have been acting strange, too.

"Rebekah, I don't want to die today. It's hard not to believe them, though, when they say it is reckoning. Dragons tear through the sky like *demons.* Who but the Lord could protect us?"

"The Lord has committed an awful sin," Rebekah said. "He's changed the dynamics of the church forever. Please," she said, trying to sway him with the same hope she had for Isaac. "Just step over the wall."

Nim shook his head vigorously. "Never. I could never leave. It's too dangerous."

"The danger is inside those walls, pastor." Rebekah walked to the gray trees to show it was safe. She returned holding the necklace he'd crafted in her hand. "I'm still the girl you knew."

Nim looked between her and the group. A bolt of lightning shocked him into a scattered panic and suddenly, he was climbing over the wall. He fell over at a second crack of thunder onto thick grass. The library pastor winced at every flash as they made their way into the forest, the lightning more frequent and full.

Isaac turned around as they approached him—quick, with his dagger in hand.

"The dragon-lover?" Nim planted his feet in the ground, slipping from her grasp. He backed behind a tree. "You let him get to you? Oh no. Rebekah, I need to go back. I shouldn't be out here."

She ignored the pastor's claims. "The notebook," she said to Isaac. "It will convince him." But when she turned back with the notebook in hand, Nim had run off.

She sprinted to find him and heard Isaac following. The confused pastor screamed for help up ahead, where the main path would lead to the field in front of the southern wall. She reached the forest edge and saw Nim marching through the open grass toward the pastors.

She felt naked leaving the forest's cover. The grass held her legs back as she ran. Lightning illuminated the dark void and the field became the main stage as the worshippers turned and pointed at her.

I'm going to save him. "Nim!" she called.

To her surprise, the library pastor stopped running, and turned.

When they neared him, each panting breath sending daggers through her ribs, the library pastor's face appeared filled with confusion and awe.

"Take this." She held out the notebook, but he shied away. "Pastor, please. You've come this far. Have faith in me."

"I..." The pastor seemed at a loss for words.

He backed away as she took another step closer.

The worshippers near the wall fell quiet. The world seemed to focus on them as she waited for Nim to either take the notebook or run.

He did nothing but stare with wide, red eyes, his gaze drifting up, over her shoulder.

Something's wrong.

Rebekah turned, reaching for her dagger, and her hand drew further back against her will. Her other arm shot back as well, wrists locking behind her and she collapsed to her stomach as a glowing blue bands locked her knees together, searing into her cloak. Itching turned to freezing burns and she couldn't help but scream.

She had landed facing Isaac, who struggled to work up and escape his own restraints.

In the distance, an outlined form emerged from Tempus's main path, larger than the group of pastors, though the form seemed collectively one.

Two red points of light appeared within the shadow.

Worshippers at the wall erupted in praise.

"You're rogues," Nim cried behind her.

Rebekah's tugs on the bands proved useless.

"I did what I had to do," Nim said. "I'm so sorry, Rebekah. So.. s-sorry..."

CHAPTER 28

SECOND ERA, 113, HIGH SILVER

Jericho

L ook at how they worship me. The swine. An effortless jaunt had carried the Lord through the forest, where no life existed in this year or any years past. Not anymore. Filled with thoughts of glory and pride, he hardly recalled the time spent walking, nor the effort of turning thousands of the holy realm's souls to his own.

In many ways, I am their God. But more so, a martyr. His soul, and the hundreds of thousands he captured, would never escape that to which all returns.

He thought back to the days when he'd been a pastor in the first-era church, so weak and obligated to take orders. That's what the church used to create, sheep.

They love me because of the power I've come to know, the power I came to be, and spread to them so graciously. That *is peace.*

Everyone must bow to something greater than them.

That is me.

Nobody else could fill the burden that was Jericho's role, bringing the Spirit of the dragons to humanity. If the rogues understood the amount of time and effort this operation took, perhaps they'd have even a little sympathy for his position.

The Lord emerged from the shadows of the forest basking in cheers of praise, holding the rogues captive from a distance. It cost no more than a sliver of effort to manipulate a portion of this middle realm, infuse it with his wealth of Spirit, and bind the disobedient beings in chains. *Their souls will be mine, the last of their rebelling culture, but first, I will have the luxury of crushing the boy's final defense.*

Jericho reached for the limitless reserves of Spirit inside him, and transferred a drop from the vast ocean to the worshippers at the wall. Their cheers and shouts lessened in the night, and their power matured.

I would like to see Abraham's face now. The boy's father would've appreciated this display of draconic Spirit used so effortlessly by the Lord, after a mixture of fear and disgust, of course.

Jericho couldn't blame the last confused believers. They didn't understand. They were asleep, yet moving throughout the world, acting according to ways outdated, taken by the ideas of ancestors who were passed down the same uninformed beliefs. Jericho had shown truth to the last of them himself; first the father, now the boy —the incompetent mother was no worry, her soul filling with infernal forces on its own.

Jericho grew eager, unable to stop himself from tightening the grip of the bands around the two rogues. To his enjoyment, they screamed their first pleas for mercy.

Where are the notebook's holy forces to help you now?

Before he knew it, Jericho had walked halfway across the clearing. The souls trembled; one soon would be revealed to him for the first time, the other devout since her very first day, trying to escape his clutches at the influence of another. *It is amazing how contagious the holy forces can be.* He remembered his father calling them viruses of the mind.

I knew the sacrifice of the Chrysos would suffice, he thought. *Deep down, I knew everything would go my way if I focused on my most important tasks, to the dismay of all else. This is the way of the Spirit. You knew too,* he thought, directing his attention toward that dark, secluded presence in his mind. *Didn't you?*

Yes, he let the ancient dragon speak, deflecting feelings of sad sincerity. *I knew this would occur.*

The Lord found it funny how puny Tiamat's power seemed now, recoiling at the burning power of the Chrysos fused intricately with the Lord's soul, so strong he had to store a portion in the Daemonus sword for it to cool. The magnificent creature knew its fate, having surrendered its neck to the Lord.

The forces Abraham bestowed upon the notebook were bound together in such a twisted, roundabout way that Jericho could never penetrate its complexity. Now, a slight tug at the pages in the poor boy's cloak loosened its shield like a beginner's knot.

Patience, he told himself, feeling giddy as the power exposed what was left of the notebook's imbued spirit for the taking. The Lord wanted to convert it all and tear the boy's soul to pieces just then, destroying that fake conception of the world and any presence of the holy forces in the middle realm for good.

And there he is. Tied up and helpless with his little girlfriend on the ground next to him. The girl—her meaningless, defiant expression almost caused Jericho to laugh. *Such passion would have taken her places and still may, once she is cleansed.*

In truth, the rogues had helped him. The Lord would take their thoughts and experiences one-by-one, dissecting them so he knows what he must do to never have such insubordination again, even in the most defiant of life paths. Once there was nothing left but their outer ghost, then he would rebuild them in his image and set them on an infernal path.

It felt as if he inhabited only his skin, floating slightly above as a supernatural being that commanded his body like it was nothing more than a container of endless Spirit. He hadn't needed the help from his ancestors to keep the Chrysos tamed, as he thought he might. It was as if the dragon knew it had lost. Jericho's body burned a thousand degrees and with his eyes he knew he could emboss the moon.

If only the rebellious filth could comprehend such a feat as he accomplished, if they knew the years of work that culminated to make this moment, perhaps Isaac would appreciate the symbolic nature of his death; or perhaps, he was simply too dull.

Jericho focused on the dimwitted pastor who did the service of leading the rogues out into the field where everyone could see. He had been quite easy to manipulate given his lack of blessings.

"You did well." His breath had the temperature of hot coals. As Jericho reached into the soul of the library pastor, he removed the accumulated, instinctive fear inside of the man and added a touch of draconic spirit, enough to allow for a purer form of manipulation. At the act, the pastor Nim of Vitria went stiff, the fat on his body and cheeks thinned and white melted from the roots of his hair to the tips.

"Nim, come back," the rogue girl cried.

"Could I have silence?" Jericho seared her hands and wrists with fire from the secure bands.

She screamed.

"You must not have heard me." He increased the intensity and the worshippers went quite as his voice boomed through the Great Spirit's presence in this land, to the sea. It seemed the more accustomed he became to the Chrysos' power, the stronger it flowed. Any action's effort was significantly lessened.

He returned the chains to their original heat and nodded. "Good. It seems you're once again capable of obeying. A shame we had to visit such extremes." The girl's soul still wasn't defeated, he could tell by the defiant way she rose back up to her knees after his punishment. Maybe she was enamored with the boy after all.

He muted his speech from the worshippers, not wanting them to hear his more forgiving side. Father told him followers must never see weakness in their leader. "I know you have the capability to be great, this you showed to me." Jericho remembered to try and sound forgiving. "I could use two souls as intelligent as yours. That is why I brought you to this church, despite your sinful ways. You show potential, but waste it worshipping hundreds of other souls who hide power from you, when you could have that power and only bow to only one. Me, a kind Lord." Jericho allowed this one offer, giving them a final chance and figuring the soul who refused to take it rightly deserved a painful route of disintegration. "What do you say?"

Silence...

Their souls were on the brink of turning, but they had to be pushed. To his surprise, he had to call forth more of the infernal Spirit, flooding their minds like rushing water toward a breaking dam.

"Your friend, Boyd, has joined me," he said. "As we speak, he progresses through the infernal realms. A gifted one, he is. Inclined toward the natural way."

"Boyd would never bow to you!"

Jericho reared back and kicked the dragon-lover in his jaw, unable to restrain himself given the years of sheer insubordination. Blood spattered across the grass. It felt good, but even better was the resulting surge of Spirit, a burst of passionate flame almost strong enough to escape his body. "I *will* have silence," he said.

I must destroy the notebook first, the boy's main outlet to the higher realms. Without it, he will be nothing.

"Stand," he said, ridding infernal cuffs locked around the boy's ankles. He laughed as Isaac struggled to his feet. "The dragon-lover of Windhaven, always a fighter. I suppose you learned that from who, the dragons?"

The boy stepped forward as if to attack and Jericho seized control of his muscles at the last moment, locking Isaac in a striking position, the fear just forming on his expression.

Jericho circled the boy, who followed only with his gaze. "A painful feeling, it is to be trapped." He removed the notebook from the boy's beaten white cloak.

Isaac may have cried, it was hard to notice.

When Jericho held the leather a sudden rush of ice filled his fingers and he had to direct Spirit into his trembling hands as they turned, gray, black, orange and then red. In an instant, the notebook picked up in flames, burning as if doused with some flammable oil.

Jericho couldn't stop the grin from reaching his face as it piled into ashes in the grass. *I've done it.* Now he heard the boy's cries, feeding into the notebook's beautiful transition from a weakened force to strength commanded by the Lord.

"You thought you could end me?" he asked the boy, reaching for the longsword strapped tight across his back.

If they didn't convert, it may be worth slaying the rogues now, before everyone, capturing their power as it left their ghosts and personally ensuring they entered the infernal realms below and remained there for eternity.

The worshippers sang in praise once again, psalms of his creation. Some called out, "Kill him! End the rogue!"

The Lord raised the Sword of Daemonus for a second time, overcome by a surge of power hotter than any flame. He felt giddy, wanting to laugh.

The moment was too great.

He could not reel the power of the Chrysos back.

He felt himself shrinking away from his body as the Spirit he accumulated flowed uncontrollably from his mouth, eyes, his pores.

A bystander, outside of his skin, Jericho watched as he dropped the sword and lost control. The reserves of the Chrysos flowed out past his will and that of his ancestors.

Hope will never end, a voice said; light and wise, as if whispered behind him.

The light poured brighter from his eyes, drowning him in a sea of shining white and he watched the power swirl as wisps through the air, toward the boy.

Cold, a witness, Jericho swam in what he realized was a seemingly endless dark ocean. *Ancestors, save me,* he thought.

BLUE STREAKS CONNECTED through clouds in the dark, starless sky. The grip on Isaac's wrists and ankles loosened and he fell forward, drained of all strength. *Free,* he thought, trying to get up and run, but his muscles were too weak.

Jericho had dropped the sword, it wasn't more than a few feet away. The Lord seemed to be fighting himself as his head cocked and shook, focusing on Isaac. A bright, golden glow of wisps swam and grew from the Lord's eyes like a plant, curling through the air over to Isaac.

When they reached him, a gripping suction pulled Isaac forth. The wisps entered in a breath and he choked, swallowing the light, and it became everything as his body fell away.

Within seconds the world changed from the dark and stormy landscape to a realm of snowy white, and Isaac's arms—*wings*—extended great and large, carrying him up through the cutting wind of a blizzard. A guttural shriek escaped through his gaping mouth—a roar loud enough to collapse the Daemonus church—and Isaac found himself an onlooker in a dragon's body once again.

A second flap led him up through cool clouds, breaking into a smoother air. To his left was the peak of the Breath of the World, except it was more like a flattened plain than anything. An oasis of lakes stretched well past Isaac's view as if not supported by the mountain at all. Wings carried him over a palace shining with a calm silver and golden sheen. The mist of the waters provided a blanket of comfort over the land. The air almost seemed to carry him further with each flap, the undercurrent sweeping and swaying in his intended direction. Dragons walked amidst the castle's opening and the other massive structures built in a distinctive, staggered pattern atop the amidst fresh grass, snow, and blue and yellow flowers blooming next to bubbling springs. A gray path extended straight through the mountain, past it all, rising even higher to lead into a rocky range.

Isaac flew over spiked rocks marking a drop off. If the dragons resided here, that meant this was the highest holy realm, according to his father's notebook. But Isaac didn't understand what brought him here. A horrible thought struck him that he wanted to immediately cast away.

Isaac feared he was dead.

Stones stood in stacked formations on the outskirts of a flat ledge, extending out from the mountain, still high above the clouds. Without wings Isaac would've fallen to his demise, but the draconic form he inhabited lowered with grace. Dragons of all kinds stood next to the erected stones; Isaac soared over Wyverns, Drakes, and Wyrms. His form reached the ground and claws sunk into the soil to stabilize him.

His head suddenly filled with dozens of scattered whispers heard from every direction. One of the lower voices continued to grow in volume, and soon Isaac located the source directly in front of him.

The head of Isaac's dragon raised.

Three great dragons stood amidst the circle, their chest plates proudly held forth in a boastful posture. It made sense how a pastor could be terrified and label the creatures as dangerous. The crevices in their armor showed the colors of their true scales. Nothing seemed casual about the demeanor of the diamond-scaled Chrysos, edging apart from the others. This was the voice Isaac heard loudest despite the fact its mouth didn't move. The pressurized, deepened voice had completely cleared the others from his mind.

Do you have the boy? It asked.

Isaac's head nodded.

From the left, two dragons carried out a slab sparkling like fresh snow, balanced between them with a string clenched by their jaws. On top of the slab lay an unconscious boy, no older than five solar cycles, and as the slab lowered onto the ground, Isaac recognized himself.

The father, the voice ordered.

This time there were no dragons. Isaac watched as his father Abraham walked out from underneath one of the stone formations. Head down, he looked like an ant next to the creatures.

He lied to me, Isaac thought. *What the Dyra said was true. He had gone to the peak all along.*

Great sacrifices are required for great blessings, the foreign voice whispered. The diamond-scaled Chrysos was not the largest of the creatures, but it had the undivided attention of the rest.

Today, we have before us, a human balanced in the Spirit. He vows to demonstrate the meaning of our higher realms, so he may walk the way of the seventh sooner than the rest, and aid in our fight against the infernal realms.

A Wyrm slithered up on its green belly, a longsword held in its mouth, dropping the weapon before his father.

A sword?

His father bent to pick up the steel.

Isaac wanted to shout for him to stop, ask what he could possibly be doing. But he was no more than a bystander in this body.

He watched his father approach the slab.

A flash of lightning erupted; the storm picking up in the clouds.

This can't be the higher realms, Isaac thought. *The dragons would never ask for this.*

Demonstrate your vow, Abraham of Windhaven, the draconic voice said.

"He was your gift to me," his father screamed.

The dragons had nothing to say in return. They didn't move.

Father isn't any better than Jericho.

But... I'm alive, Isaac thought suddenly. *He couldn't have done it if I'm still alive.*

His father raised up the sword.

Abraham screamed, and the sword fell.

But before it could strike, thunder boomed, and a more detailed, loud, and beautiful streak of lightning than any Isaac had ever seen reached down from the sky, striking his young body on the slab.

The bolt remained in one place, a strange wave of pumping electricity, striking with a whopping jolt that seemed to shake the whole mountain.

Abraham fell in despair, the sword dropping to the ground, as it had with Jericho.

It worked, one of the whispering voices said, and the other voices joined in fascination as the blue streak of lightning pulsated, flowing into Isaac's seizing body.

His father screamed next to the neverending strike.

You've demonstrated your loyalty, the voice said. *The Spirit has blessed him instead.*

The draconic form Isaac currently inhabited spread out its wings, stretching, and flapped. Isaac was drawn up and away from the scene as the lightning continued to flow, growing in intensity. He flew toward the thundering sky as the dragons below spread out, back to the oasis where it had been safe. Isaac caught one last glimpse of his father on his knees before the slab.

He sacrificed me...

Isaac's form speared through the lightning filled sky. Blue streaks circuited around him, connecting with one another while a tearing rage disintegrated the only truth that Isaac held onto over the years.

He betrayed me, gave me up. It doesn't matter if he regretted it. It's too late. Electric shocks took hold of his body, forcing his wings in convulsing patterns.

The Spirit has blessed him, said the thick draconic voice from the diamond-scaled Chrysos below. With the words, Isaac began to fall out of the vision, out from the illuminated darkness, back and back until he was a spectator under a black and blue sky in a void of purple and black; yet the strikes of lightning hadn't faded from around him. The light stung deeper, harsher, and Isaac found his own body seizing in front of the damaged Lord.

An all too real shock spread out to his fingers, down to his toes, and a world of white surrounded him growing brighter and blinding. As his muscles tensed, his neck cranked back, gaze forced to the sky.

What is happening to me?

He let out a wordless scream, tearing at his cloak when he had the chance, trying to rid himself from the pain. The burning heat rose in intensity with each second's pulse, and Isaac was forced to keep staring up, into a white streak.

From where the bolt emerged, a tear opened in the sky, and the more Isaac peered into it, unable to look away, the more he saw the tear widening.

The night sky and its black clouds shrunk back to reveal a clear and starry night.

Then again, the starry sky tore, revealing a realm of green.

Then again, and again, and again. Isaac had the sensation of falling upward through the sky, the terrible burn of light intensifying with every new entry.

I can't take it anymore, he thought, but his body survived.

A heavenly silver glow illuminated after the last tear, where lightning patterned the clouds. A single bolt leapt out from these depths, subsiding through every one of the realms to where Isaac stood.

When the bolt reached his own, the burning connection's power became too much to bear, and Isaac let himself go in the flood of pain.

The next thing he knew, Rebekah tugged at his wrists, and he looked down to see his skin filled with scarred streaks lining every one of his veins.

"We have to go," she said. "Before he wakes."

She's still alive, he thought, comprehending their danger in full.

He tried to stand and collapsed. The ground seemed to pull against him. His body ached everywhere, as if tacked with a thousand needles.

Isaac rolled over and saw Lord Jericho's body a few feet away, dripping a red and purple liquid from the robe that partially covered him.

A shriek sounded from above. Isaac looked up to see Helios moving through the starless purple sky, the draconic form of Haskil following behind. The dragon screeched, and a tear opened within the void to expose a starry land in which Helios entered. The pudgy flying form of Haskil could barely keep up.

"Helios needs help," Rebekah said.

"Let's follow him."

A sadistic, cackling laugh sounded from the Lord.

Jericho stood, slowly, the Sword of Daemonus within reach. His head snapped forward. The red had fully returned. "Good trick," he said. "One I didn't see coming. The Chrysos was smart to use me as a way to transfer its power." The Lord laughed as they ran. "You won't make it far."

The harbor, Isaac thought. He led Rebekah in a run for the wall. The Lord's worshippers jumped the stone border and followed after them.

They veered into Tempus, tripped over dead sticks and fallen branches.

"Here," Rebekah said, darting along the dry river that led to the beach.

"There aren't any ships." Isaac reminded her between breaths. They wouldn't have a second chance if they were caught by the Lord again.

Shrieks called from above as they weaved through the hollowed trees. Their strides grew minuscule as they trudged onto the white-sanded beach. The sea extended to forever.

The battle between Helios and the servant became clear in the sky. It remained longer and longer in this realm, when suddenly

Helios entered a tear that Haskil didn't seem to catch, re-appearing behind the servant and descending upon him. With Haskil clutched between its claws, Helios crunched its jaw around the servant's upper body and tore it in half.

Black wings upon a headless, round body splashed into the ocean.

"Here!" Isaac screamed as he ran. "Helios!"

The dragon swooped toward them. At the sight of the creature, the Lord's followers retreated back into the forest.

Isaac grew worried when Helios didn't slow as he neared the beach. The dragon flew overhead drenching Isaac and Rebekah in a dark shadow, looking familiar in the face and even the shape of its wings, but stronger. Helios screeched, and entered a tear in the world that shimmered in the form of a door, hovering just above the sand.

They ran toward the escape. As Isaac neared, a faint hum picked up that reminded him of the Dyra, and on the other side he saw the world was snowy and white.

Rebekah entered before him, and he stuck a foot into harsh wind just as the Lord stumbled out from the forest; larger, skin pulsing red like coals of a fire.

Jericho tensed and screamed a gutteral shout toward the sky. Wings sprouted from his back. "It's too *strong*," he screamed as the Lord's face elongated. Two red horns sprouted from the top of his head. "I must become it, father. There is no other way." Another resounding scream, and the Lord faced Isaac, his head the shape of a dragon.

The Lord scrambled toward them like a bull, and had almost reached them when Isaac stepped through the shimmering tear, the giving sand replaced with a hard crunch, and suddenly there was dull silence. He spotted Helios, heard the flap of wings in the air as the dragon soared high above a nearby mountain range. Waves with white caps had been replaced by gray mountains capped with white.

"We have to follow him," Isaac said, noticing what he thought may be the Breath of the World. Even if it wasn't, he knew where they had traveled.

This isn't another realm.

A glance behind him confirmed the shimmering gap Helios created had disappeared.

CHAPTER 29

SECOND ERA, 113, UAIR
ONE OF FALLING SILVER

Rebekah

"We're not safe here," Rebekah said. The world of white they entered was so different from her home in the third district of Lothal and Daemonus. Those were the only two places she'd ever been, despite her hopes with Priska to see the world. The Lord never mentioned anything about other realms. She would never forgive Jericho for many things, and that was one. But if this was another realm, was it holy or infernal?

She wanted nothing more than to get away, for the fleeing to end and to be done with this fight, yet they had to push on. It felt as if the war had just begun. "We have to run while we can." The bitter wind bit at her exposed face. *This place has to be infernal.*

Isaac stared out toward the mountains, blending with the terrain in his white cloak, helplessly watching the dragon flying amidst the rocky towers no more than a few hundred paces away.

Rebekah still couldn't believe what happened to poor Isaac, and how he stood here now after being struck by thousands of bolts of lightning. The way the sky opened up, she thought it might have been the heavens that saved them. Whatever happened had changed Isaac, morphed him into a shell of his former self. Scarred tendrils like tiny lightning strikes covered his skin.

She reached out as he swayed too far right, but he managed to catch himself. "Can you walk?" She felt like they were back at the cathedral, when she so desperately urged him from the cave.

His eyes were suspended over dark bags.

She reached out and ran her fingers softly along the deep blue and black scars running up, under his sleeve. She lifted the sleeve to reveal more of the lines over his arm and shoulder.

The lightning.

He pulled away.

The blizzarding weather must sting.

It had been a perfectly timed strike, more than a coincidence. Isaac somehow lived after being burned alive a thousand times over by a bolt that never seemed to end. And it had loosened the Lord's hold, allowing them to escape. If it weren't for Helios, however... it made no sense, but then again what did in a world entirely new? The Lord never taught her about different realms, so of course it was a surprise to see dragons moving between them. The project of saving the dragons seemed easier and impossible at the same time, though they were safe for the time being, and that was all that mattered right now. The Lord had yet to figure out how to navigate the realms as easily as Helios.

Isaac raised his hood. "I received another vision back there."

She was able to get him walking. "Like the first-era? You mean the dragons spoke to you?"

He pointed off to where Helios flew, to the tallest mountain, and she made the adjustment to their path.

"That's what the Spirit was that left the Lord," he said. "I don't know exactly, but I think it the Chrysos was too strong for him, once I looked into his eyes."

"It lived on," she said, amazed. If only she'd seen the notebook, she would have always known how great the dragons were. Never would she have fell for the Lord's cheap tricks. "What did you see in the vision?" The question felt intrusive, and she regretted asking it immediately. "Don't worry, we'll get you safe. Then—"

"I saw the same thing as before," he said, bending near the funny smelling trees on the mountain—like orange and lemon, but the branches had little green spikes as defensive leaves, and the flowers were the color of ice. He picked up a stick, using it to walk. "The vision I had from Helios at the harbor continued. I reached the Great Mountain, saw a bunch of other dragons, and..." He looked at her through the shadows of his hood, then up the stone path. "My father, he... He did something to grant me access to other realms, I think. I heard the dragons say so, a diamond-scaled Chrysos. While the lightning was striking my body, it was like I saw into all the higher realms, to where the dragons stayed on the Great Mountain, and once that happened, I'm back to normal."

She couldn't help but laugh, carried off by the wind. "Yes, normal."

This was no longer the boy she humiliated at training, but the one who almost defeated the Lord and watched his best friend fall into flames. Meanwhile, she'd given everything away she once thought to be true. They did all of this together.

"How could we be normal?" she asked. "We battled with our fists against the most powerful Lord in all the land. We did as the Elder told us, and had hope. We lived on."

Isaac shook his head. Hope would be something he had to work on.

The worn path wrapped around the mountain, the wind whipping it free of snow.

To their left, Helios flew down with a quiet grace, given how massive his amber wings were, bringing the dragon to rest on a flattened ledge. Out of instinct, Rebekah looked away.

Isaac lowered his tone. "I have to do this by myself."

It took everything she had not to tell Isaac to walk closer. The fear had been so conditioned within her.

As Isaac approached the dragon, a yellowish glow radiated off him.

Rebekah reached inside of her cloak for the Elder's amulet.

CHAPTER 30

SECOND ERA, 113, UAIR ONE OF FALLING SILVER

Isaac

I saac had known they were safe when the world returned to
white.

Helios, come. The thought replaced a mantra he'd been
holding in his mind as the sting from his scars solidified in the cold.

Hope, hope, hope.

He hadn't looked into the dragon's eyes after it'd grown. Helios
snorted, sending frozen air across the ground. Wet snow reached his
ankles but he trudged on, the dragon's presence being enough to fill
the air with hope.

He is grown.

Isaac's reflection grew larger in the amber scales and the person
who stared back seemed much older as well. The dragon huffed
guttural clicks that resonated in Isaac's gut, extending its wings,
bronze-colored in the underside. Unlike the dragons of the Great
Mountain, Helios wore no armor, and his chest exposed smooth skin.

Helios, it's me, Isaac thought in his mind, like the dragons had on the peak of the Breath of the World. The amber creature seemed to calm, snout lowering to sniff Isaac's trembling hand as he reached out and touched the outer scales; armored and coarse, they were called *Taliosa* in his father's book. Haskil's blood still showed on a portion of the claws, three jutting out from the wing's tip as well as the talons on its feet.

The dragon snorted, backed away.

He doesn't want me to be close. Maybe it is my thoughts.

Isaac catered to only the purest of his intentions, trying to remember what it felt like in the realm of the Dyra.

The dragon's head lowered.

He inspected the minor cuts on Helios's orange neck; the snout and caved, hazel eyes that brought him so much excitement and made him feel as happy as the days he used to dream. The pain from his scars lessened, soreness and fatigue melting away as Isaac left his body behind once more, trading it for a vision.

Windhaven in the fall was a dying place where trees traded their leaves for snow, but there is a type of beauty in death. Isaac used to love one particular tree because it had leaves when all the others didn't. *Hope.* It stood outside their handbuilt cabin home with red-brown petals, and he watched now as the last leaf wavered but didn't fall when a man in a long lumber coat hurried by. He recognized the man, had just seen him about to drive a sword through his stomach atop the Great Mountain.

His father limped differently, though, and his demeanor was more sad and rushed than happy to be home—as he always remembered it. The white in his beard and frailness of his body seemed well-developed. Isaac didn't remember that.

The door to the cabin opened and the face of his mother smiled out like a beam of sunlight. Streaks of tears pathed their way down her face, layered with ash from the chimney. She ran up to Abraham and jumped in his arms.

"You're home," she said.

"Sarah.... I've made a mistake."

She separated from the hug. "Is he okay?"

Father's head slowly shook. "The rumors are true."

This is after he left me at Daemonus.

She stumbled back onto the bed. "What, about the Lord?...." She sighed as if she didn't believe it. "No, they can't be. No one is powerful enough to overthrow the dragons. There must be eternal balance, or... How could Isaac have been born?"

"He is an exception," father said. "The holy spirit finds a way, but it won't for long. I must return, free my son of the hell I trapped him in."

She stood and wrapped her arms around him. "Take me with you. Don't leave me here again... I can't stand being alone, not with this news. If you care for me, you'd let me save my son as well. Let me help you." Her words were almost indistinguishable through the sobs.

"And watch the only two people I care for die at my hand? I cannot risk your life, Sarah."

Father swallowed and stood straighter. "It was my fault for sending him there. I should've trained him myself. But I have to get him back, my flower. It's not too late, I don't have to sail all the way to the island. They may be able to do something at the mountain."

Her clouded eyes looked up. "Haven't they been defeated already?" A longer silence filled the room with grief, and the scene's corners had started to give way to a terrible blizzard as Isaac fell back... back...

He found himself soaring over Windhaven's mountainous landscape.

Overlooking the island, he descended into the thick of the mountain range. The snow fell hard—Windhaven in mid-winter.

Again, he knew the man walking on the path alone, despite his bundles. The sled he pulled was one Isaac rode on occasions—and on other occasions, one he pulled.

Two other forms were there as well, further down the path,

walking close to the rocky wall, donned in gray-and-white garb nearly invisible in the storm. The Breath of the World loomed high over all. Isaac knew the exact route his father walked, a little further than where he'd been allowed to go, still only the beginning of the path up the mountain.

Like a bird diving for prey, he drew closer to his father at the same time the two black cloaks approached. His father didn't notice. Isaac wanted to scream and warn him but he had no voice here.

When father turned it was too late. He'd been one to fight, and nearly took out his assassins even after fetching his sword from the sled. One of the black-cloaks—which they clearly were—threw a dagger to connect with father's leg. When Abraham collapsed the black cloaks closed in. The scene faded out, up and up as they continued to stab, then bury his father with snow, and Isaac knew exactly where the murder occured; a few feet from where his real body was in the present-day. He even saw the ledge Helios had been perched upon. Just then, the sore, burning sensations of his body returned, and the next moment he averted his gaze from the orange dragon Helios.

The dragon clicked, deep and unsettling. Its wings stretched wide. Flaps knocked Isaac backward as it lifted into the air, flying off over the mountains, headed in the direction of the Breath of the World.

Tears filled Isaac's eyes as he looked around, somehow hoping to find his father's body, to save him. *No, he's gone.* He thought of Boyd, the idea of false hope, and knew that he'd avenge them both.

The emotion was too much for Isaac to take. The snow numbed his scars but he needed something for the pain. *Why would Helios show me such a thing?*

But even as he placed the stick into the ground and lifted himself up, he knew. It wasn't the second vision of his father's death that mattered, but the sight of his mother. He wasn't supposed to go up the mountain and find his father's body. That was probably long gone. But he needed to go down from the mountain, back home.

"I'll follow you anywhere," Rebekah said from somewhere next to him. How she knew the effect saying something like that had was beyond him, but she seemed very capable of understanding him on a level nobody else ever had.

"Part of me will never leave Daemonus," he said on their way down the path.

"Which part of you is here now?"

Isaac turned and looked into her eyes. "Whatever made me strong enough to stick around."

The stars above shined clear and bright. So much took place under that sky. Isaac questioned what happened to Boyd on that far off island. He wondered if Helios would ever return. He'd never felt so connected with a creature, and now it was gone, just like his friend.

As they walked on, Rebekah pointed out the fading of his scars. Once he looked at his hand, regular and filled with life again, he lifted the sleeve of his cloak so she could see where else the scars lie.

"Your entire back and arms," she said. "But as I speak, it fades. Gone, gone, and... wait. It stopped."

"What do you mean?"

"The scar stops at your neck, and spreads down to your shoulders. Like the roots of a tree or something."

He put his cloak back on. They walked in a brisk silence, only disturbed by the subtle chime from Rebekah walking with the amulet of the Dyra. He thought to ask her why she put it on, but didn't, assuming everyone mourned differently.

"The Lord has overtaken Daemonus," he said. "But his sacrifice didn't stretch all the way out here. Windhaven looks just like I remember it." What feared Isaac most was what the Lord became before the door back to St. Daemonus shut behind them, and how he vowed to find and end them. He'd seen the power of what a promise could become.

"Where is it we're going?" Rebekah asked. "We've been walking for quite a while. Are you sure we're safe here?"

"I'm sure. We're headed home," he said, knowing by the long, open road it wasn't long before he could point it out to her.

The cabin hadn't changed much since he last saw it in the vision. The same logs held up the structure, and but a few of the auburn leaves had fallen.

He keep himself from rapping on the door.

A look at Rebekah proved she understood, her eyes wide and hopeful.

Footsteps approached, the sound of creaking wood.

The door cracked open to show a woman with light red hair, and at the roots, hints of what had once been a darker shade. Her face contorted as it studied btween them, not comprehending the sight before her, and Isaac could see the years of worry and loneliness in her shock. She wore fur robes of an intricate weaving, though the color had left them long ago. Isaac had been there when she made them herself.

His heart broke for her.

After a gasp, she had caught her breath, extending her arms out for a hug.

CHAPTER 31
SHEYOL PURGATORIO, THE INFERNAL REALM

Boyd

Compelled to stand, Boyd tried to lift himself up, though he had not the strength.

Frigid, he thought, remembering the eternal descent into darkness.

But it wasn't cold now, the sound of molten rocks and bursting flames made sense as Boyd managed to lift his head. He'd given in, and was a product of the Lord.

Red.

Lava burst in cresting waves; a sea of fire falling onto nearby rock, crashing onto bodies that lay along the shore and dragging in their torched corpses. If he hadn't woken up fast enough, the tide would've soon reached him.

Up, something inside of him commanded, and he couldn't resist the urge to plant his hand onto the rock, and rise. *It should be hot.*

I should be dead.

Yet Boyd felt empty inside, a single will granting him the strength to *stand*.

Everybody around him did the same.

Something has taken control of me.

It lived inside of him, a disturbing passenger leeching onto his own mind. The feeling was unsettling, though it'd always been there... Boyd had only just realized.

Up.

He rose to his knees without choice. Standing, screaming while he tried to resist, Boyd was joined by the bodies that lay near him on the shore of hot coals, screaming their own story of pain and agony —most consisting of praise.

All at once, the skin on Boyd's back tore open. Pressure released from inside of his chest, out of his back. A weight lifted from his shoulders and he found himself in shade.

This time, the scream was against his will—more like a screech into the fiery depths as his nails grew out into claws, and hundreds of thousands of the Lord's other followers mimicked the call.

ACKNOWLEDGMENTS

I would not be the writer nor the person I am today if it weren't for my writing group based out of Brandon, Florida. Thank you to everyone who read my early work and told me to keep writing.

DEAR READER,

Thank you for taking the time to read this story.

The process of writing this book was tough. I don't think writing a book will ever get easier, just different. This particular time was rough, though, going through COVID and the death of my grandmother. Major shifts in the family made it hard, but everyday I managed to sit down and write, thanks to great family members and an amazing wife. I wouldn't have been able to do it without them.

And I wouldn't be able to do this without you. One of the main ways that authors can gain recognition for their books is through accumulated reviews. So I have to ask, if you enjoyed and finished this book, please take the time to write and leave an honest review. I read all of my reviews and love to hear what readers say, taking things into account for later books.

Happy reading,
Austin Valenzuela

P.S. I love to converse with my fans. Please visit me at any of my social media pages (Instagram - @valenzuela.austin; TikTok -

@valenzuela.au) and ask me any questions you have about my book or upcoming projects.

Milton Keynes UK
Ingram Content Group UK Ltd.
UKHW041907240823
427419UK00005B/276